I0618325

Copyright © 2019 Nichole M. Bridges

ISBN: 978-1-7343416-0-7

Ember's Shadow – Into the Darkness

an Ember Summers Novel, Book 2

by Nichole M. Bridges

Contents

Chapter One

A throbbing pain in my head told me I was too tired and too hungry to be sitting in an airport with a vampire who was cranky on his best of days. My only hope was for the third member of our party to arrive before the plane left for Phoenix, or I was going to have to spend two hours packed like a sardine on an airplane with Marek.

While Marek is a powerful master vampire who could keep me safe from any number of attackers, I didn't think he would be the best person to provide moral support for my fear of flying. My Guardian James would be the better choice. Unfortunately, James was running late due to an emergency at The Council of Guardians, and I was afraid he wasn't going to make it.

I searched the crowd of people milling about for his tall blonde presence, but I didn't find him. James had been my constant companion for weeks, and I've come to rely on him for everything from my safety to moral support. He could wrap me in his arms and make me feel safe with nothing more than his embrace.

Maybe it's his height and muscular stature, but there is certainly something that draws me to James much more naturally than to anyone else I've ever met. From the moment I first saw him, I knew he was important.

A hand slid into mine, and I looked up into Marek's bright blue eyes. They made me feel like I was drowning. It was startling yet compelling at the same time. I pulled my hand away because I didn't want to touch him.

Marek's features were a little too sharp to be called traditionally handsome, but his face has grown on me. It may have something to do with him saving my life and sharing his blood with me. It also could be his dark hair that fell just past his ears and his athletic build. The package was impressive if you ignored his personality.

Marek glanced at me with soft eyes as if he knew what I was thinking. He did that from time to time now that we had shared blood. Based on my research, which I've done a lot of in the past week, when vampires share blood, a bond forms between them. That bond allows them to know where the human is and to feel their emotions.

He and I have had a rocky start to our acquaintance, but he has proven I can trust him. He intrigues me and being intrigued by a vampire is a dangerous thing, according to James. While I'm not convinced Marek has feelings like the rest of us, I'm not scared of him like I used to be.

A call to start boarding broadcast over the PA system, and I felt myself begin to panic because James was nowhere to be found. Marek stood, seemingly unconcerned. His exterior calm at odds with my inner alarm.

When I was going to call James to make sure he was in the terminal, my phone rang.

"I'll be there soon," James said.

"You better run because they started boarding," I said.

"I'm almost to the parking garage. I should be there in less than ten minutes." James said.

"James, you don't have ten minutes even if you get through security quickly. DIA is a huge airport. You're not going to make it." I said.

"I'll get there one way or another, even if I have to take another flight. Don't worry, Em." He said, then hung up.

I dropped my phone back into my purse and looked up to find

Marek standing next to me. He put a hand on my shoulder and turned me to face him.

"Do not worry. James will make it," He said.

I nodded my head in agreement even though I didn't feel it. I needed to be on this plane to get to Natalie, and I needed James to be on it with me. I wasn't about to take on this quest without him. Having Marek with me was good, but something in the back of my mind told me that a human would be better able to deal with the desert heat of Arizona than a vampire.

Our boarding group was called, and Marek and I got in line. I was searching the area for James and crossing my fingers at the same time. I was a nervous wreck all knotted up inside and feeling frantic. People were steadily boarding in front of me, and soon only five people separated me from the gate and the walk down the jet bridge.

"Just walk," Marek said from behind me and placed his hand at the small of my back to push me forward.

I handed the lady my boarding pass then felt the heat of Marek's fingertips through my t-shirt as he propelled me down the terminal bridge. My heart was racing so badly I couldn't swallow. I'm sure I looked like a terrorist with a bomb in my shoe because the flight attendant gave me a concerned look when I stepped onto the plane.

"She is nervous about flying," Marek said as an explanation to the woman. "Come now, my love. Take a deep breath. It will be alright."

I blinked hard at him and took a deep breath. It helped a little, and the flight attendant let me pass with a look of pity. Marek kept his hand on my back all the way down the aisle. He helped me into a window seat then settled in next to me. I looked over at him, and he locked eyes with me.

"He will make it," he said then turned away.

"You called me your love," I said, feeling confused.

He turned back to me and said, "You were behaving strangely, and people believe when a man and woman are traveling together, they are a couple."

"How did that work exactly?" I asked, confused.

"A man can calm his wife when she is nervous about flying." He said, pulling my hand into his.

He kissed my palm then looked up toward the front of the plane. My hand tingled where his lips had pressed onto it, and I was so stunned that I was in a haze for a few minutes. Marek was never nice, and his odd behavior threw me enough that I briefly forgot about James and my panic.

I looked out the window and watched as the ground crew prepared the plane to move away from the gate. I checked my phone and noticed that James had tried to call. The message was brief but precise. He wasn't going to make it.

"Maybe we should catch a later flight," I said and started to stand.

Marek wouldn't budge and gave me no choice but to sit back down. He gave me a look that said I was crazy. All I knew was that it would be mad to be alone on an airplane with a vampire. I needed James to hold my hand and tell me everything would be alright. If he were sitting next to me, saying reassuring words, everything would be okay.

The panic continued to rise in my body, and it was all I could do to stay seated. Running my hands through my hair and wringing my fingers wasn't taking the edge off at all. I could feel the beating of my heart speeding up with each breath I drew. I could feel tears well up in my eyes, and it was only going to be a matter of seconds before they fell down my face.

"*Milaya moya*, you must calm down. They will remove you from the airplane. I can hear them discussing it right now." He said in a firm but soothing voice.

I looked up toward the front of the plane, and sure enough, they were looking at me and speaking urgently. I blinked hard and tried to clear the tears from my eyes, but it was too much. I couldn't calm myself down.

"Help me," I whispered to Marek, but I knew there was nothing he would be able to do to help.

I was coming apart at the seams and completely unable to put a lid on my emotions. Marek realized it and smiled. Of all the things he could do, a smile was not going to work. I looked at him, confused. Then he leaned in and kissed me. I was so completely shocked by his lips pressing into mine that I gave in to the sensation.

I would have expected the lips of a vampire to be cold, but Marek's were warm and soft as velvet. He slipped his fingers into my hair and tilted my head back so that he could deepen the kiss. He ran his tongue along my bottom lip, and I shivered in his arms. My breath came faster, and I realized that I was kissing him back, and it was...amazing.

While caught up in the moment, I slipped my tongue between his lips and moaned when he pulled it deeper into his mouth. His grip tightened on my hair, and he kissed me more urgently. I was distantly aware of movement as the plane taxied away from the terminal, but I didn't care. Marek consumed me while his kiss made my body burn for his. It was the kind of kiss that leads to more.

My body was filling with desire, and every touch from Marek fueled my passion. I slid my hands up his chest feeling the hard muscle under his shirt and marveled at how good it felt. His embrace tightened around me, and my fingers trailed a path up to his neck. His skin was smooth and warm, and all I could think about was ripping the clothing away from his body so I could feel the length of him pressed against me.

His kiss was passion and sensuality mixed with power as our lips danced together. The rush of his power felt almost as pleasant as the press of his lips on mine. I didn't need to breathe as long as he was holding me, kissing me. His power would breathe for me.

Before the thought completed in my mind, he pulled back, ending the kiss, then he smiled. I had never seen him smile like that. It was a genuine smile, and it was a rare gift from a man that was always so serious. It softened his features, and I realized for the first time that he was truly handsome.

I smiled back at Marek and pushed down the panic that was just under the surface. The thought of having made out with a vampire was a hysterical bubble ready to explode if I let it. He succeeded in calming me down, but I wasn't sure if it was by sacrificing himself or by taking advantage of the situation.

Marek looked me in the eye and asked if I was okay.

"I'm fine," I said lamely.

He smiled then turned away. "James will catch the next plane. There is a direct flight leaving shortly after this one. He will not be too far behind us."

"Why did you do that?" I asked, but it sounded breathless and weak.

"Would you have preferred to be removed from the airplane?" he asked but turned away as if that was the end of the conversation.

"No, but you didn't have to kiss me..." I started, but he interrupted me.

"Your need for James to be near you is unwarranted. Besides your own power, I am more than adequately capable of protecting you." He said in a voice more accented than usual.

I suspected he was a bit annoyed.

"That isn't the only reason I panicked, and you know it," I said.

"I know." He said and pushed my hair back over my shoulder. "You should rest."

The sudden familiarity was foreign, yet after that kiss, I wasn't sure what to expect. Right now, I was just thankful to have the caring side of Marek showing instead of the hardness he usually exhibited.

I took several deep breaths to calm my still racing heart and put out the fire that Marek had kindled. I stared at his profile for a few minutes before finally turning away and looking out the window.

This vampire was more than I could handle. The last thing I wanted was to be attracted to someone who I knew could be cold and uncaring. I had seen him treat people callously before, hell he had treated me that way, and I wasn't stupid enough to think he wouldn't do the same thing again.

He didn't look at me even though I knew he could feel my emotions. I wasn't going to be fooled by his sudden warm behavior. Marek had managed to wiggle his way into my good opinion lately, but that didn't mean that I trusted him the way I trusted James.

I was more than a little curious to know if Marek would handle another panic attack in the same way. There were indeed other ways to calm someone down. I found it interesting that he chose to kiss me.

I let myself relax, knowing there was nothing I could do about James. Being stuck on an airplane for a few hours with Marek was unavoidable at this point. My thoughts began to wander as I relaxed and let go of the anxiety that was pent up inside me. My breathing smoothed out, and I soon fell asleep.

A sudden bump of turbulence woke me and I grabbed Marek's hand so hard he winced. What could make a vampire wince? He looked at me in awe, and it scared me.

My heart started to pound so hard I could feel it thumping against my chest. My face started to tingle, and I felt a little dizzy. There is something utterly helpless about being thousands of feet in the air and having no control over your fate. It was too similar to the reality of my life as a whole.

"It is a bump like the one you drive over on the road." Marek said.

"When I run over a bump on the road, I don't plummet to my death from ten thousand feet in the air," I said with venom.

Marek raised an eyebrow and smirked. Apparently, he thought I was cute.

Marek leaned toward me and said, "I would never let you fall."

I paused, looking at him, and felt his sincerity through our bond.

"Somehow, I believe you," I said, knowing that if anyone could do it, Marek could.

Marek stared at me for a moment as if he was shocked. He recovered quickly and squeezed my hand gently. The corner of his mouth turned up slightly, and his eyes sparkled. A warmth slipped through the bond between us, and my breath caught at the feeling.

I wasn't used to the bond between us and experiencing another person's feelings was surreal. In a moment like this, I recognized his feelings separately from mine, but at other times they got confused. I wondered if he had bonded to anyone else before and if he knew how to handle it better than me. I assumed he did.

I realized I had no idea how old Marek was, but asking him seemed like a dangerous question. While he was currently polite, I knew he could snap at me at any moment to become the unfeeling version of himself. I didn't want to provoke the vampire, so I turned away to watch out the window.

Chapter Two

We arrived on a rare cool evening at Phoenix's Sky Harbor Airport and proceeded to make our way to the bus that would bring us to the rental car pick-up center. As we walked, I frequently glanced at Marek but didn't see any sign of the man that had kissed me senseless on the airplane. In some ways, that was a relief because I didn't know what to do with him if he had an interest in me romantically. I hadn't been out of a relationship long enough to want someone else, especially if that someone was a vampire.

Of course, my traveling companion is more than just a vampire; he is a member of an elite group of supernatural watchers that call themselves The Council of Guardians. The first of whom I met back home in Denver. Their organization is secretive, but I have learned during my association with them that the Guardians are selected to watch humans and other creatures that show signs of the paranormal to the extent that could be dangerous.

Until I realized that I had powers beyond clairvoyance, I didn't see my value or the need for a Guardian. Somehow, they knew even though I had to learn the hard way about my own abilities and that not only were supernatural beings walking this earth, but some of them wanted to use humans with paranormal capabilities for nefarious schemes. I wouldn't take their protection lightly again.

Marek was another story, but his presence was more of a serious nature. I was enjoying his silence while we went through the mundane task of renting a car. I knew my free time was limited because he was determined to have me train so that I could better protect myself. Apparently, one of the most dangerous things in this world was an untrained fire starter like me.

I watched Marek walk in front of me. His movement was smoother than a ball bearing on glass, and no matter how much time I spent with him, it still unnerved me. In the dark of the night, he looked like any other man, but I knew he wasn't a man at all. His blood could heal, and he was stronger than any human on the planet.

"Your thoughts are slowing your footsteps," Marek said in his slight Russian accent.

I shook my head and quickened my pace as he walked toward our car. Marek was ever vigilant for danger, and that was both a relief and an annoyance. I missed James' playful nature and pulled out my phone to check if he was able to make a later flight. It would be great to have him here sooner rather than later.

As much as I have grown to trust the vampire, I preferred the company of my human Guardian. James was someone that could fill the hole left by my ex-boyfriend's betrayal on a level that was friendly but could move to romance if I let it.

I was perfectly happy with my boyfriend Nikko until I found out that he was not only cheating on me but that he wasn't entirely human either. Taking a chance on giving my heart to another man made me nervous at best.

Having my heart figuratively ripped out of my chest was something difficult to overcome. If I could set aside my fears and let James in, he was the type of man that could help heal what was broken. He was duty-bound to protect me. Starting up a romantic relationship with him would not be the brightest move, nor was it a sanctioned activity by the Council.

Pulling up my voicemails revealed that James had indeed called and left a message. I listened to it while Marek loaded our bags into a plain mid-sized sedan. The scowl on his face showed clearly his distaste for such a vehicle. I'm sure that if he had his pick, he would be driving a classic muscle car like his own 1969 Chevy Chevelle, but rental agencies like this one don't offer beautiful cars, only functional ones. I listened to the message James had left then let Marek know when to expect him.

"James was able to get on a flight with another airline that is only an hour behind us, so he should be here soon," I said.

Marek gave me a look that said he had heard the message himself and didn't need the replay. So much for thinking Marek would even act human; I'd have to remember he was all business.

We rode in silence to our hotel, and I didn't have any reason to speak until Marek was checking in, and I realized we only had one room. The thought of sharing with Marek was too much.

"I'm not sharing a room with you," I whispered.

The look he gave me could have melted steel. It was clear he didn't think I was using my brain, nor did he think I should be thinking for myself on this one.

"The room is a suite. The bedroom is separate from the living area." He said as if that would be the end of it.

My stomach twisted as I thought of him sharing a room with me. The feeling of unease would not go away, and unlike the visions I usually had, this feeling wouldn't pinpoint exactly why it wasn't a good idea. I just knew it would end badly.

"I'd rather have my own room if you don't mind," I replied.

"That is not acceptable...from a security standpoint." He said, and it was evident by the tone of his voice that there was no point in arguing.

I shut my mouth and stepped away from him while he finished checking in. After taking several deep breaths, I was able to shake the bad feeling I had enough to take a look around. The hotel was a five-star establishment, something that was above my usual station and seemed to be somewhat extravagant. I guess the Guardians are well funded.

The main room was softly lit by strategically placed chandeliers and filled with dark woods and leather. The masculinity was broken by several large floral bouquets of white flowers. The effect was stunning, and I couldn't wait to see what the rooms looked like, even if I had to share.

The bellhop led the way to a shiny bank of elevators, and we followed in silence. More opulence met us in the elevator car and again in the hallway upstairs. The color palette changed on the seventh floor, where our room was located, soft grays with a touch of purple. Each room door was ebony black with brushed silver hardware. It was beautiful.

When we arrived at our room, Marek directed the man where to put the luggage, and I wandered further into the suite. The grey theme continued throughout but was altered in the bedroom. The bed was white with butter yellow pillows and a puffy white duvet. It was modern and feminine and looked like a cloud. I couldn't wait to get into it.

"Will this be suitable for you?" Marek asked with just a touch of annoyance in his voice.

I didn't hear him approach, and the sound of his voice made me jump. I resisted the urge to roll my eyes at his comment then turned with a smile on my lips.

"It's gorgeous, and the bed looks very comfortable," I said, sliding my fingers along the silky fabric.

He paused for a moment as he looked at the bed himself. I could have sworn his lips quirked.

"If you look at the menu and select something, I will have it delivered to the room," he said, then turned and walked away.

The abruptness of his leaving had me curious. I felt a flutter of desire roll through the link between us, and I smiled as my eyes followed his lean form into the living area. Just as my eyes rested on his ass, he turned, and I was shocked to find myself staring at another part of his anatomy. I closed my eyes and moved to find the menu. I could feel the flush on my cheeks as I fumbled around looking for the list of options for my dinner.

I closed my eyes just as a sharp pain shot through my head. I gasped and grabbed my head with my hands. I pressed my fingers into the pain, but it did nothing to make it go away. I felt Marek move toward me. He wrapped his arms around me just as the images hit. The distant sound of his voice didn't stop the vision.

Natalie screamed in pain as Viktor bit into her neck. Her body shuddered as he pulled her closer and drank deeply. Her cries turned to moans as what he was doing evolved from pain to pleasure. After a moment, Viktor pulled back and laughed at her glazed look then turned his head to look right at me. Only I wasn't really there for him to see.

"Ember," he sneered with my sister's blood dripping from his mouth. He smiled as I tried to yell for him to leave her alone, but either he couldn't hear me, or he refused to react to my words. He turned away from me and resumed his attention to my sister, who was now compliant with his wishes. She didn't fight him when he started removing her clothing. In fact, she was trying to help him.

I heard Marek's voice pulling me out of the vision and back to reality, but the images were slow to fade. No matter how much I wanted it to end, one image clung to my mind. Viktor's teeth stained with my sister's blood.

I didn't want to see what he was about to do to my sister any more than I already had to, so I clung to the sound of Marek's voice. His voice was a promise that this vision would end even if the reality had still occurred. As the last of the images faded, Marek's voice finally came together with coherent words.

"What did you see?" Marek asked. His voice was urgent yet soothing at the same time.

"It was Natalie, we don't have much time. Viktor is...playing with her." I said through gritted teeth.

"He will not hurt her..." he started to say, but I interrupted him.

"Won't hurt her? He was sucking her blood and tearing off her clothes, Marek. He has already hurt her!" I screamed and pushed away from him.

He grabbed me faster than I could get away and spun me around. The intensity in his eyes stopped me from fighting him off.

"As I said, he will not hurt her because she is the only link he has with you. You are his target, not your sister. That is why you need to think about what you just saw." He said.

I shook my head, but he wouldn't let me get out of it.

"I don't want to think about it," I said weakly.

"You must, or we will never find your sister. In your vision lays the clues to her exact location." He said.

My heart was pounding, and my breathing became erratic as his fingers wrapped around my arms. His hands tightened around my biceps until they were just on this side of hurting. I looked down at those fingers, and he let go, but he didn't step away from me. His body stayed pressed to the front of mine.

He touched my cheek and said one word, "Please."

It was said softly and in a voice that was so tender. This vampire was an enigma. I had a sudden feeling that he was going to be important in my future. It was one of those non-specific feelings that felt like a premonition.

I closed my eyes and took a deep breath.

"You do not need to tell me, show me the vision," Marek said.

"What?" I said, confused.

"Use the bond between us to push the images into my mind." He said. "No words needed."

"I don't know how to do that," I said, feeling confused. Was that even possible?

Marek took my hand in his. I let him do it even though it felt weird.

"The bond between us has weakened. It will be easier for you if we renew it before trying." He said in a perfectly logical matter of fact tone.

"Whoa, I don't think we need to do that," I said, stepping back and trying to walk away.

Marek stopped me and said, "If you can feel the bond fully, it will be easier to share your vision. After that, you will not need it." He said as if renewing the bond was no big deal.

"I can feel it now," I responded. Being bound closer to Marek was not a good idea. I knew it, but he was insistent.

"It is but a thread now. You need a clear pathway." He said while pulling a knife from his pocket.

He pushed up the sleeve of his jacket. Then he brought the knife to his wrist and made a small incision. Blood beaded to the surface and with it a vanilla scent that reminded me of the last time I had his blood.

I took a step toward him automatically, and his usually stoic face showed a hint of a smile. He was going to enjoy this. I knew it, but I also couldn't help myself. I remembered how good it tasted the last time and the rush it gave me. Without further hesitation, I grabbed his arm and brought his wrist up to my lips. I felt him tense slightly before I closed my mouth over the cut. He shuddered as I began to pull on the wound and take his blood into my body.

Like before, it didn't taste coppery like I would expect blood should taste. It was a warm caramel flavor, but unlike before, it was like it was begging me to consume it. I drank deeper, but the wound was closing, and the supply disappearing. I leaned into Marek and tried sucking harder, but it wouldn't bleed anymore.

Before I knew what I was doing, I had bitten him. As my teeth sunk into his skin, Marek gasped. The sound brought a wave of pleasure rippling through my body. Almost instantly, I felt my back hit the wall, and Marek's body press hard into mine. It was everything I wanted at that moment. He was warm and hard against me, and his taste was magic on my tongue.

"No more, Ember. That is enough." Marek said, but his voice sounded distant, almost as if he was speaking from far away.

His voice did nothing to stop me from sucking harder on the wound. I was rewarded with a rush of sweet ecstasy that filled my whole body. My limbs were tingling, and I was getting aroused by the press of Marek's body against mine. I could suddenly feel how Marek felt with me pressed against him. We were one, and it was exquisite.

I grabbed the bond between us and pulled it toward me, wrapping it around myself. The feeling was like velvet and silk. I wanted more.

"No, Ember do not..." Marek urged me to stop, but it was too late.

I could feel his panic and under it all his desire for me to keep going. It felt right in a way that I couldn't understand.

A voice next to my ear pulled me out of my thoughts. "You need to let him go Em."

It was James, he was talking to me and interrupting my thoughts. When did he get here?

His distraction broke the seal of my lips on Marek's skin. I dropped his wrist and instantly felt its loss even though Marek's body was still pressed against mine. In fact, it wasn't just his body that was pressed against me. I could feel his teeth graze my throat too.

"Oh God," I gasped and pushed him back, but instead of using my hands, I used my power. It was pulsing strongly at that moment and so easy to use.

Marek was gone in an instant, and I felt cold from his loss. I could still feel him in my mind, but differently than just moments before.

"Use it. Show me the vision." Marek said. His voice was husky, even from the far side of the room.

Before I thought of anything else, I recalled the vision and pushed it down the lines of our bond, opening it up completely. I didn't grab the connection this time; instead, I just poured the images down the pathway.

I opened my eyes and found Marek seated on the floor in the corner of the room. His head was in his hands, and he was shaking. He didn't look well.

"What just happened?" James asked.

Marek looked at him for a moment, and James gasped. He looked at me then back at Marek.

"Let's take a walk," James said, pulling me out of the room.

"What's wrong with him?" I asked, trying to look back at Marek as we went through the door.

"You are. Let's go." He insisted, yanking me by the arm into the hall.

As soon as the door closed, I felt more lucid, and the realization set in that I had done something wrong.

"What did I do?" I whispered and looked up at James.

"I didn't think it was possible, but you rolled him," He responded.

"Rolled him? What do you mean?" I asked, confused.

Marek was an old vampire with lots of power. It couldn't be what I thought.

"Here, sit down," He said as we came to a bench near the elevator.

I sat and looked up at him while I waited for him to answer.

"You took control of the bond. It shouldn't be possible with a vampire that strong." He said. He looked half proud and half scared.

"That can't be a good thing," I said, knowing that a powerful vampire like Marek would not want to be controlled.

Although, as soon as I thought it, I could feel him again. He was angry but not with me, and there was also something else. Something that he wanted desperately. I dropped the thread between us. I didn't want to know what it was.

"No, master vampires don't give control willingly to just anyone, and I think he may have done it by accident. He doesn't usually make mistakes like this." James said.

"So, you are saying he gave me control?" I asked. Although I was confident that wasn't what happened. I kept that thought to myself.

"Yes, it's the only way it could have happened. I had to step in, or he would have..." James shook his head but couldn't finish the thought.

"He would have what?" I insisted.

"If he had bitten you back, the bond could become permanent." He sounded like he didn't want to tell me how close I had come to becoming irreversibly connected to a master vampire.

"Crap," I said, cringing when I felt Marek respond through our bond.

He wasn't happy that James was telling me and I wasn't pleased he could understand what was going on.

"More than crap. That kind of exchange only happens to bonded mates or those preparing for the change." James said. "That isn't something you want to do without a full understanding of what you are getting yourself into."

The thought of binding yourself to a vampire forever was hard to imagine. It obviously happened but not to anyone I knew or had ever heard of. Granted, I was new to this life, so my experience was minimal.

"What were you doing, Em?" James asked, shaking his head in disbelief.

"Don't judge me, James. Marek wanted me to try sharing my visions directly with him, but the bond was too weak. He made it sound like it was no big deal to renew it." I said.

"It's a big deal," James said, stating the obvious.

"Clearly," I said, feeling angry with James.

What happened wasn't his fault, but I couldn't help but feel if he hadn't missed his flight that James would have been there to stop this from happening in the first place. Maybe that was my real problem. James wasn't there for me, and I had to rely solely on Marek.

"Shit, I need to talk to him," I said and stood up to go back to the room.

"Ember wait," He said, grabbing my arm.

"Let me go," I said and put the force of my kinetic power into it. He dropped my arm instantly, wincing like it hurt. That was interesting...I could get used to that.

When I opened the door, Marek was still on the floor, but he looked better. His eyes were closed, and his head was tipped back against the wall. When the door closed behind me, he looked up. His eyes piercing with emotion that I couldn't comprehend. I'd never seen him this way before.

"Are you okay?" I asked tentatively.

The look in his eyes at that moment told me he was both happy and angry. I could feel the emotions simmering along with our connection, but it wasn't clear to me yet how to interpret those signals.

"I'm sorry, whatever I did..." I said lamely.

He smiled, which stopped me from thinking clearly. I blinked hard to make sure I saw that right. Marek didn't smile often.

He stood without effort and walked over to me. He took my hand in his lifting it to his mouth. He kissed my palm, and a zing of heat flooded through my body. At that moment, his presence overwhelmed me. I couldn't think of anything but the warmth I was feeling and the intensity of his stare.

"You may regret what you did one day, but I do not." He said.

I knew he was telling the truth. He wanted me to be bound to him forever. I took a step back, and he laughed.

"You already do," He said, closing the distance between us again.

Marek touched my cheek lightly and ran his thumb along my jaw. The movement sent waves of pleasure through my body. It felt somewhere between the warmth of a hug from someone you love and a sexual invitation.

He said, "It is late. You should go to bed. You need your rest."

All I heard was "bed," and I felt a blush on my cheeks. I turned my head and closed my eyes. I had to shake this feeling and get my brain to function again. At that moment, I realized that I really was exhausted. Whatever had just happened confused me, but I wondered why Marek was so intimate with me. Was it the bond?

"You'll understand soon enough." He said, answering my thought.

I gasped in shock, and a quirk of a smile showed on his lips before he stepped away. The distance allowed me to take a deep breath and clear my head. James chose that moment to come back into the room. I didn't know what to do next, so I followed Marek's suggestion and went into the bedroom. Talking to either of them further felt like it would be even more exhausting.

Chapter Three

My fingernails got caked with dirt from crawling under bushes, not my usual kind of activity. I'm the one usually sitting at a desk all day researching for a legal firm. We hired private investigators to do the dirty work, but this wasn't for the practice. I was searching for my sister. I was trying to be sneaky and see into this building without being seen. James was playing lookout. We were on our own yet under strict orders not to enter the building.

Marek wasn't here due to what you could call a fatal sun allergy. He could stand more sun than most vampires, but Phoenix, Arizona wasn't called the Valley of the Sun for nothing. Marek couldn't risk prolonged sun exposure unless we were sure of Natalie's location; thus, our present reconnoiter without him.

While I slept last night, Marek did some recon on his own and narrowed things down to a few buildings that James and I were currently checking out. I was supposed to use my powers to determine if Natalie was in the building, but that attempt backfired. I couldn't figure out how to use my gift and try as he might, James couldn't get me to use it either.

I cursed under my breath as I scraped my knee and wished I was wearing jeans. It was too hot for that, but a girl could hope. I approached the window carefully, and the muck covering the glass combined with the embedded wire within the glass made seeing anything in the interior of this building sketchy at best. I strained to hear as much as I could, but the building's air conditioner was roaring nearby, cutting off any sound that might be there.

I risked a look down the wall trying to find another possibly cleaner window, but they each looked just as bad. What I needed was to get inside to take a look around.

"What are you doing?" James whispered.

I appeared out from under the bushes and brushed more dirt off of me.

"This isn't going to work. I can't see a thing through those dirty windows." I said.

He looked up and down the building but must have come to the same conclusion as me because he shook his head.

"We can't go in now. We'll have to go back to the hotel." He said.

I was unconvinced that we were done, and I told him as much. Maybe I could use my skinned-up knee to our advantage.

"No way, you are not going in there, especially not alone," James said, making a slicing motion with his hands as if that would clear the thought from my mind.

"I'll pretend I took a spill while jogging. Then I can go in and ask to use the bathroom so I can clean up." I said while pulling James back toward the car.

James pulled out his phone, but I grabbed it before he could dial.

"Don't call him," I said, pleading with my eyes. "I need to do this."

"Marek will not be happy about this. It isn't a good idea." He said, shaking his head from side to side.

I put my hands on his chest to draw his attention then slid them up around his neck. His eyes met mine, and I stared into them, willing him to agree with me. His hands touched my hips in response, and I was surprised to not feel a surge of heat. It was underhanded and completely taking advantage of him, but I needed this.

"I can do this, James," I assured him.

He nodded then stayed quiet as I pulled away and tied up my t-shirt in the front to reveal my stomach. I was going for a look that said I was someone out for a run. It also helped to emphasize my breasts through the V-neck of the shirt, which would help distract any men that might be inside. If the heat in James' gaze was anything to go by, my outfit was right on point.

My knee must have been up for the charade because blood started dripping as we walked back to the front of the building. I smiled to myself and tried to think of what I would say if anyone inside questioned my story. Hopefully, if it were a man, he would be too distracted and not worry about it.

"You go in, go into the bathroom, then come right back out, understood?" James asked.

"Yes," I said, crossing my fingers behind my back. I couldn't promise that would be it.

If he was suspicious that I wasn't honest, he didn't say anything. I jogged in place after pulling my hair into a ponytail. When I had enough of a sweat to look convincing, I practiced a limp while walking toward the building. It wasn't that hard considering my knee hurt like I had actually taken a spill and not just pretended to take a fall.

James held back, and I could see his agitation. It made me a little nervous about what I was about to do, but I reminded myself that if I found Natalie, we would get her back that much quicker. I was doing this for her. Besides, there was no telling whether this was the right location anyway. The other buildings we had checked out were both duds.

When I was within view of the front door, I bent down to look at my knee. I figured that would both look like I was concerned for the injury and give any men inside a view down my shirt. It felt a little degrading, but if it sold the con, all the better.

The door was locked when I tried to push it open, so I took a moment to see who was inside. Two guards or front office types were behind a desk of some sort, so I waved at them and smiled. They hesitated so long I thought this wasn't going to work. Then the two men looked at each other and smiled.

One got up and walked toward the door. The man moved slowly but smoothly, and a sudden surge of fear threatened to paralyze me. The man's smile was creepy, and he licked his lips when he noticed my bloody knee. I hoped he wasn't what I thought he was.

The door opened, and the man leaned out.

"Whatcha want girly?" He said with a scratchy voice that made my teeth hurt.

"Um, I fell and was wondering if you might let me use your bathroom so I could get cleaned up?" I said.

"Why would I do that?" he said, and his smile grew.

"Well, I hoped you would help out a woman in need," I said uncomfortably.

His eyes moved down my body ending in a flare of his nostrils. He inhaled deeply and smiled a yellow-toothed grin. If he was scenting the blood from my knee, then he was certainly not human. My stomach rolled, threatening to send my breakfast back up.

"I cannot let ya in wittout ya give me sometin'," He said in barely enough English to understand.

Anger mixed with fear flowed through my body at his words, and I realized I had to make a decision. Either I turned tail and run or try to play dumb. I sucked up my courage.

"What is it you want? I don't have anything with me. I was jogging." I said, looking behind me, trying to see if James was close enough to hear this.

The man behind the desk barked something I couldn't understand. Yellow teeth turned around and shook his head.

"Fine," he said, turning back around. "Ya can use da can."

He said, looking disappointed and opening the door wider so that I could come in. I hesitated long enough that the other man inside got up and started walking toward us. I figured he was the guy in charge, so I should act thankful and hurry.

I took a few steps inside and smiled up at the other man. "Thank you. I'll just be a minute."

"Take your time." He said in a deep voice that sounded much nicer than the man with the yellow teeth.

He pointed me toward a door across the room and told me there was a first aid kit in the cabinet. I walked to the door remembering to limp then closed the door behind me. I leaned against it for a minute listening in case the men said anything. I couldn't hear their voices, so I looked for the first aid kit and started cleaning up my knee.

A quick look around the room showed me that I wouldn't get anywhere other than back to the lobby from this room. My mission to learn something was going to be cut short. I fought the urge to kick the wall and instead splashed my face with cold water. It did little to calm my temper.

I took a moment to try reaching out with my power. Since I made it inside, the hope was that proximity would help me find Natalie. I took a deep breath and tried reaching out. I felt a buzzing in my head and pushed out like I did when I shared my vision with Marek. I was hoping to see something, but after a few minutes, I realized nothing was happening.

My brilliant plan to infiltrate Viktor's lair wasn't working. The only thing I succeeded in doing so far was to get frightened by a creepy guy, a guy who bore a shocking resemblance to a vampire who made the situation all the more troublesome. Somehow, I had to get out of here without drawing any more of their suspicion.

I fixed up my knee with three bandage strips. Once they were applied, I trashed the supplies I had used and readied myself to leave. I listened at the door before opening it but didn't hear a thing.

When I stepped back out into the room, I noticed one of the

guards was by the front door, and the other was casually standing near the bathroom door. I smiled at both of them and started toward the exit.

"Thanks for letting me in," I said, stepping toward the door.

"Leavin'?" Yellow teeth said.

I turned around to find that he had moved from the bathroom door to just a few steps behind me. His nostrils were flaring, and I tried to ignore it.

"Yes, thank you. I'm all bandaged up." I said, pointing at my knee.

His eyes didn't dip down to check out the wound. Instead, he stared into my eyes. I felt my body stop moving as I looked at his eyes, and the shock of it pulled me out of whatever he was trying to do. I turned and strode toward the door.

"But we didn't even catch your name," guy number two said, stepping in front of my only exit.

"Oh, well, that was rude of me. My name is Sally." I said, reaching out my hand to his.

He took it, then brought my hand to his lips. I tried to pull my hand free, but he wouldn't let go. As his lips touched my skin, our eyes locked, and I felt myself getting dizzy. Unlike with the other man, I wasn't able to pull myself away.

"Sally, is it? What are you really doing here?" he said softly.

I fought the compulsion at first, but then I couldn't stop myself from speaking. "I was out looking for someone that is lost."

"Who is lost?" he asked.

I hesitated then started to say my sister but was interrupted by a loud knocking on the door. The man cursed under his breath and let my hand go. He turned and cautiously opened the door.

"I'm sorry to bother you, but my girlfriend called to say she fell on her run and that she was going to stop in one of these warehouses to clean up. Have you seen...?" James saw me at that moment and stopped midsentence.

He held out his hand, and I practically ran to him. The feel of his hand in mine cleared my head enough to know that I was in grave danger before he showed up. The smile on James' face disappeared as soon as he saw my face and realized that something was wrong.

"Well, there she is." He said and pulled me past him and out the door.

I kept moving until I reached the sun then waited for James. His words were too soft for me to hear, but whatever it was, he was steaming mad when he joined me.

"What did they do?" he asked, speaking softly while ushering me ahead of him back to the car.

"I'm not sure exactly, but whatever it was, I'm glad you stopped it," I said.

James pulled me into his arms and hugged me tightly.

"Jesus Em, that was reckless." He said, pulling me back to look at me.

He kissed the crown of my head then let me go and pulled his phone out of his pocket. I assumed he was calling Marek, and that was confirmed when he started talking.

"I think we found the right warehouse. You were right, Ember got herself into some trouble, but she's okay." He said, glancing at me.

He unlocked the car and waited for me to get in before he finished his phone call. I could feel anger coming from my connection with Marek. I tried to block it, and it shut off immediately. Well, that was interesting.

James wrenched open the driver's side door and dropped into the seat like a reluctant prisoner. Understanding dawned on me a little too late regarding who was going to pay the price for this incident. I immediately pulled out my phone, but James stopped me from pulling up Marek's phone number.

"It won't help. Nothing you can say or do right now will take away the fact that I agreed to let you go in that building alone." James said.

His voice was soft and resolved to accept his fate. A fate that I made him accept by my rash actions.

"It's my fault. I didn't give you much choice. I can talk to him..." but James wouldn't let me speak.

"No, Ember. I'll drop you off at the hotel. Marek will speak with me later." He said, then started the car and drove.

Panic fluttered through my chest thinking about what would happen to him. What would he do to James? The last time James got into this much trouble; Marek beat him within an inch of his life. I didn't want that to happen ever again, especially when it was my fault.

I pondered the possibilities on the drive back to the hotel. There had to be something I could do or say to persuade Marek that It was my fault.

James drove the rest of the way without saying a word. The closer we got, the more relaxed he became, and the more worried I got. He was going to take whatever punishment he received, and I couldn't let that happen.

When we arrived, James pulled up to the front door then got out but left the car running. He wasn't going to come in with me, and that made tears well up in my eyes. He shook his head when he saw me and drew me into his arms.

"It will be okay, Ember. I'm stronger than you think." He said and smiled down at me.

"But..." I started, but he stopped me with a finger to my lips.

"No, go upstairs." He said, then kissed me on the forehead and got back in the car.

My legs felt frozen like I wouldn't be able to walk. Marek stepped out of the elevator as I approached it. I should have known James would not have left me to go in on my own without knowing I would be protected. I stopped abruptly and looked around to see how many people were in the lobby.

"It does not matter how many are here to witness. I am *vampyre* and can make them believe anything I wish." Marek said while walking toward me.

He took my arm and pulled me over to the waiting elevator. Once inside, I was sure he would yell at me or maybe even hit me. It wouldn't be the first time I was afraid of him.

Instead of reacting the way I thought, he simply stood there waiting for our floor. He was deceptively calm, and yet I could feel a glimmer of his emotions boiling under the surface. He was so angry I wasn't sure if the man standing beside me was the same man I was connecting to the feelings.

The elevator arrived on the seventh floor, and once again, he led me by the arm as if I would run away. I knew better than to think I could get away without speaking to him. He pushed me into the suite, but as soon as he had the door closed and locked, he moved in front of me so quickly I barely saw it. He grabbed me and started searching me for what I assumed were wounds since he was particularly upset about my knee.

"Why is it still fresh?" He asked.

"I cleaned it up, but wounds take time to heal Marek." My voice was a little snippy, but he didn't seem to notice.

Before I could say another word, he lifted me in his arms then placed me on the counter of the little bar we had in the corner of the suite. My heart raced from the shock, and it pained me to admit that it was a bit exciting as well. He was so unpredictable.

He looked me in the eye as if he had heard that last thought. He lifted my knee and pulled the bandages off.

"Ouch!" I yelled and tried to pull my knee back.

"It is still bleeding." He said, looking up into my eyes.

"Well yes, I just injured it less than an hour ago," I said sarcastically.

He shook his head at me, "No, it should be healing already."

I thought of the words James had spoken to me not long ago about the reasons a vampire would share blood with a human. One of them was for healing.

"It's fine, although it would be better had you left the bandage on," I said, not hiding my annoyance.

Marek ignored me and pulled a pocket knife out of his pants. As he wet a towel in the sink, I got a bad feeling about what he was going to do. I was not in the mood to take more of his blood.

"I said it was fine," I said, my voice a little shrill.

He ignored me, slapping my hands away from my knee and giving me a look that begged me to give him a reason to take action. It was the kind of look that made you comply, and I did what he asked. He wasn't someone I could resist, and that scared me even more.

He inspected the wound and found a few pebbles that I had missed. He cleaned them out much to my dismay. The pain was nothing compared to the shock of seeing him take the knife to one of his fingers. He sliced what appeared to be a large gash down his index finger, but no blood came to the surface. He swore under his breath, or at least I thought he did. He was speaking Russian.

He took the knife to his palm next, and blood swelled into his hand. He seemed pleased and proceeded to smear the blood over my knee. I jerked back before I could stop myself. The thought of someone rubbing their blood on my open wound was more than I could comprehend. All reason said that was a terrible idea.

Marek appeared to understand and patiently said, "My blood is not like yours. It will heal and protect your wound."

I nodded my head, and he repeated the process until he was satisfied. He washed the blood from his hand. I was surprised to see that the large gash in his palm had already healed. After a few minutes, he used the wet cloth to clean the blood away from my knee, and I gasped when I saw the perfectly healed skin revealed.

"That's amazing!" I exclaimed.

"That is a minor repair compared to what may have happened today. Why did you do this?" He asked.

He was still acting so calm, and it was confusing me.

"I know you're mad," I said.

"Mad is hardly how I would describe it." He said through gritted teeth.

Great, now I'm antagonizing the vampire!

"I'm sorry, but I knew I had to go in there to know where my sister was. If I didn't do it, we wouldn't have known for too long, and that could be deadly for her."

He stared into my eyes for a moment, and I saw something pass beneath his crystal blue gaze. It was a decision of some kind, but I wasn't sure if it would be good or bad for me.

"You are not skilled enough in your powers to be alone on a mission such as that. James was sent with you to deter you from acting in a way that would put you at risk." He said.

It was strange to see a man who was usually so cool and calm be on the verge of yelling at me. I pushed down my fear.

"I understand your anger but..." He didn't let me finish.

"I do not think you understand anything. You are but a child on this earth compared to the creature that has your sister. If you want her back alive and unharmed, you must also be unharmed!" He said the last with such intensity that I shuddered and pulled as far back from him as I could while sitting on a counter.

"Marek I..." but again, there was nothing I could say or rather nothing he wanted me to say.

"No! Your words are poison. They destroy the thinking of skilled Guardians and make them but pawns in your game. It will stop here and now, or we leave your sister to her fate." He said with venom.

Tears fell silently down my cheeks, but there was nothing I could say to refute his statement. James knew better than to let me go in that warehouse, and I convinced him otherwise. It was my fault entirely that James was in trouble and that Marek was so angry.

"I'm sorry. I didn't, I should have..." but there was nothing I could say.

Marek moved toward me and cradled my face with his hands. I could feel the tension in his fingers. He could so easily snap my neck and be done with my drama and problems. I could see it in his eyes. I braced for it as if it was what should happen.

He shocked me again by pulling me into his arms. It was so gentle compared to the hot flood of emotions I could feel coming from him.

He cradled my head into his neck and whispered into my ear. "You are my poison too."

He struck so quickly I didn't have time to defend myself. I felt his teeth enter my skin, followed by an instant burn that made it feel like my neck would catch fire. I cried out in pain only to be pulled out of pain and thrown into bliss. Each swallow of my blood down his throat had an echoing pulse in my body that could only be described as near orgasmic.

My arms moved from trying to push him away to pull him closer to me. I wrapped my legs around his waist, and he lifted me off the countertop. I felt him carrying me but didn't know where, and I really didn't care. Distantly I felt my back push into something soft followed by the weight of his body on mine. I ground my hips into his and felt an answering thrust from him.

Our clothes were in the way, but I couldn't seem to move enough to take them off. The pleasure changed shortly after, and I had a moment of clarity. A vision of me lying dead with my family weeping beside me gave me enough strength to try to push Marek away. He didn't budge and sucked so hard on my neck that I almost wanted him to keep going.

With my last ounce of strength, I placed my hands on his chest and told him to stop. His drinking slowed, and I realized that his teeth were no longer in my neck. I didn't waste any time. I summoned my power and unleashed it into his chest.

Marek flew from the bed and hit the wall. I realized after using my power that I was too weak to move. I had lost too much blood.

"Do you understand now?" he asked.

A cold coil of truth pooled in my abdomen. This wasn't Marek going out of control. This was my punishment. It wasn't the first time he chose a demonstration to make me see something.

"Yes," I said through gritted teeth.

He walked over and sat beside me on the bed. "Do you have the strength to fight me now?"

I shook my head no, and he smiled.

"So, if I decided to take advantage of the situation, you could not stop me?" He said with a wicked smile.

"You know I can't," I said with gritted teeth.

He stroked a path from my temple to my breast, and God help me, but my body wanted him to keep going. My body was still thrumming with desire from before.

"This is what they can do to you. This," Marek said, running the tip of his finger around my nipple, "is why you need me."

Tears fell from my eyes as I used the last of my strength to push on his chest.

"This is why you should stay away from me," I said and funneled all my power into that one hand.

He was not only pushed off the bed, but we would have to explain a hole in the wall. He laid in a heap, not moving, and I was able to pull my phone out of my pocket. I texted James that I needed help and hoped that he would arrive before Marek woke up.

Chapter Four

My vision swam as I sat up to get a better look at Marek. He still wasn't moving as I struggled to prop myself against the headboard. I didn't feel as bad as I thought I should and almost believed I could stand. I strained my ears for any sign of breathing, do vampires breathe? Or any sign of movement that might tell me Marek was conscious.

What I heard was the door to the hotel room open, and James yell my name.

"I'm in the bedroom," I said with a much too raspy voice that almost gave out.

He was at the door in a blink of an eye. I felt too terrible to be shocked by it.

"What happened?" He asked, rushing to the bed.

He stopped before he got there when he saw Marek's half-hidden body. Part of him was actually inside the wall.

"He attacked me," I said, fighting off angry tears.

James stepped over Marek cautiously then sat on the bed to gather me in his arms. He kept looking at Marek as if he would explode at any moment.

"Tell me what happened." He said, lifting my chin so he could see in my eyes.

As I started to speak, Marek stirred. "She will do no such thing."

Marek sat up slowly, rubbing his chest where I had used my power on him. I flinched but stayed where I was. I knew I could defend myself. If I could knock out a vampire as powerful as

Marek, I could do anything I needed to survive.

"I want you out of here," I said and was proud that my voice didn't waver.

Marek looked at me then at James and smiled. "You can be sure that she will be better able to defend herself next time."

My confusion was temporarily shattered by the sight of a burn mark the shape of a hand on Marek's shirt. It obviously hurt because he touched it tenderly.

"What did you do?" James asked quietly.

"Nothing she did not need to learn." He said, then tugged off his shirt.

I'm not sure if I was more shocked by the perfect imprint of my hand on his skin or by the sight of his naked chest. The view was better than I expected, and the sudden surge of lust made me uncomfortable.

Marek met my gaze and smiled. Leave it to him to make an already uncomfortable moment even more uneasy. I didn't know where to look after that until I met James' gaze. He was looking at me like I was an alien. That's when I got mad.

"What?" I shouted at James.

He lifted his hands and backed away from me. Marek just smirked and leaned against the unbroken section of the wall crossing his arms casually across his stomach. A stomach that was tight with well-defined muscles. The smugness on his face made me angrier, and I jumped off the bed to come at him. I was there before I had a chance to think about what I was doing.

Before I could do anything, Marek said, "You recovered quickly."

There were so many things that I wanted to say to him, but nothing came out. All I could do was look at the shiny red burn marring his beautiful chest. The rest of his skin was creamy white and smooth, but the mark drew my eye more than anything else.

Before I could stop myself, I reached for it. Marek flinched slightly, and I held my hand about an inch away from his chest. The mark was a perfect match to my hand, and I could feel the heat coming from it. I lowered my fingers onto it and felt the shiny welt. It was warm to the touch.

Marek's breathing became ragged, and I met his gaze. Touching it was hurting him, but he didn't say a word to make me stop. His stomach muscles were clenched tightly, and his fists were balled.

"You could tell me to stop," I whispered.

His lips turned up on one side in a half-smile, but he didn't say anything. I lifted my hand from his chest, but he stopped me by grabbing it. His hand clamped around my wrist like a vice, and it reminded me of the unbelievable strength he possessed.

"Do not move." He said.

"But I'm hurting you," I said, confused.

Our voices were soft, but James was close enough to hear us if he wanted to. Marek's eyes darted toward James then back to me. He tightened his grip on my hand briefly then let it go. I dropped my hand to my side and took a step back. He didn't move or say a word. His reticence confused me.

"Why did you do it?" I asked.

The smile left his face so quickly I thought I may have imagined it in the first place. It was with a blank look that he spoke to me.

"You must learn to control your powers and resist the compulsion of a vampire. What better way to learn than with a real-life situation?" He said.

I blinked back the tears that were threatening to overtake my resolve. Crying would not be appreciated by Marek, and I needed him to see strength from me right then.

"An exercise could have been done with my knowledge and in a safer way than what just happened," I said and was proud that my voice didn't crack.

My fingers traced the wound on my neck and found that it was mostly healed. No puncture marks were evident, just a trail of blood was left to show what had happened. Marek caught my hand and brought my fingers to his lips.

"If I had not made it safe, you would not be standing here now with nothing but a smear of blood on your neck." He said, then licked my fingers clean of blood.

I should have been appalled and disgusted by it, but my traitorous body throbbed in pleasure, remembering how it had felt to have him drawing my blood into his mouth. I recalled the feel of his tongue as it encouraged the flow and how his lips moved in time with his swallows. The thrust of his hips against my body, and the strength of his arms as he held me made my entire body hum with the memory.

I was ready to throw myself back into his arms. It was that knowledge that allowed me to pull my hand free and turn my back on him. James looked at me and the expression on his face was one of disappointment and pain.

He moved toward the door and said, "I'll leave so you can get cleaned up."

He closed the door when he left, leaving me alone with Marek again. His action was reckless for a Guardian, and I realized that I knew that only because Marek was thinking it at that moment.

I felt Marek move behind me, and I froze as his hands touched my shoulders. He pushed my hair away from my neck.

"What are you doing?" I asked him.

"You do need to get cleaned up." He said then started to lick my neck.

I stayed still and tried not to enjoy the feel of his tongue on my skin. My body wasn't listening to my mind, and my brain wasn't able to protest.

"I can clean it off myself," I said but didn't step away from him or push him away.

"You could," he said as he licked a path up to my jaw, "but you would have to remove your clothing."

Looking down, I saw that my shirt had blood on it too. How did I not notice that before?

"My shirt has to come off anyway," I said.

Marek pressed closer against my back and moved his hands to my waist. His fingers found their way to the edge of my t-shirt, and they slid under it so slowly that it was a few minutes before I realized it had happened.

"Then, take it off," Marek whispered.

I moved my arms, and he pulled up on the fabric at the same time. Within seconds he had my shirt off and turned me around with my hands resting on his chest. His skin was warm, and the mark I had made was almost gone.

"It's almost healed," I said, moving my fingers to the few marks that remained.

"The blood of a powerful Seer can do many wondrous things." He said.

A stab of pain in my chest from the thought of how he used me sobered me up. This intimacy between us needed to end. I didn't have to be a Seer to know any sort of relationship with this man would be suicide.

"It wasn't just a lesson," I snapped and tried to pull away from him.

He pulled me back against his body so hard that I lost my breath. My breasts and stomach met his bare skin, and molten warmth that felt like hot caramel sliding down my body hit me instantly. It was exquisite and yet painful at the same time. This wasn't a man I wanted to be attracted to.

"No, but you do not wish to know the reasons for the things I do. You would not be able to cope with that sort of truth...yet." He said, then released me and left the room.

My body shivered from the sudden chill, and I wrapped my arms around myself. I needed to get myself cleaned up but couldn't bring myself to move. There was something about the way Marek spoke to me that triggered something in my subconscious. It was a part I couldn't access directly, but it triggered my power none the less.

The sincerity of Marek's words brought with them a vision that I didn't want, but like any Seer, I was a slave to the power. I had enough presence of mind to reach out for the wall to steady myself.

As my vision came, I found myself standing in a large room full of people I didn't know. They all moved with a similar grace that I had come to expect from Marek, which meant they were most likely vampires. I expected to feel panic while in the presence of so many otherworldly creatures, but instead, I felt calm and protected.

A voice next to me startled me into turning to see who it was. Marek stood in a pose that could only be considered regal and spoke with a blond man of a height that was at least four inches more than Marek's own height. His hair was long but not feminine at all, and he kept nodding in such a way that felt like a bow.

I couldn't understand any of the words they were using since it was a language I didn't know, but what I could surmise was that this tall blond was going to do a favor for Marek. He was happy to do it from the way he was reacting, and I was more than a little curious as to why. Marek pulled me to his side, and my shock at the physical contact mixed with the blur of the vision had me wondering why I was experiencing this.

My eyes drifted around the room, looking for anyone I might know but came up empty. The only person in this room that I was familiar with was Marek.

"Alone at last," Marek said, and I turned to look at him.

He was smiling in that way that told me he was pleased to be looking at me. It was a smile I had only seen once before, and my breath caught at the emotion that poured through our bond. It felt like love, but that wasn't possible. A vampire doesn't love. They manipulate. Marek had proven that to me just moments ago.

The vision shattered, and I was once again in the hotel room. I stumbled a bit and walked into the bathroom. Instead of a shower, I drew a bath so that I wouldn't have to stand longer than necessary. My balance wasn't precisely right after the attack or what Marek called a lesson. The thought sent a surge of anger through me.

After stripping off the rest of my clothes, I got in the tub and started to wash. Most of the blood was cleaned off me, and the thought of how it had been done made my body quake. I shook off the feeling and relaxed into the bubbles. I had more things to consider than how a vampire could elicit a sexual response from me.

My mind got stuck on that vision and how it didn't seem to have any relation to our current search for my sister. Marek was very comfortable with all those people, and it appeared that even I had a place there, which was quite odd. I couldn't imagine a time when I would be comfortable around that many vampires, especially since I didn't think that many even existed.

My dream journal is where I would file that vision. I used to write down all the dreams I had so that I wouldn't lose any detail after the initial vision faded. Now I use it to write down all my visions, awake or asleep. The last notation I had made was about my sister.

She was in hell with an evil vampire, and I was in a posh hotel having lustful feelings. I should be the one in hell.

A knock at the door made me jump and kicked my heart to race. I called out instead of going to the door. I didn't want to be naked in front of either of the men in this hotel room.

"What do you want?" I yelled.

"Are you okay?" James asked from behind the bathroom door.

"I'm fine," I said with more confidence than I felt.

"Are you sure?" He asked.

I got out of the tub and opened the door a crack. "I'm fine, James."

His eyes were filled with worry, and it might have been my imagination, but I thought he was on the verge of tears.

"Are you really?" he asked.

I pushed the door open and walked back to the tub. As I sunk back into the water, I remembered the last time I had been in the bathtub with James in the room. It was after I shot my boyfriend, ex-boyfriend now. Nikko is a werewolf, but I didn't know that at the time. He had lost control and started coming after me. If the Guardians hadn't been there that night, I might have been killed.

James was important to me, and if what he saw happen earlier changed things, it would hurt.

"Thank you," James said from the doorway.

"For what?" I asked.

"For letting me in," he said.

I turned to look at him. He looked scared. I reached my hand out to him.

"Stay in here with me?" I asked and hoped like hell he would do it. I really didn't want to be alone despite my earlier behavior.

"Em, that's not a good idea," James said, drawing back out the door.

"Please, James. I don't want to be alone right now." I implored him.

James wouldn't look at me, but he also didn't leave the room.

"James," I said with more urgency.

He looked out toward the living area. Whatever he saw decided things.

"For a bit," James said.

He walked over and sat next to the tub. He took my hand in his, and I felt better instantly. I needed his support.

"Thank you," I said, smiling up at him.

He was quiet for a while before saying, "you exchanged blood with him."

It was a simple statement, but it brought me to panic. James had said that having Marek take my blood after I took his blood would mean something.

"What does it mean?" I asked, trying to hide how terrified that statement made me.

"Do you feel different?" He asked.

"No, why didn't you answer the question?" I asked.

James dropped my hand and stepped toward the door. He looked hurt, but somehow it amplified my panic.

"It isn't my place to discuss that with you, Ember." He said, then left the room.

Although I was in a tub full of hot water at that moment, I felt cold. I needed James in a way I didn't understand until that moment. He was the humanity and warmth now that I had shut Nikko out of my life. James was starting to fill that hole for me, but Marek complicated it all.

Thinking of Nikko brought a tear to my eye, and before I knew what I was doing, I had connected with him, mind to mind.

"Shit, Ember, what are you doing?" Nikko said, out of breath.

"Sorry, I was just thinking about you, and then there you were," I said, confused. How did I do that?

"Are you okay?" He asked, sounding concerned.

"I'm okay. Well, sort of anyway." I said.

He was at the gym. That explained the heavy breathing.

"You could have called," he said, laughing.

"I'm sorry," I said, pulling away.

"Wait! Don't go." He said.

I could feel his love pouring through the connection. He still loved me deeply. More tears fell down my face.

"You're crying." He said softly.

"Yes," I admitted.

"And you reached out to me?" He asked, tentatively.

I could feel him trying to be gentle, but he was so happy inside it actually brought a small smile to my face.

"I did, but I'm not sure how," I said truthfully.

"I'm sure your Guardian can help you figure that out, but I'm glad you did. I miss you, Em," He said.

I cringed at the mention of my Guardians, they are both acting strangely, and I needed someone I trusted. Although he hurt me, I realized I still trusted Nikko.

"They aren't making things easy for me. I just needed someone I knew to calm me a bit. Thank you." I said.

"I love you, Em. I'm here any time you need me." He said, and I believed he was sincere.

"I shouldn't have reached out to you. I'm not sure how or why I did." I said, and I could feel the hurt coming from Nikko.

"No matter what has happened, I will always be here for you." He said.

"I know," I said, confident that it was true.

"But Em, maybe next time you can call me? I almost dropped a dumbbell on my foot." He chuckled.

"Sorry..." I started.

"No, no, Em, it's okay. Please don't apologize. I can't believe you can do this, but I'm happy you did that you connected to me." He said with such warmth, more tears dropped from my eyes.

"Thanks, Nikko," I said glad that I wasn't really talking because I

would have had a hard time forming words while crying.

"Where are you? I know you quit, but my father told the team you took a leave of absence from work. I've been worried." He asked.

"It's hard to explain," I said, trying to think of what to tell him. It was interesting that his dad didn't say I quit, which I had.

"You can tell me anything." He assured me.

"I don't want to burden you, Nikko. I should leave you alone." I said.

"Hey, Em, call me later?" He asked.

"Thanks, Nikko, take care," I said and broke the connection.

Being in his head was eye-opening. He did still love me, and more than I thought. I wasn't sure I should be leaning on him right now, so I hadn't answered his question. We had broken up. I couldn't talk to him about issues with James and Marek. It felt too much like talking to my ex about my love life. That was a sobering thought. Was this my love life?

I left the bathroom clean in body but not in mind. I sat on the bed in a towel and pondered what my life had become. I went from a life I loved with the man I loved to chaos and supernatural powers I couldn't comprehend, let alone control. I just connected mind to mind to my ex-boyfriend who cheated on me. My life had become insane.

Chapter Five

"**E**mber Summers, you need to pull your head out of your ass," Sam said.

I sighed. Sam was right, but I still didn't want to hear it.

"I know, I know!" I said, agreeing that I shouldn't be contacting Nikko.

"That man probably thinks you are going to get back together with him. It's sad, really." She said.

"I couldn't help it. I accidentally dialed Nikko's number and couldn't bear to hang up on him." I said, not telling her it was actually a mind to mind type of call. She would never understand that.

"Butt dialing him is no excuse. I know you have a hard time letting people go, but you have to give the man some time to reflect on what he did before you act like friends again." She said.

"I hear you," I said.

"You have plenty of other people who love you, including guys who would kill to date you. What about James? I know you are attracted to him." She said.

"It's complicated," I said, thinking about how it was even more complicated with what happened with Marek. I hadn't thought about James romantically in a long time. Something changed.

"You know the best way to get over a guy is to jump on another one?" She said, laughing.

"You mean literally jump on one?" I laughed.

"Yes, that is just like me," I said sarcastically.

She was behaving silly, which was making me laugh, and it was exactly what I needed. There were so many intense emotions going through my head, having a moment to chat with my best girlfriend was a much-needed event.

"I'm just saying that if the opportunity presents itself don't overthink it. Let it happen." Sam said.

"I'll keep it under advisement," I said.

"Although Greg will be disappointed if you find another man. The two of you have chemistry, and Todd and I love you both." She said wistfully.

"I know Sam," I said, feeling a tinge of guilt.

Greg lives with Sam and Todd. They have been roommates since college and the best of friends to each other and to me. Greg and I flirt like we should be dating. The problem is that neither of us is ever single at the same time, so we have never actually dated.

After what happened with Nikko, I was reluctant to ruin another great friendship. Greg was off-limits for now. If it ever happened between us great, otherwise I was glad to count him as a good friend.

"I love you, Em. Take a breath and do something fun. Promise me you will take care of yourself?" She said.

"I promise Sam. Love you too. Send my love to Todd and Greg. I'll call you later in the week." I said and hung up the phone.

I thought about calling my parents to give them an update on Nat but chickened out and sent a quick text to my dad instead. There was nothing new to report, but I had to let them know I was still on it.

I missed my friends, but I had to get my head on straight and think of my sister. I could feel a constant unease anytime I thought of her. I pushed aside my feelings and went to find James. We had a date to train today, and I wanted to get it done so we could move forward.

Marek, James, and I got in the rental car and headed out of the city. If all went well with this training session, I expected to be included in taking down the warehouse where my sister was being held and getting her back. I'd had enough of the attack style training Marek preferred.

It turned out that when the three of us were in the car, James had to ride in the back seat. His long legs were scrunched up, and he didn't look happy at all to be there. I guess when your boss is a vampire, and he claims the woman you are guarding is a higher rank than you, there is no other seating arrangement. Poor James...

We drove out beyond civilization near the White Tank Mountains. Marek avoided any hiking trails or signs of life pulling onto a dirt road that led us to no road at all. I was surprised the rental car made it all the way out there without getting stuck.

"We will start with your kinetic power. Up until now, you have only used it when threatened, but it has been inconsistent." Marek said.

"I think I know where to start," I said and pushed with my power against Marek's chest.

He was pushed backward but not far. He stayed on his feet and laughed.

"Is that all you have for me?" He said, smiling an evil grin.

"Honestly, I was hoping for more," I said, frowning.

I really did think I was going to throw him down on his back at the least. After what I had done before, I had much higher hopes.

"Maybe she needs to tap into her emotions?" James offered.

"Indeed," Marek said and motioned for me to try again.

I took a deep breath and thought about how angry I had been with Marek yesterday and how scared I was about him taking my blood. A surge of unease went through my body, and I used it to push more power into my command.

Marek was knocked over and landed inelegantly on his ass. I couldn't help my laugh.

He was up and in my face in an instant. I tried to push him again, but before I could, he had me on my ass. He was the one laughing now.

"Not fast enough, Ember. You must use more power and make it hurt. Pushing a vampire down only delays them. It will not incapacitate." Marek said.

He held me down on the ground, his hand pushing down on my chest to keep me where I was. I could tell from our bond that he wasn't going to go easy or worry about hurting me. He was sure that our blood exchange would keep me from being hurt too badly. Interesting revelation...

I tried to pull more information from Marek, but he shook his head no and shut down our connection.

"No cheating, Ember," He said with a growl.

I pushed him off me and got to my feet before he got up. As he ran toward me again, I didn't hesitate and pushed more power into him. He flew backward ten feet and landed on his knees.

"Better but not good enough," He snarled and ran at me again.

He moved faster than I could see, and I hit the ground, my breath whooshing out of my lungs all at once. It hurt...bad. I laid there stunned for a moment, and Marek took that as an opportunity to fully incapacitate me. He had me on my stomach with my arms pulled painfully behind my back quicker than I could imagine.

"If I wanted to kill you, you would already be dead." He whispered into my ear.

My body shivered at the light touch of air against my ear. Marek had his knee in my back with my arms pulled up at a severe enough angle he could have snapped the bones with a flick of his wrist. Somehow my body still thought his whisper was pleasant. My body could suck it!

I screamed, throwing my power back at him and adding a little something extra. Just pushing him back wasn't working, so I tried pinning him down like he did to me.

"Ember, no!" James yelled.

It was too late, I had Marek down and jumped onto him, trying to grab his arms. I should have known it was stupid. Marek's elbow connected with my head, and my vision went black.

"Em, can you hear me?" James said.

He sounded far away, but as my brain woke back up, I realized my mistake. I thought Marek wouldn't hurt me. I was wrong.

"Shit, why did you do that?" I yelled, trying to find Marek.

"Coddling you will not teach you to fight." He said.

James offered me a hand. I took it, and although dizzy, I got back on my feet.

"If I may, I'll show her some basics of self-defense. She doesn't know much yet." James offered Marek.

He inclined his head to James in the affirmative and stepped back to watch the show.

"Let's go over a few basics before you get knocked out again," James said, glaring at Marek.

He showed me how to stand so that my weight was balanced and where to look. He also showed me how to make a fist so I wouldn't break my hand if I hit someone.

"Now punch me but push the power through your elbow instead of thinking about your fist. When it comes from your bicep and shoulder it will make your punch land harder." He said.

I threw the punch and it landed right in his stomach. James grunted slightly, but it didn't really phase him.

"Sorry," I said.

"You need to punch harder, Em," He said, motioning me to punch again.

"I don't want to hurt you. It's easier to hit Marek knowing I can't really hurt him." I said.

"You won't hurt me either." He assured me.

I looked at him doubtfully but threw another punch. This time I trickled in some kinetic power with it, and it knocked him back about a foot.

"Sorry!" I said, cringing at what I just did.

James shook his head like it was nothing.

"Let's try a few other punches." He said. "Landing a punch is one thing but targeting a weak point on the body will make your punch a lot more effective."

James said to target the eyes, throat, stomach, kidneys/liver, or groin. Those are areas that, if hit, double the pain and increase the likelihood of incapacitation. He had me practice aiming for those spots (I was careful not to injure him regardless of what he said), and I found that my aim was actually pretty good.

He showed me a series of punches and jabs and had me repeat them over and over until sweat started to pour down my face.

"Good, now let's add in some kicks. A front kick is good for keeping your opponent in front of you and far enough away that they are less likely to be able to throw a punch. You can also use this one for a groin kick." He said and demonstrated the technique for a good front kick.

After practicing that kick for a while and trying not to kick him in the groin, we moved on to other kicks.

"Your shin can be as powerful as a baseball bat when used as the striking point in a sidekick. Combine that with hitting the liver or kidneys, and you can drop a large male with little effort. Watch me use that on Marek, then you try to kick me." He said and proceeded to kick Marek how he said.

Marek found it amusing that he was the dummy in the demo, but his face showed no sign of it. I only knew because I could read his emotions.

"Your turn Em. I'll let you kick me once or twice, then I'll start blocking. Try to kick me hard enough to drop me to the ground." James said.

"I don't think that is a good idea," I said.

"I'm tougher than you think." He said with a wink motioning me to begin.

I took a few soft kicks with my right leg aiming for his side then he started blocking me. I threw in a few punches and jabs that he taught me between kicks. I landed a few good ones that made me wince.

"Harder Ember. You won't know how much force you need unless you go all out. You won't hurt me. It's okay." He said with a smile.

"Famous last words James," I said.

I kicked him and punched him and then landed a perfect kick. My shin connected with his left kidney, and he fell to the ground.

"Wow," I said, shocked.

Then I dropped to the ground pulling him onto his back.

"Ow," He said.

"I thought I couldn't hurt you?" I said, concerned.

"I'll be fine in a minute." He said, smiling.

"Why are you smiling? I just kicked you in the kidney." I said.

"That's why I'm smiling," he said with pride. "You're a quick learner."

"I'm sorry," I said and helped him up.

"More hitting, less talking," Marek said.

I looked up at the vampire, and he motioned me to come at him. Hitting him would be a lot more fun but try as I might, I couldn't catch him. He moved way too fast.

"Use your Sight, Ember. You can anticipate where he will move and be there before he even knows where he is going." James said.

James was holding his side. I felt better seeing him upright, but the distraction cost me with Marek. He punched me in the stomach, and I doubled over with the pain.

"Shit!" I yelped.

"This is more than training Ember. This is your life on the line." Marek said, scolding me.

"Okay, okay," I said, trying to stand back up straight.

"Use what James showed you but put all your power into each movement instead of physical strength. When you fight a vampire, you cannot get in close like you did with James. If you get close, you die." Marek said.

I thought back to when I had faced Viktor Ivanov not that long ago. I had kept him at a distance for a while, but when he moved in close, I did almost die. A flash of searing pain on my chest and throat dropped me to the ground. I could hear Viktor laughing and feel the blood dripping from my wounds. I had summoned all that I had to take him down. I thought I killed him, but he was alive and taunting me. Tears fell from my face. The pain was more than I could take. It was going to kill me.

"*Milaya moya*, he is not here. You are not hurt." Marek had me gathered up in his arms within seconds.

"I can feel it," I said, my teeth chattering like I was losing too much blood.

"Feel *me*," Marek demanded. "Listen to *me*."

I clung to the sound of his voice and felt his presence. It was so intense I could feel him through my entire body and mind. He had saved me then, and he was saving me now. Our bond was strong. I could feel his concern and his, not love, but something like it.

"And me," James said, brushing the hair out of my face.

I opened my eyes and saw then both leaning over me, caring for me. I took a deep breath and cleared my head of the memory.

"Why did that just happen?" I asked, tears still trailing down my cheeks.

Marek said, "Your power is growing, and you slipped into the past."

"I what?" I said, sitting up.

"As a Seer, you can look not only into the future but into the past as well. You got caught in a memory." He said.

"That is not something I ever want to do again," I said, shaking my head and clearing those thoughts out.

"You may not have a choice. Ember, you must learn to recognize when you are in a vision so you can pull yourself out. If we had not been here, you might not have made it out." He said.

The thought of getting stuck in a memory of the past made me shudder with fear. It was terrifying to be pulled somewhere against my will.

"I think she needs a break from training," James said.

Marek gave James a dirty look. It was clear he didn't feel the same way. Marek was of the mind that pushing harder made you stronger. Weakness was for when you were dead.

James didn't back down, though. "You can't push her like she is a vampire whether she has had your blood or not."

The look Marek gave me told me he wouldn't be cowed into going easy on me. I hadn't even been the one to say it, but somehow, I got the blame.

"I'm fine now, James," I said, grabbing his hand to assure him.

He squeezed my hand and shook his head. "I don't want you to get hurt."

"I'll be okay, James," I assured him.

He tilted my head up, so I looked him in the eye. I thought he was going to kiss me or something, but then he pulled back.

"Every mistake in training saves me from making the same mistake in a real fight. I'll be okay." I told James and turned to face Marek.

Chapter Six

Many hours later, I was regretting telling James I would be fine. My thigh was bruised deeply, and I couldn't put much weight on it. My eye was swelling shut and dripping blood from being slammed face-first into the dirt too many times to count. I was sure I had a few broken ribs and some internal injuries, not to mention having blacked out a few times.

I was exhausted after a full day of training but clung to the fact that I had kicked Marek's ass as much as he kicked mine. I thought that was a win, especially when his injuries looked as bad as mine. His were healing on their own, though. He didn't need the healing treatments that I would need.

On the ride back to the hotel, James worked on my wounds as best he could while glaring daggers at the back of Marek's head the whole time. Some of my more severe injuries would need a little time to heal, but the minor ones he fixed quickly and efficiently.

James said vampire blood would be the only help for what was left. I could tell that it didn't make him happy.

I leaned into James in the backseat and tried to hide the pain every time we hit a bump. Marek kept glancing back at me in the mirror because I couldn't keep the pain from him. I would have to work on that, especially if this bond between us was as permanent as I suspected.

"Is there any chance we could stop for something to eat? I'm starving." I said, catching Marek's eye in the rear-view mirror.

His eyes crinkled up briefly, then he nodded. He must have remembered that I was human and required food. He dropped James and me off at a restaurant down the street from the hotel and left. It was abrupt and confused me but I shook it off and followed James from the car.

James took my hand, and we walked in to find a table. It was a small place with about six tables. We sat down, and the waitress came over to get our drink order.

"Water for me. Thank you." I said, taking the menu and searching for something that looked good.

James ordered a beer, and I raised an eyebrow at him.

"Alcohol doesn't affect me." He said.

Curious.

"It's good to be out of that car and alone with you for a change," I said, smiling.

He smiled, but there was a lack of joy in his eyes.

"You aren't happy,' I said.

"I just watched you get your ass repeatedly kicked and had to heal your wounds. That is not my idea of a good time." He said.

"I'll be fine," I assured him.

"I know you will be, but I'm cautious." He said.

"Why?" I asked, trying to see what was bothering him.

"You belong to him now. It changes everything." He said.

The look on his face was serious, but I didn't understand it.

"I don't belong to anyone," I said defensively.

"Whether you agreed to it verbally or not makes no difference. I can't ignore that you let Marek take your blood. A lot of it from how well your wounds healed on their own." He said, avoiding my eyes.

I hadn't realized it myself, but the cuts and minor bruises had healed faster than I thought possible even with healing treatments from James.

"Hey," I said, grabbing his hand. "It was a demonstration. You know how Marek is. He rather force me to face something than talk to me about it."

He gripped my hand back, which was a good sign. I could tell he didn't believe me though.

"I know what Marek is, and there is always a reason he does something. That incident after the warehouse was more than training Ember. I think you know that." He said.

I thought back to what Marek had said to me before he bit me. That I was his poison. Admitting to James that I thought Marek had feelings for me didn't seem wise.

"Maybe," I agreed. "But I don't think it was planned."

"Not possible. Marek is one of the oldest creatures I've ever met, and he is always in control." James insisted.

I didn't argue with him. He knew more about vampires than I did, and I had to trust his judgment. Marek didn't strike me as a being led by his passions anyway.

"Speaking of Marek, the two of you seem to be getting along better today," I said.

James shook his head and sighed.

"He didn't punish me for what happened at the warehouse if that's what you mean. I don't know why exactly, but I think he understands." James responded.

"What do you mean?" I asked, unsure of what he was talking about.

"He knows you are irresistible." He said, smiling.

"Stop. I am not." I said.

"You are. I'm undone simply by the look in your eyes sometimes. Then your body touches mine and..." James shook his head.

"What are you saying?" I asked, laughing.

"Then it's like you've put a spell on me. I'll do anything you say." He said with a straight face.

"You can't be serious, James," I said, smiling, but he didn't look amused.

"Your friend Todd said to me one time that you had no idea the effect you had on men. It's true. You bewitch everyone you meet and walk away, blissfully unaware." James said.

"If that were true, I surely would have noticed. I'm not completely blind." I said.

"No, you are not, but you can be naive." He said gently.

His words stung as if he meant I wasn't smart enough to see it. I pushed it down and tried to ignore it.

"I guess it's a good thing you have my back then," I said.

"My duty is to your safety." He said, smiling.

"I'm glad," I said.

I smiled and withdrew my hand as the waitress arrived with our drinks. I watched him as he ordered. He isn't your typical blue-eyed blonde. James' features are more masculine and sexier than any boy next door type. He had grown a scruff of a beard lately, and it looked good on him. His hair was disheveled, but it was in a wind-tossed sexy way. It was distracting and beautiful at the same time.

The waitress cleared her throat, and I reluctantly looked away from James to give her my order. When I looked back, he was smiling, and this time it reached his eyes. He was delighted that I had been staring at him. It reminded me of the first time I had seen him. In a room full of people, my eyes landed on him. There was no one else to see. Why hadn't I remembered that the past few days?

When we got back to the hotel room, I could feel Marek's temper simmering under the surface, but he didn't say anything. He had looked at James and me for a moment and then looked away.

Marek had a bunch of papers covering the coffee table, and he was drawing something on them with a red marker. They looked like architectural plans, but I couldn't tell of what.

"What are those?" I asked, walking over to him.

"The plans to the warehouse you found." He said, leaning back so I could see them better.

"Where my sister is?" I asked, knowing that was the place.

Excitement at finally being able to get her back filled my thoughts.

"If she is there, yes." He said, clearly implying that she might not be there after all.

"Where did you get them?" I asked curiously.

He looked at me like I was an idiot. Maybe I was.

"I requested them as soon as you saw vampires in the building. They arrived earlier today." He said.

I wondered how they had arrived and with whom. Marek lifted his eyes to mine, and I understood that he had ways he would not explain to me now. The how or why wasn't important anyway. All I needed to know was where Natalie was and how we were going to get her back.

"What have you learned?" James asked, sitting down on the floor across from Marek.

"There are three levels below ground. There is a wing likely to hold prisoners and another section that could be used for either more prisoners or as a stronghold to protect residents." Marek said, pointing out each location on the plans.

"You think Natalie is in one of those locations," James stated.

It wasn't a question. Marek doesn't waste time on a conversation. He was telling James the plan, but I didn't understand it.

"How do we get in?" I asked, looking over the entry and exit points.

"I will test their defenses tonight then decide on a strategy,"

Marek said.

"And we go with you," I said, indicating James and me.

"No, Ember. You and James stay here tonight." Marek said.

"Why? We need to go in and get her. If we all go, we have a better chance of getting Nat." I said.

Marek shook his head no. "First, I test their defenses, then I decide what we do next. I will not risk your life before I know how well they are equipped to defend themselves. You made progress today, but you are still learning. I will not put you in danger unnecessarily."

"I need to go, Marek," I said with spiking anger.

"You will stay with James this evening. I will return after assessing the risks." He said and pulled the warehouse plans off the table.

"No! I have to go with you." I insisted.

"You will stay here like I said. No more, Ember!" Marek said with such vehemence that I sat down hard on the couch.

Getting the vampire angry was stupid, and if the look on James' face told me anything, I needed to shut my mouth. Tears welled up in my eyes, but they didn't fall until Marek left the room. The sound of the door slamming shut had such a sense of finality to it that I broke down.

James was there in an instant holding me and rocking me. I could feel Marek getting further away, and no matter how many times James stroked my hair, I felt like Natalie wasn't coming home because of it. He was leaving me behind when he should be taking me with him. We wouldn't get Natalie back unless I was there. And Marek wouldn't trust me to survive it.

"He's making a mistake," I said.

"He knows what he's doing. Viktor won't have your sister in a place without fortifications. We have to know what we are dealing with before going in." James said.

61

His argument was reasonable. Had I been an ordinary human, I probably would have trusted what he said. Unfortunately, I am not ordinary, and every instinct I had was screaming at me to go with Marek. Something terrible was going to happen if I didn't.

"I can feel it, James. I need to be there." I said through gritted teeth.

"He won't change his mind. He never does." He said, trying again to soothe me.

I looked into his eyes and let the rest of my tears fall. They fell because of my sister. They fell for what she was going to have to endure because of an arrogant vampire who wouldn't listen to me. What good was it to have powers if I couldn't use them to save my own sister?

My anger rose to the surface as I stared into the beautiful blue eyes of my Guardian. He was going to keep me from my sister too. He would follow Marek's orders and keep me in that hotel room because he thought that was the right thing to do. James was in my way too.

"Marek doesn't know what his actions will affect," I said.

James shook his head. "We will wait for Marek then put together a plan for getting your sister back. Rushing in without recon would be too dangerous. We will get her back after he checks things out."

I took a deep breath and made a decision that might make James hate me, but it had to be done. I put my hands on his chest and closed my eyes. Letting my anger go was hard, but with every breath, I was able to release a little bit more. This wouldn't work if I couldn't control my emotions.

James must have felt the tension leaving my body because he lifted my chin. I opened my eyes and gave him a small smile. He leaned his forehead against mine.

"It will be okay," He whispered.

I nodded my head yes, as if I agreed. After a deep intake of breath,

I let go of the last traces of my anger. We had time before Marek would do anything. The sun hadn't fallen yet. Marek wouldn't make a move until the cover of night; I was sure of it.

"At least we are finally alone," I said.

James pulled me in closer to him, wrapping his arms around me. I let him hold me for a while before I looked up at him.

He brushed the hair back from my face and ran his fingers along my jawline. It felt good, but it didn't make my heart race like I thought it should. That confused me because I had been attracted to him since the first time I saw him. If anyone could make a woman's libido rise, it would be the man in front of me.

"So much has changed since we first met," I said, thinking back to the way we used to flirt and how I was so attracted to him.

Maybe it was a matter of wanting what I couldn't have. I was dating Nikko then, and it was exciting to have attention from a handsome man like James. I didn't think I needed a lot of excitement in my life. Now that I have it, I'm not sure what life would be like without it or if I would want to live without it.

"You have been through a lot, but you've handled it well." He said, stroking my back.

"You make me feel safe," I said and wished it could be more.

James is the type of man fathers could trust to treat their daughters well. He is genuine and kind.

"I want to want you," I said, looking into his eyes.

"I know you do." He said and gave me a sad smile.

He tucked my head in under his chin and hugged me tighter. It felt safe and warm and helped me calm down more. He was becoming a big brother to me.

"How about you go get cleaned up, and I'll order us some dinner?" James said.

I nodded my head yes and got up. I was sore from training, so it was more of a groan and push process. I was also sure that I didn't smell great after sweating my ass off all day in the desert.

As I walked into the bathroom, my thoughts traveled to Marek and what he might be doing right now. I could imagine him sneaking about outside the warehouse, testing the security of the building. He wouldn't be seen or heard unless he wanted to be, and anyone getting in his way would be removed swiftly and efficiently.

Seeing a vampire in his element must be a sight to be seen. I've witnessed Marek's ability to move quickly and appear to walk as if gliding on glass. I wondered what else he was capable of and if I would ever see it myself.

I peeled off my clothes and turned the water on to get it warming up in the shower. I caught my reflection and saw a hint of the bruises I had from my training session. I reflected on what I had learned today and felt ready to handle just about anyone physically. My powers were still a work in progress, but I could hold my own. I had, after all, knocked Marek on his ass enough times to be proud.

I knew I could take on Viktor's horde of lackeys, and I would do it with Marek. I just had to distract James somehow, so I could get out of here without him knowing.

I stepped into the shower and allowed the water to soothe the tension in my body. I cleaned off the muck and grime and instantly felt better.

The hot water felt good drumming into my skin, but it couldn't wash away the feeling that my sister was slipping away tonight. A surge of anger shot through me, and tears pooled in my eyes. I washed the tears away with the spray of the water. There was no use crying when I needed to be acting.

I shut off the water and dried off. I towel dried my hair, then pulled on a robe and went into the living area. James was sitting on the couch with his head in his hands.

"Are you alright?" I asked, coming over to him.

He looked up, and his face was stricken for a split second before he turned to hide it. It was as if something terrible had happened.

"James, what is it?" I asked, moving closer to him.

"It's nothing," He assured me and patted the couch for me to sit next to him. "The food should be here any minute."

I looked at him with narrowed eyes as if squinting would tell me what was going on.

"Tell me why you look like your dog just died," I said, sitting next to him.

He was quiet for a moment as if he wasn't sure if he should tell me.

"It's really nothing. I'm just tired." He said, smiling.

"Did I kick your butt too hard today?" I asked, smiling.

"Something like that," He said but didn't show any humor.

My eyebrows wrinkled as I wondered what his issue could be. He was typically in good humor most of the time and often the one encouraging me to look on the bright side. If James was upset, something had to be really bothering him, but I didn't want to push it. I needed to focus on getting my sister tonight.

"Well then maybe we can relax for a while, maybe watch a movie. How about that?" I asked.

He smiled and agreed.

"Good. Let's see what our options are..." I said, picking up the remote and flipping through the menu.

I settled in next to James on the couch after choosing the movie. He seemed to relax a bit, so I leaned into him. Cuddling up next to him was a habit, so when I laid my head on his shoulder, I expected him to reciprocate. He didn't. He stayed sitting the way he was, not making a move to put his arm around me.

That's when I knew that I was the problem. What James said earlier came back to me, that I belonged to Marek. It made my anger rise again, thinking about it. I sat up straight and fumed. Vampires were going to drive me insane in this life.

Just as I was about to say something, a knock sounded at the door. I jumped like a child caught doing something bad. James gave me a look then went to the door to let the room service attendant in with our food.

I sat down at the dining table that was tucked into a corner of the room while James tipped the guy. James had ordered enough food to feed a crowd, but the selection was a good one. I started in on a juicy steak with a loaded baked potato. It was divine.

"How many people are we feeding?" I asked, teasing him.

"I'm starving, and with as much energy as you expended earlier, I figured you would need to refuel as well," James said.

He was right. I polished off the steak and went in for some chicken shortly after that. I hadn't realized how hungry I was until the first bite of food hit my mouth. It was like I turned into a zombie craving brains only not gross and infinitely tastier.

"Why *am* I so hungry? We ate not that long ago." I marveled, shoving more food into my mouth.

"Using supernatural powers can lead to a larger appetite. You need more calories for your body to support all the extra energy you're using." He said.

It made sense. I didn't realize how tired I was until I perked up from eating. I was going to need that energy tonight if I was able to slip out and join Marek.

We ate in mostly silence with an occasional comment about the food. I hated it. James and I had never been so awkward with each other. He was someone I trusted, and I couldn't take the distance.

After we ate, we went back to the movie. This time I didn't let James sit rigidly next to me. I pulled his arm around me and dared him with a look to pull back. He smiled and shook his head but kept his arm where I put it. I snuggled closer and enjoyed the warmth of his body next to mine.

A few minutes into the movie, I started to doze. I had planned to stay awake and figure out a way to get out of the room without James noticing, but that plan was quickly becoming difficult.

"You should go to bed, you're exhausted," James said softly, running his fingers through my hair.

"Mmmm, that feels good," I responded.

He stopped abruptly.

"What the hell James? Why are you acting so weird?" I asked, angry.

It was one thing to think you couldn't be with someone, but it was entirely something else to behave like you didn't care.

"I'm sorry." He said but didn't elaborate.

"Nothing has changed," I insisted. "Don't deny me affection because you think I'm off-limits."

"I wasn't," He started saying, but I interrupted.

"Yes, you were. There is nothing wrong with caring for one another and showing it. If you pull back, I have nothing, and that will hurt too much." I admitted.

He pulled me into a hug and said, "I don't ever want to hurt you."

"Then stop overthinking this, whatever you think this is," I demanded.

He pulled back and nodded his agreement. He still looked a bit pained, but he seemed to be making a decision. I hoped he decided to pull his head out of his ass and be himself.

"Good. Now I really am tired. Are you going to decline if I ask you to lie down with me? Because we've slept in the same bed together enough times now that it would feel weird if you don't." I said.

His brow furrowed, and I grabbed his chin so he would look at me.

"Jesus, you really are upset about something. What is going on, James?" I asked.

He looked like a lost puppy, it was pitiful and made my heart-ache.

"We should have healthier boundaries." He finally said.

I let out a breath in a sigh. Maybe James was right.

"How about you start your boundaries tomorrow?" I suggested with a smile.

He shook his head like I was acting silly, but he grabbed my hand and walked with me into the bedroom. He laid down fully clothed as usual and pulled down the covers for me. I smiled and grabbed something to sleep in.

I dressed in the bathroom, brushed my teeth, then laid down next to him. He pulled me into a spoon position like he usually did. I realized at that moment that I needed the physical connection with him not in a sexual way but in a way that allows one human to comfort another.

Chapter Seven

James was sound asleep when I crawled out of bed just after midnight. I dressed in the living room and took his keys. If I hurried, I might get to the warehouse in time to catch Marek before he went in. I didn't think he was going to just scout the perimeter, not after the way he was studying the plans for the building.

It took less than twenty minutes to make it to the warehouse. I found Marek's rental car a few blocks away from the building but no sign of Marek. Luckily, I had the inside track on finding him, all I had to do was use the bond. Unfortunately, that was easier said than done.

While I sat in the car, I thought about Marek. I thought of his scent and his presence with his commanding personality. I thought of him standing before me with his leather jacket and the ever-present scowl on his face. His piercing blue eyes and dark hair staring back at me as if he needed me to be there.

I felt a tug coming from the warehouse, and I knew he was already inside. What I also knew was that he felt me too. There was so much anger coming from him that I was afraid of what he would do when I found him. It was worth the risk, though, because finding my sister was the only thing I could afford to care about.

As I approached the entrance, I looked for any sign that Marek had come through. The door was slightly ajar, and there was a light flashing in the lobby. I ran up to the doorway and peeked through to see if anyone was there. No one was in view, so I entered the lobby looking around.

The last time I had been in this room, two vampires were guarding the way into the rest of the building. Today there was nothing but a smear of blood on the floor. Blood was a bad sign, but I didn't hear or see anything else to stop me from going in further.

I entered the next door and walked down a hallway following the trail of blood. A foot was sticking out of a room just up ahead. I walked softly, trying not to make any noise at all as I approached it. When I got there, I was shocked by what I saw.

"Shit!" I said, then slammed my hand over my mouth, hoping no one heard me.

There was a body on the ground, and it was missing its head. I felt sick, just thinking about what must have happened. Looking at it and smelling it made my stomach roll. I fought back vomit as I stepped back out of the room into the hall. I would have felt vindicated regarding Marek doing more than just scouting if I didn't feel so sick by the evidence.

As I moved down the hall, I heard muffled voices. A surge of fear filled my body. It was one thing to think you could face hostile opponents and something else entirely to be presented with them.

The sound of something crashing through a wall came from up ahead, and I rushed forward. I felt Marek nearby and hoped it wasn't him being thrown through the wall. I didn't want to risk talking into his mind in case I startled him. It could be deadly for both of us if he was too distracted.

I turned a corner and saw what the noise was. Marek had a vampire by the neck and pushed up a wall. The vampire was familiar. In fact, he was one of the ones I had run into the other day when I was here last. It was yellow teeth, and he wasn't cooperating with Marek.

"Where is she?" Marek snarled.

"Not here." The vampire choked out as best he could.

Marek turned his head as I approached.

"Damn it, Ember! Go back to the car." He said.

"I'm here, and I'm staying," I said, stepping closer.

I tried to project an air of confidence but wasn't sure I pulled it off.

"Ah, chicky wit a skinned knee." The vampire smirked.

Marek stilled and asked, "Is this one of them?"

"Yes, he and his buddy were here the other day," I said, knowing what he meant.

Within seconds of my confirmation, Marek had ripped the vampire's throat out and thrown him to the ground. Blood sprayed in an ark across the room and splattered over Marek's already bloody clothing.

A squeak from the other corner of the room drew his focus, and I instantly felt sorry for that guy. After one look at me, Marek knew he was the other vampire who had compelled me.

"Your only hope of survival is to tell me where her sister is." Marek spit out while looming over the other guy.

"She isn't here. The boss moved her." He said.

"What?" I yelled.

Marek looked at me, and I knew to let him handle it. I couldn't help my surprise though. I knew Viktor expected me, but I thought that was part of his plan.

"Moved where?" Marek asked.

"Don't know. Boss doesn't tell us." He said.

Marek pulled the vampire close by gripping his shirt. I could see him starting to tremble, but Marke didn't have any mercy.

"Try again," Marek said through gritted teeth.

"Can't...tell you." He said hesitantly.

Marek let out a snarl and hit the vampire across the face. I heard a crack, and I imagined the guy's cheek was cracked or his skull

71

or both. The guy screamed in pain, and I shuddered at the sound. Marek threw him down and ran at me.

He backed me up against a wall and said. "I told you I would handle this. What did you do to James?"

"Nothing. I left after he fell asleep." I said cringing.

Marek said something under his breath that I couldn't understand. I think he cursed, but he was once again speaking Russian. As he did that, the vampire got up from the floor and rushed us. I flung my kinetic power at him and threw him through the wall.

Marek looked at me, and I thought he was going smile before he disappeared after the vampire. I scrambled to keep up only to find the guy losing his head, literally. Marek pulled it right off. The amount of blood and guts that came after had me gagging and fighting to breathe air that didn't smell like blood.

"Suck it up. If you are not willing to finish it, you should not be here. We need to move." Marek said and walked past me down the hall.

We came to a staircase leading down, and I followed Marek as he descended. I tried to avoid the blood drops that were dripping from him as I took each step. I didn't want to slip or track the blood more than we already were. It was hard to keep the gross factor out of my mind as we moved, but as Marek said, I had to suck it up.

Using my power, I reached out to see if I could tell if anyone was coming just like I had trained for. Someone was up ahead, but I didn't have enough experience to know how many or if they were human. I tapped Marek on the shoulder and pointed. He seemed to understand because he nodded sharply and pushed me behind him.

We approached a turn in the hallway, and that was where I thought someone was waiting for us. I moved to tap Marek again, only to be startled by my phone buzzing in my pocket. Marek looked at me like I was an idiot, and he was probably right because right afterward, a group of thugs came around the corner. They were moving faster than I could track, and before I knew it, one of them had me pressed against the wall.

I was having a hard time breathing since the guy used my neck to hold me back. I could hear Marek snarling and fighting the others, but my vision was quickly going black. It happened faster than I expected, and almost too late, I remembered to use my powers.

I put my hands on the guy's chest and funneled all the power I could muster into him. It flung him backward into the opposite wall taking a huge chuck out of it. Unfortunately, he had such a good grip on me that I went with him. Thankfully he took the majority of the blow for me, and I scrambled to my feet.

Just as I stood up, another guy grabbed me from behind. This time I was prepared and used what James had taught me to throw the guy over my shoulder. Putting some power behind it. He didn't just roll over but was thrown down hard enough to knock him out.

I turned to see how Marek was fairing just as he broke a guy's neck. He didn't rip the head off the guy this time, which was good except that he chose that moment to rush toward me. At first, I thought he was going to break my neck too, but instead, he grabbed me and stared into my eyes. The message was clear, I was an idiot, and he was distracted by my presence.

"I'm sorry," I said.

"No, you are not." He said, shaking his head.

Satisfied that I wasn't severely hurt, he checked on the two guys I had fought. He made sure they wouldn't follow us and then led the way down the hall again. I tried not to dwell on how he broke everyone's neck. I understood they were vampires, but I couldn't help feeling sorry for them.

Marek held up a hand as we approached a door with a keypad on it. It must be the secured area he had pointed out on the map.

From what I remembered, there was a way around this section that would take us down to what we assumed was the prison level. I looked around and found it.

"Over there," I pointed.

Marek nodded and led the way. We passed through another hallway before finding a door that led to another set of stairs. He hesitated before going down.

"Check if anyone is there," he told me.

I did but didn't sense anyone was near the steps. A few people were moving around further out, but we could make it through. I told him what I felt.

"Can you sense your sister?" He asked.

I tried but didn't find any trace of her. "No."

"Then she really has been moved." He said, shaking his head. "Stay vigilant, and do not hesitate if you see someone vampire or not."

I nodded my agreement and followed closely behind him. We came upon a gate of sorts that was sitting ajar as if someone had cleared out so fast, they didn't have time to close it. It gave us a way to slip in, so we took it.

About halfway down the hall, I looked into a familiar room. It had been the room my sister was held in. It matched the visions I had where Viktor was tormenting her or taking advantage of her. The bed was rumpled, and the sheets dirty. I could see blood on the pillows and on the sheets, but not a lot of it.

Marek doubled back to me and saw the room.

"Is this it?" He asked.

I nodded as tears came to my eyes.

"Hold it together. We are not clear yet." He said.

I gathered myself up and walked further into the room. There had to be a clue in here that I could read. I ran my hands over the bedding then picked up one of the pillows. Putting my fingers into the bloodstain, I thought of my sister. Instantly I felt her, but she wasn't close. In fact, she was on an airplane. She was sleeping, and I couldn't tell who was with her. I poked around in the vision as much as I could, but no clues were leading me to where she was going.

A crash behind me had me spinning around to see what was happening. Six guys were beating Marek to a pulp, and one had just noticed me. He came at me, but I pushed him off into the wall before he could get close. I grabbed two of the others with my mind and pulled them off Marek before sending them down the hall in a flying heap.

By then, the first guy I had thrown was up and coming at me again. He tackled me, grabbing my hands and immobilizing them above my head. He rammed his knee into my stomach, and it knocked the wind out of me. He smiled and leaned in like he was going to bite my neck, but I didn't let him get that far. I was angry, and with my anger rose my fire.

Within seconds the guy lit up like a log coated in lighter fluid. I pushed him back with my kinetic powers and held him still while he burned. At that point, the others I had pulled off Marek were back, but they were backing away from me. I guess they didn't want to be turned into a BBQ.

"Put the fire out, Ember," Marek said from the hall.

I dashed the flames, but the guy was still crackling, and the smell was horrible. I turned away, trying not to puke but ran right into Marek. He steadied me then pulled me into his arms.

"Good work," he said then kissed me on the forehead.

I tried to shake away my shock and refocus on the task at hand.

"Where are the others?" I asked, trying to breathe shallowly to keep the stink out of my lungs.

"Dead," He said. "I chased down the ones that ran away."

"Right," I said.

My phone chose that moment to buzz again. Marek nodded, letting me know it was okay to check it. It was James.

"Where are you? Why haven't you been answering your phone!" He yelled.

"I'm at the warehouse with Marek," I said and cringed at his response.

"I knew it. I'm almost there. Are you hurt?" He asked.

"No, I'm fine," I said.

"Tell Marek I'll be outside in five." He said, then hung up.

The hurt in his voice came through loud and clear. He probably wasn't going to trust me again. I knew the consequences of my actions before I took them but knowing them and feeling them was acutely different. My chest hurt, and it felt difficult to breathe.

Marek just looked at me while I pulled myself together. He had no sympathy for me. He hadn't wanted me to come either.

"Come, we will go meet him. I can use his help in clearing the rest of the building." He said and walked away.

I followed behind him, keeping aware of my surroundings but not wanting to move too fast. Seeing James was going to suck. I took advantage of him. It was a low blow.

James walked through the door just as we got to the lobby. The raw hurt and pain were evident on his face. I dropped my eyes to the floor and internally kicked myself for being such an ass.

"Is she here?" James asked Marek, ignoring me.

"No, but she was. We need a crew sent over to clean this up." Marek said then turned to go back into the building.

James walked over and put his arms around me. I hugged him, but he felt stiff to me.

"You scared the crap out of me." He whispered.

"I know," I said lamely.

He released me and followed after Marek pulling his cell phone out as he went. I stayed behind him and watched as he moved through each area efficiently, making sure there was no one left alive. I hadn't seen him move like that before. He was like a Navy SEAL or Special Forces elite soldier moving through the building. I stayed out of his way as he made quick work of searching every room.

We caught up to Marek and found him leaning over a table in the room where Natalie had been held. As I got close, I saw what he was looking at. There was a necklace with a note addressed to me.

Chapter Eight

Marek warned me not to touch the note or the necklace. He would have someone check it out before he let me look at it. He sniffed the air, and the look on his face told me it was Natalie's.

"The scent is the same as the blood," Marek said.

"How did he know we were coming and that I would be here?" I asked no one in particular.

"He has taunted you in your visions. He must have understood that you would come for Natalie." James said.

Always the realist and so practical, James pointed out what I should have already known. Of course, Viktor expected me. He took my sister to lure me here, but why leave before I got here?

"If he expected me, why isn't he here?" I asked.

"Something changed," Marek said, and he didn't look happy.

If something changed, it could greatly affect my sister. I hoped it wasn't related to her. I'm not sure what I would do if he harmed her. I've allowed the guys to distract me, and I've relied on them to know when to go get her. Not again. This is my fight.

Marek noticed the change in me. The hard look he was giving me chilled me a bit, but I didn't let it chip away my resolve. Not even he could dissuade me from getting my sister back. I have never allowed someone to stop me when I put my mind to it.

"What are you planning?" Marek asked softly, walking over to me.

James had stepped away and was explaining to someone on the

phone what we had found. He left to go upstairs before I responded.

"What do you think?" I said defiantly.

"Don't do anything stupid, Ember." He warned.

I gave him a hard look of my own. He was going to try to control me and the situation. It was what he did.

"I'm done letting you take the lead on this. We lost Nat because I listened to you. I won't let it happen again." I said.

He shook his head, but I knew he understood. If he kept trying to protect me as if I couldn't defend myself, he was going to lose. My will was too strong for that bullshit. I promised myself right there and then that I wouldn't ignore a feeling I had again. I knew this was going to happen, but I let it play out instead of acting. It was my fault.

I let that revelation sink in for a moment then walked over to what Viktor had left for me. Before Marek could stop me, I picked up the note and tore it open. The writing was in an exquisite hand as if it had been done with calligraphy. It was the kind of handwriting you saw from the 1700s on old documents and letters. The beauty of the letters was spoiled by the fact it had been written in blood.

It read:

Dearest Ember,

Please let me start by apologizing that I missed you today. I had intended for us to meet again, but unfortunately, that was not possible. You see, there was an incident, and I had to take your sister away to a safer location. Did you know that I am not the only one interested in your more unique qualities?

I fear it has caused me to do something I did not intend, and now we must delay our meeting. When the time is right, I will come to you. It is best if you do not try to locate your sister. I know that it will be difficult for you, but please know that until she is ready, the meeting would not go as you expect.

Ever yours,

Viktor

I handed the letter to Marek before he could tear it from my hand. He cursed immediately, most likely from not only the content but also because it had been written in blood.

"Is it my sister's?" I asked, referring to the blood.

"No, this is vampire blood." He said, sounding confused.

"What is it?" I asked, scrutinizing his blank face.

"It isn't something a vampire gives freely. A vampire's blood is powerful. We guard it, not give it away." He said.

"He gave me a way to find him," I said.

"More than that. Victor gave you his power." He said.

"What do you mean?" I asked, looking into his cool blue eyes.

"A vampire gives his blood to only those worthy of the gift. Giving it to you in this way is an old tradition. This is how a vampire marked his intended. It was a sign of trust and respect to give your blood on a document such as this." He said with reverence.

"His intended…what does that mean?" I asked, thinking of how Marek had freely offered his blood to me many times.

"He wants you as his mate." He said, and the cold dread that I felt from him panicked me.

I looked around to see that no one was there. James was waiting for the team upstairs, so we were alone now.

"Marek, you've given me your blood. What is your intention with me? You've had my blood as well." I said, holding my breath.

He looked at me like I was his air to breathe, and I gulped. He wanted me as his mate too. I could feel it in every fiber of my being, but he didn't say it. He was trying not to want me.

"I have a responsibility to keep you safe, that is all." He said.

"Marek," I said.

"No, not now." He said as he turned to leave the room.

Just then, James walked in, and by the look on his face, he knew something had happened. It was probably clear by the fact I held the note open in my hand, not to mention the tension between Marek and me.

"What did I miss?" He asked, walking up to me.

"I couldn't wait," I said, handing him the note.

He read it silently, and the look he gave me after chilled me even more. He knew what it meant too.

"This is Viktor's blood, isn't it?" He asked me.

I nodded, and he swore so long and so hard I thought he wouldn't be able to stop. This meant more than I knew, and I needed the details ASAP.

"Tell me everything I need to know about this. Why are you and Marek so freaked about this?" I demanded.

Marek wasn't as forthcoming as I had hoped, but James didn't seem to leave anything out. Not only had Viktor proclaimed that he wanted me as a mate but putting his blood on paper with that intention was a warning to everyone else. If anyone got in his way from this day forward, their life was forfeit. It was vampire law and a tradition that stood the test of time. It didn't matter what my thoughts were on the matter, it was a master vampire's right to make a claim.

"Is there a book I can read about all this? I have a serious lack of knowledge on this topic for someone that has been declared the intended mate of a master vampire." I said, hoping James had a resource or that he could teach me himself.

"I'll get you everything you need," He said.

The look on his face scared me, but I didn't ask. I had enough shocks today to last me for a while. I didn't need to explore what he was feeling too.

A master vampire had marked me as his mate by sending me a letter written in his blood. Why did vampires think they had the right to claim people as theirs in the first place? It isn't like I had a choice, according to James or Marek, but becoming someone's mate had a permanence to it that I didn't like.

The language in the letter suggested a level of familiarity we didn't have. Calling me his dearest and signing it "ever yours" had me thinking I wouldn't be rid of the vampire by merely telling him no. He already demonstrated an obsession for me that was psychotic at best.

I tucked the letter into a pocket for safekeeping. If nothing else, I could use Viktor's blood to help me find him. His letter would be useful and hopefully lead me to my sister as well. Ultimately that was what I had to focus on. A weirdo vampire penning me love notes as if we were long lost lovers couldn't get in the way of what I had to do.

"James," I called, and he turned around. "I need to get back to Denver."

He nodded his head sharply and moved to talk to a few of his team that had arrived. I wandered back upstairs while he was busy. As I passed through the halls, I saw where Guardians had removed bodies and started cleaning up the evidence. I ignored the door where my sister had been held and hurried up to the ground floor.

Marek was arguing with someone and pointing toward the door I slipped through. I knew he felt me enter the room. Marek's shoulders tensed slightly, and his head turned just enough that he would be able to see me in his peripheral vision. He could stop me if he wanted to, but he let me pass.

I didn't stop walking until I got to the car. I leaned against the door and turned back toward the warehouse. Besides a few vans parked along the road, there weren't any signs of what had happened tonight. Vans in a warehouse district didn't stand out, so all looked calm and normal in the neighborhood.

I pulled out my phone and made a call while I waited for the guys to wrap things up inside. Although I had quit my job, I was sure Bob would let me come in to use the database for some of my own research. He was a reasonable guy, and since he told the staff that I took a leave of absence instead of quitting, I was sure he wanted me back.

As I finished my call, Marek exited the building and made a beeline for me. He moved faster than any human could possibly move, and I took a sharp intake of breath. Before I could let it out, he was standing in front of me.

I thanked my former boss and hung up the phone. When I got back home, I had a place to start. It gave me a sense of purpose and a direction to head in. It was what I needed right now.

"Why do you need access to your work?" Marek asked.

"I want to dig up everything I can on Viktor. His real estate holdings, his finances, everything I can possibly find." I said.

"I have people to do that for us," Marek said.

"People that don't care about the outcome and people that may miss something because they aren't as deep in this as I am. Besides that, I know my shit, and there isn't anyone that can do a better job." I said proudly.

The corner of his mouth quirked up at my attitude. His feelings flowing into me were hard to miss. He liked it when I was cocky and confident.

"I will have James escort you back to Denver. He can connect with the Council resources while you do your research." Marek said.

"I don't think I need his protection, Marek," I said.

It made me angry that he couldn't trust me to protect myself.

"You need backup. I know your strength, but even I leverage

backup sometimes." He said.

"Fine, but bringing him to the office with Nikko, there could go badly. He is going to jump to conclusions and make it awkward." I said cringing imagining how that might go down.

"He would be right. James is in love with you." Marek said deadpan.

I was struck dumb by the comment. I tried several times to say something back but failed.

"Why do you say that?" I asked, finally managing to find words.

"He cannot take his eyes off of you and will do anything you say. If he wasn't the best Guardian I have, he would be reassigned to eliminate any chance of a problem." He answered.

I studied his face as I searched his feelings. He wasn't happy about it, but he didn't seem to be too upset. I knew James had feelings for me, but I didn't think it was as serious as Marek has made it out to be. James was right that we needed to have better boundaries.

"If that is true, it isn't his fault," I said, feeling guilty about how I had encouraged his affections.

"You have been affectionate with him, and he was warned not to let it go any further. Although he was told to keep you at the hotel tonight at any cost. I am surprised he didn't take the opportunity to seduce you." He said.

My anger peaked at the thought that James would sleep with me only to keep me in the hotel. I'm glad he didn't. I don't think I could forgive him if he did.

"Apparently, I need to learn to read a situation better," I said.

"Take this opportunity to learn how to handle James and Nikko, and before long, others will fall at your feet. With your power, you are capable of anything. One day you may even be leading your own Guardian team." He said in a voice that sounded almost proud.

Marek moved to walk away, but I grabbed his arm before he did and slid my hand into his. He looked down at my hand then up at me. I let go of him, and his crystal blue gaze held a warmth that made my body tingle.

"Where will you be?" I said in a voice that was softer than I intended.

"Wait for James. I will send him out to you." He said with a small smile and stepped away.

I watched him glide back to the building. It was too smooth to call it walking. The man, well the vampire, was a cool cucumber. A bubble of envy lifted in me at how he was able to hold it together so well. I needed a dose of his calm and control. It's like I am fire, and he is ice.

I didn't even get upset that he left without answering my question, and I should have been. He exuded that control over everyone around him. He was able to quench my flames, which was rare.

James came out a short time later and found me scrolling through flight times on my phone. I needed to get back to Denver, so I could get started on researching Viktor's life and thus find my sister. Taking charge of the plans helped me relax enough to wait for him and not leave him behind.

"Are you ready to go?" He asked.

"Yes. Do you want to drive? I'm a mess." I said, looking at my blood-splattered arms, hands, and clothing.

"Sure," He said, taking the car keys from me.

He watched me walk to the other side of the car and get in. It took him a moment to get in, and when he did, he gave me a look that got me wondering what he was thinking.

"You seem fine," He said as he started the car.

"I am," I said.

"After what I saw in there, I thought you might be more upset."

He said.

I looked down at the blood splatters on me, but it didn't bother me as much as it probably should. I felt accomplished at having worked beside Marek to take out so many enemies. It was like I felt a rush of power from having fought.

"I'll be glad to get cleaned up, but other than that, I'm good," I said.

"Good." He said.

I told him about the flight times I saw, and he gave me a phone number to call his travel team. They booked us on the first flight out in the morning, which was only a short wait since it was already well past midnight.

Chapter Nine

J ames had his car at the Denver airport, so we loaded it up with our luggage and headed out. Our first stop would be my office, even though James thought I should get some more rest before tackling any research. I had slept on the plane and was feeling pretty good, so it wasn't necessary.

James sent in a request for information from the Denver based research team he used and had them send the file directly to me. I was itching to read the contents and to get my hands on my work computer so I could dig through everything. I had a feeling I would be able to find out more than his team was able to. I wasn't just good at my job, I was great. That's why my boss was hesitant to let me leave.

"If you quit your job, why are they letting you use their systems?" James asked.

"Because I asked nicely. And Bob wants me back. Nikko said he didn't tell the team I quit, just that I was taking some time off." I responded.

"When did you talk to Nikko?" He asked.

Shit, I hadn't told him about that little nugget. I looked over at him, and he was glancing my way, waiting for a response. I suppose not answering quickly would make it sound more suspicious than it was, and it was something I should have told James and Marek about. Somehow, I hadn't found the time.

"That is something else entirely." I started, "I probably should have told you right after it happened, but there was so much going on, I didn't mention it."

"You didn't mention what Ember?" He said, giving me the side-eye.

"I sort of connected to Nikko mind to mind. It was an accident because obviously, I didn't know I could do it, but we chatted briefly. That's when he told me Bob told the team I took a leave of absence." I said.

"Have you done it since then? Connect mind to mind that is." He asked.

"Only with Marek," I said, cringing at the effect it would have on James.

He was a grown man who could take care of himself, but I didn't want to hurt him. It seemed like an intimate thing speaking within someone's mind like that. I suspected it would hurt him.

"That's to be expected. Does Marek know about what happened with Nikko?" He asked.

"No," I said.

"Your connection to Marek is part of the bond. I'm not sure if what you did with Nikko was a side effect of taking Marek's blood or power you already had." He said.

"Can vampire blood give you powers?" I asked curiously.

"It can and it does." He said.

Having an ability like that could come in handy like it had when Marek and I were going through the warehouse searching for my sister. I didn't know if I could do it without the influence of vampire blood. I hadn't been able to do it before taking vampire blood, but that wasn't definitive proof of where it came from.

Thinking of Marek conjured up a vision of him covered in blood.

"Oh my God," I gasped.

"What is it, Ember?" James asked concern evident in his voice.

"A vision…" I said, then got lost in the images.

I saw Marek shut himself in the hotel bathroom. He leaned against the wall and shook his head. Then he rubbed his hands over his face. He shook his head again. It looked like he was trying to clear whatever images were there.

He leaned over to turn on the water. As the spray filled the shower, he peeled off his blood-soaked clothing. His body was covered in cuts and bruises. I couldn't tell how much blood was his and how much came from others. The damage was extensive, and it shocked me to see him that way. He hadn't let on at all that he had been hurt.

Maybe it was a vampire thing, but his injuries didn't detract from his muscular body at all. Somehow the blood looked good on him as if it belonged there. That thought should have grossed me out, but instead, it ignited a small ball of desire in my belly. He could not only survive more than a human, but he was healing so fast I could see it happening.

Now naked, he stepped into the shower and rinsed off as much of the blood as he could before soaping up his body. He winced a few times as the soap got into the scrapes, cuts, and what now looked like punctures. Were those knife wounds? He must have been hit harder than I thought.

For the first time, I was seeing him react to pain. I suppose it was only logical that he would feel pain, but prior to this, the thought hadn't occurred to me. My heart hurt, watching him get cleaned up. I wanted to help him or comfort him, but he was all alone.

When he rinsed the soap from his body, most of the injuries had healed enough that they didn't look too bad. In fact, he didn't look bad at all. I tried to pull myself back, but the vision wouldn't let me out. I was stuck staring at him while hot water sluiced over his body. He stood under the spray for a while, letting the heat of the water beat into his back and shoulders.

Marek turned off the water and pulled a towel from the rack. Then he wiped the moisture from his body, and my eyes followed that towel everywhere it went. They tracked down his torso, over his abs and down lower. He moved the towel over his long legs then back up again. If I didn't know he wasn't aware of me, I would accuse him of doing it on purpose.

He ended the torment by wrapping the towel around his waist, covering himself from further prying eyes. A few rogue water drops fell from his hair as he moved, and they ran down his chest. I couldn't help but watch them as they made a wet trail down his body. Although he was covered up a bit, his lean muscular body was still very much on display.

Marek leaned over the counter and splayed his hands out on the cold marble. His head drooped down as if he was in deep thought. He looked decidedly better now that all the blood was washed away, but I could tell that his mood had only improved a fraction from where it had been.

I wanted to put my hand on his shoulder and turn him around to look at me. Maybe if I willed him to see me?

His head snapped up and looked into the mirror.

"Ember?" He asked the empty room.

I cursed to myself then tried our link to talk to him.

"*Are you okay?*" I asked.

"*What did you see?*" He asked, nonchalantly.

"Enough to know you were hurt in that warehouse and didn't say anything," I replied.

"I heal, my injuries are not important. I thought you flew back to Denver. How are you speaking to me?" He said.

"I am in Denver. I had a vision, then somehow, we connected real-time. I'm not sure exactly how it happened." I answered.

"If you are in Denver, this should not be possible." He said.

"I don't know how I did it," I said.

"Have you had any sign of Viktor since you returned?" He said.

"No. It's been uneventful." I said.

"Keep his letter with you at all times. Any vampire that sees it will know what it means. You can use it to protect yourself if you need to but promise me you will only do that if there are no other possibilities." He said, adamant that I not show the letter unless I had to.

"Is it really that important?" I asked unsure if a piece of paper could really mean that much.

"It is. Promise me," Marek said with vehemence.

"I promise," I said.

"Good. Are you with James?" He asked.

"I am. We are in the car driving to my office." I said.

"Stay with him Ember, do not let him out of sight." He urged.

"I will. When will you be back?" I asked.

"Soon. I have a few more things to do here before I can leave." He said.

"Okay," I replied lamely.

"Be vigilant, Ember. Do not think you are safe, not even for a moment." He said, then he disappeared.

The vision blinked out like Marek had changed the channel. Maybe he had.

When I opened my eyes, James was there. He had pulled over to the side of the road and come around to my side of the car. He was sitting on the edge of the seat facing me. When I looked up, he thanked God. It was too much, so I pushed him back.

"Give me a minute," I said short of breath.

"What happened?" He asked.

"I had a vision then somehow linked to Marek. It was weird, but I'm okay. Why did you pull over?" I asked.

"You looked like you were having a seizure or something. I thought it might be a vision, but it was different than when you had them before." He said, stroking my cheek.

I grabbed his hand and smiled up at him. "I'm fine, it was different, but no harm done."

He smiled at me. I reached out and rubbed my thumb across his bottom lip. Then I pulled my hand back, remembering that I needed to have better boundaries with him.

Something about the vision made me stop and think. I had forgotten about Viktor.

"Viktor or one of his lackeys could be following us. We should get moving." I said.

James acknowledged the possible threat and went back to the driver's side of the car. We were almost to my office, and I was suddenly glad the vision had occurred before we got there.

"He's going to be there," I said, thinking about all the ways we could possibly avoid it.

"Who Nikko?" He asked.

"Yep," I said.

"We don't have to go." He offered.

"I can't leave it alone, James," I said.

I was going to have to face him some time or another. It might as well be now.

"He might not be there," James offered.

"No, it's Wednesday. That's his office day." I said.

"What do you want to do?" He asked.

"We go directly to my office then get to work. If Nikko comes in, let me handle it." I said.

James nodded his head in agreement as we pulled into the parking lot for the law firm. Nikko's Porsche was parked in his spot just like I thought it would be. A fluttering of nerves filled my stomach, but I pushed it aside and got out of the car.

I led James into the building and over to the elevator. We road up in silence, but when the elevator dinged and the doors opened, my nervous feeling returned. My instincts said avoiding Nikko would be for the best.

Unfortunately, the receptionist saw me and ruined any chance of me coming in without anyone knowing.

"Ember dear, so good to see you back. Mr. Manetti told me to expect you today." She said loudly.

Her words were for me, but her eyes were all for James. I couldn't blame her; he is super handsome.

"Thanks, Margaret, we'll be in my office," I said, pulling James along.

Margaret beamed at me and winked. I tried not to laugh, but it was hard. I succeeded in only snorting, which wasn't very dignified. I got it under control as we went down the hall.

Nikko's office was down the opposite hallway making it easier to come and go without him seeing us. If he had a client in his office, he wouldn't have heard Margaret, but if his door was open, he knew I was here.

I closed the door to my office as soon as we were both inside and got to work. While I booted up the computer, I asked James about what he knew of Viktor.

"He is as secretive as most master vampires. I know very little. He has a nest of vampires in Denver, and he has an association with a coven of vampires the Council pays to handle the bounty cases they need to be resolved. He has held esteem on the Council for years." He said.

My eyebrows pinched together; I had more questions than answers now.

"What does it mean to hold esteem on the Council?" I asked.

"While he isn't a full member of the ruling board, he is a master vampire which affords him sway and influence on the board." He said.

"So how do we know what he does and doesn't already know? Could he have found me because of the information he got from the Council?" I asked.

"While it's possible, it is also highly unlikely. Only Marek knows all the details of who we are guarding and why. He runs the Guardians." He said.

"Marek runs all of it? Then why is he in the field? Shouldn't he be in an office somewhere?" I asked.

James laughed, "Could you really imagine Marek sitting in an office doing paperwork?"

"No, I guess not," I admitted smiling.

The image of Marek sitting behind a desk in a suit and tie was hilarious. He was an action-oriented man with little time for sitting around.

"The supernatural world doesn't operate the way the human world does. We don't have the same stereotypes or standards. If Marek wasn't in the field, he could appear weak, and that is a big problem if you are in power." James said.

"Appearing strong is really that big of a deal?" I asked.

"Yes, it can mean the difference between life and death, but Marek doesn't just appear strong, he is strong. Other vampires tremble in his presence. Viktor must not know Marek is involved, or I'm sure he would back off." He said.

"Something must have changed. In fact, Viktor mentioned in his letter that someone else was interested in me. Who could that be?" I asked.

"I don't know, but we will be ready for them if they make a move. I know Marek. He didn't return with us for a reason, and it wasn't because the ground team needed help at the warehouse." He said.

"You think he has a lead?" I asked.

"If not, he will before he comes back," James assured me.

James looked into my eyes and said. "He is the best there is, Ember. If there is something to find, he will find it."

His confidence in Marek warmed me. The vampire could be annoying and an asshole, but there was something there that intrigued me. He was super intense but often didn't show what he was thinking. The fact that I had access to his feelings was a gift I valued.

A ding from the computer brought my attention to the computer. I logged into my email and pulled up the file the Guardians had sent. It was a link to a secure server where I could retrieve the information. I had to electronically sign a non-disclosure agreement, then I was in.

I reviewed everything they had, which was extensive, but there was still a lot I thought was missing. They had a comprehensive list of his business and financial holdings, but it lacked anything personal. He had to have personal property and assets associated with him somewhere.

Sorting through everything a second time, I came up with a plan. I gave James the public information items to review, and I dug into the more complicated pieces. I started by running each of Viktor's known aliases in each database to find any additional information I could. I ended up with about 30 more possible properties to search for. It was going to take a while to get through everything.

James and I had been working for a couple hours before a knock sounded at the door. I knew who it was without opening the door. I answered, telling him to come in.

Nikko walked in with a big smile that fell quickly when he saw James. Then he looked nervous and a little angry. His eyes darted between us as if he suspected something.

"Margaret said you were here, so I wanted to say hi. What are you doing?" He asked, sitting down in one of the guest chairs.

James was sitting next to me behind the desk, so there was only one other chair left in the room. I didn't usually have many visitors in my office, so there weren't many seating options.

Nikko eyed James with a wary look. It was clear he hadn't expected him to be in here with me.

"Your father said I could use the office when I needed it so here I am. James is helping me with some work I'm doing." I said with a tight smile.

"I expected you to be alone." He said.

"I can see that. Were you just saying hi, or was there something else?" I asked, growing impatient.

He gave me a hard look that said I was being rude. The truth of the matter was that I probably was being rude. He was keeping me from my work, and I didn't want to have this conversation.

"You know I was just thinking about taking a break. I'm going to run down to the coffee shop in the lobby. Do you want anything?" James asked me.

I gave him a look that said I wasn't happy he was ditching me.

"We can both go. I could use a vanilla latte." I said.

"I don't mind making a run. Nikko, can I get you anything?" James asked.

Nikko ordered an Americano coffee, and James left.

"That was a not so subtle exit," Nikko chuckled.

"Cut the crap, Nikko. What do you want?" I asked.

"Shit Em, why are you so hostile? I know you aren't happy with me, but after what happened with the mind thing, I thought you would want to talk." He said.

I sighed. "There's just a lot going on. The shit hit the fan in Phoenix, and I'm trying to dig through all the crap."

"How can I help?" He offered.

"You can't," he tried to protest, but I cut him off. "Seriously, Nikko. This isn't something I can share. I signed an NDA for some of what I'm working on. James has clearance, but you don't."

"Okay." He said, then asked. "Are you back with the firm?"

"Your father wants me back, but I'm not sure when this will be over. He left the door open for me when I'm ready, but now isn't the time." I said.

"Will you tell me if there is anything I can do? You know that you can still count on me as a friend, right? Anything you need, I'm here." He said.

"I do Nikko, but I don't know how to do this. You know I've decided to move on, and it isn't fair to you if I pull you into things." I said, feeling my stomach twist and turn.

He looked thoughtful, but I knew he was upset. I knew every line and crease in his face and could read the story better than anyone else. Nikko wanted me to be his friend, but what he really wanted was to have me back as his girlfriend. He hadn't accepted my decision yet, and it would take time for him to get there.

"I love you, Em. I can't sit here seeing you in pain and not offer to help. It tears me up to think you might not ask me when you need me." He said.

"Nikko, don't say things like that," I said, dropping my head into my hands.

A moment later, his arms were around me, and I had tears in my eyes. Nikko and I had been friends for a long time before we crossed the line and made it a romantic relationship. He had always picked me up when I was sad after a breakup or supported me when I needed help. How could I live without him in my life?

I understood now why James had left me alone with Nikko. We needed to have this conversation even if it was difficult. I pulled back from him and looked him in the eye.

"Everything has changed Nikko. We can't just pick up where we were like nothing happened." I said.

"I can't change how I feel about you. You know me, Em. I don't walk away from the people I love." He said.

"I know Nikko, but we aren't a couple anymore. You need to accept it, or we won't be able to be friends long term. I don't want that to happen." I said.

"I hear what you're saying." He said, but his expression was still determined.

"It will be better if we can be just friends," I said.

He nodded, but he had a weird look on his face. Then he said, "Is James still your Guardian? You two seem close."

"Don't go there, Nikko," I warned.

"Is he why you won't look at me?" Nikko asked.

"Back off," I said with venom.

"I can tell by the way he looks at you." He said.

"What can you tell Nikko? That he cares about me? That he will protect me with his life? That's what Guardians do." I said.

"It's more than that." He insisted.

"It doesn't matter If he does have feelings for me. You and I aren't a couple Nikko. I don't belong to you!" I said loud enough that the entire law office probably heard me.

"Tell the Guardian to drop off my coffee with Margaret. She'll bring it to me." He said then walked out of the room.

I leaned back in my chair and stared out the window. Tears fell freely from my eyes as I watched the clouds roll across the sky. It was a slow release of emotion that fell drop by drop down my cheeks. Every time I tried to stop myself from crying, more tears would fall. This is exactly what I was trying to avoid when I came here. I loved Nikko, and I was angry with him, which tied my emotions up into a tight ball of pain.

As the weeping slowed, I felt resolved to set the situation with Nikko aside. I had to focus on my sister and the vampire mess I was now in. I also needed to find out what the letter from Viktor really meant and how I was going to deal with it. Being claimed by a vampire had to be bad, I just didn't know yet how bad.

Chapter Ten

James was pacing back and forth in his living room. We had spent three days researching Viktor's life, and now I was reading about vampires. We were at James' place so I could access all the materials he had on the subject. I could tell by his pacing that he thought I wasn't going to be happy.

He was right. I finished reading about vampire mating rituals and threw the book down.

"So, it's like Viktor and I are engaged? Not that he intends something, but that we already are?" I asked incredulously after reading about how vampires claim a mate.

"Sort of like that yes," He cringed.

"Why didn't you tell me this already? This is insane!" I yelled.

"And that's why I didn't say anything yet, but it isn't enforceable until you publicly acknowledge it." He said.

"Which is why Marek told me to only do that if there was no other option. He didn't say why, which is typical." I said, shaking my head.

I was so angry at both of them; I could hardly think straight. Their high-handed handling of my life was putting me in danger. They didn't see it that way, but the truth was the truth.

James sat down next to me and looked at me, pleadingly.

"The letter can save your life if it comes to it, but yes, acknowledging it makes it a legitimate claim," James said.

I closed my eyes and tried to settle my temper. A vampire had written me a letter in his blood, and somehow that meant he had claimed me as his mate. If I acknowledged it, I would actually be his mate, and that was even more frightening. Vampires didn't have human mates, that meant at some point I would have to turn into a vampire.

"He warned me, but Marek should have told me outright. What kind of messed up misogynistic culture is this?" I said.

I was seething mad. There wasn't going to be much James could say that would calm me down. Viktor had no claim on me, and I pulled out the letter he had left me. The urge to rip it up was strong, but I knew something better, fire.

I pulled out the letter and unfolded it. Then using my pyrotechnic power, I lit the thing up.

"No, Ember!" James yelled and grabbed the letter from me.

He put out the flame, but it was already charred where I had been holding it.

"If the letter is gone, so is the threat it holds." I insisted.

"Viktor will know if the letter is destroyed. Burning his blood is a signal you don't want to make." He said.

"More information you kept from me, James?" I asked seething.

"Shit Em, I didn't think you would burn it. It's vampire blood. He will feel it burning. It is part of him still even though it's on paper. It's like the vampire blood in your body, it connects you to Marek in the same way." He said.

I stilled as a realization hit me, "I've had Viktor's blood, and he took mine after he attacked me. That's why he knows where I am, where I'll be. It's how he will find me like he said in the letter."

"And why he feels you are his. He nearly killed you before, but for some reason, he now wants you as his mate." James said.

"He has always wanted me as his mate. He tried to make me a vampire after he ripped out my throat. That's the real plan, James. He wants me as one of them...a vampire." I said.

The thought rolled around in my head for a bit, and I knew that not only would Viktor try again, but it could happen. It was inevitable that I would become tied to a vampire. If it wasn't Viktor, it would be Marek. He wanted me to.

"Ember," He said, grabbing me. "You know how to defend yourself, and you have me and the entire Guardian ranks. He won't be able to get to you."

"No, James. It isn't that simple. I already have a taste for their blood. Marek's, in particular, draws me in, and I can't stop myself. What if it happens again? I can feel their darkness calling me James." I said, terrified.

He held me close and assured me as best he could, but the truth was if it happened again, I didn't think I would stop. Vampire blood made me feel too good. I wouldn't resist it, and I felt the truth of it in my bones.

If I thought about it, I could feel Marek's blood swirling around in my veins with every beat of my heart. It was a dark pulse of power that I hadn't felt before, but now that I was focusing on it, it was clear.

Someone pounded on the door, and I instantly knew it was Marek. I could feel him so close, and at that moment, I needed him near me. He would understand. He would have a plan.

"It's Marek," I told James as he moved toward the door.

My eyes locked with Marek's when the door opened, and he knew what I had been thinking and feeling. He had rushed here faster than was prudent because he could feel my distress. He was in front of me and pulling me off the couch within seconds. Our eyes held each other's and all the questions I had, and all the terror that was there was now his.

"He will not have you," Marek assured me in my mind.

"I've seen it, Marek. It will happen." I said sure that we wouldn't be able to stop this madness.

"No! He will not have you." He said with so much power, it brought

tears to my eyes.

I nodded my head and took a deep breath. I couldn't look away from him. He was so confident, and I could feel that he would die before he would let Viktor have me. I was afraid he would have to die because I was just as sure that Viktor wouldn't let Marek stand in his way.

I put my hand on his cheek and felt a sad smile pull on my face. The darkness was coming for me. Now that Marek was in front of me, I recognized it as vampire power. It felt like his energy, a vampire's energy.

"What is it?" James asked in a whisper.

It was like he couldn't raise his voice enough to say it louder. I turned my head to look at him, but I couldn't bring myself to smile. Reassuring him was not something I was capable of at that moment.

"We have another problem," Marek said.

That was an understatement. We had a dire situation if what my Seer instincts were telling me was true. I also felt that Marek had found something that I wasn't going to like.

"I don't know that I can take any more bad news right now," I said, feeling shaky.

Marek helped me back to the couch and sat down next to me. The look on his face told me he had found something in Phoenix.

"The note Viktor left you spoke of someone else who was interested in you. I believe I know why he left you the note." Marek said.

"You found something," James said, but it wasn't a question.

"I did. The Egyptian is in town." He said, and James swore.

"Who is the Egyptian?" I asked, confused.

"You think he's after Ember?" James said to Marek.

"I know he is. He was spotted entering a loft in downtown Denver this afternoon." Marek said.

"She is the only high-value target in the state right now," James said, running his hands through his hair and looking extremely agitated.

"Who is the Egyptian?" I asked again but with more urgency in my voice.

Marek and James looked at each other, and James motioned to Marek. I guess he got to tell me because he started talking.

"Asher Sanz is a contractor of sorts known as the Egyptian. He specializes in obtaining what his employers want. He has a reputation for successfully completing every mission he has been hired for, and he has been hired for more difficult missions than you." Marek said.

I let the information sink in. If someone had been hired to do something to me or kidnap me, I wasn't sure that there was anything I would be able to do to stop it. I hoped Marek had a plan.

"Is he a vampire?" I asked.

"No, he is worse," Marek said.

"What could possibly be worse than a vampire?" I asked.

Marek gave me a look.

"What?" I asked.

He shook his head. "A magician is worse."

I tried to wrap my head around what Marek was implying. I had images of a man with a long beard and a pointy hat with stars on it. Was he serious? He looked at me like I was dumb.

James helped paint a better picture by saying, "Think tattooed supernatural badass. He invokes the Gods and Goddesses of Egypt. His power is beyond our comprehension."

James was right. I couldn't fathom what that meant. If a person could channel the power of a god, how could we possibly fight them? Gods were all-powerful and omnipotent beings who could do whatever the hell they wanted to do.

Marek looked at James and shook his head. He wasn't happy about what he just said, but I was glad for it. I needed to have all the information.

Marek looked down and saw the burned letter on the coffee table. He snapped his head around to me with a questioning look. I sighed and let him see what had happened. Showing him a vision of It was easier than talking about it with him. I also wanted him to know how angry I was over, not being told critical information.

"Now that Asher Sanz is here, we cannot expect to protect you by ourselves. I will tell you what you need to know." He said.

James looked shocked. He clearly had never heard Marek agree to something so easily nor admit to not being able to protect someone. Whoever this Asher Sanz was, he was definitely a bad-ass. The thought terrified me more than anything to date. If Marek was afraid of someone, he had to be formidable.

Marek started by telling me about vampires. Our previous conversations were "need to know," but I could tell from the beginning that I was finally being told the whole story. The hierarchy was a complicated web of who was oldest and who had the most power. The ability to feel a vampire's power level was an essential part of their society and something I would have to learn if I was going to be able to navigate their world.

I could already feel the darkness coming from Marek, but I hadn't yet honed that talent to know how to compare it to other vampires. After my experience in the warehouse, I knew how to pick a vampire out of a crowd, but I needed to understand more to find their power.

"How do I gauge your power level? All vampires feel the same to me." I asked Marek.

"What do you feel when you focus on me?" He asked.

I turned to him and opened the bond. He shook his head no and blocked me. Jerk. I took a deep breath and reached out. At first, I didn't sense anything, then I poked at the darkness that told me he was a vampire. It shimmered like a lake if the lake was made of shiny tar. I pushed into it and felt a pop.

"Oh shit," I gasped as I felt a deep cold penetrate my body.

"Hold onto it, Ember. Try to find where it goes and see what it is." Marek said voice strained.

I ignored the cold and explored the black lake that was Marek's power. It was vast, and beneath the surface, it was turbulent and almost angry. It felt like if the power was released, it could destroy worlds. I was lost in the power's need to be free. I tried to withdraw, but it held me immobile.

I felt a hand on my arm, and it grounded me. I pulled back again, and after another pop, I was out and back into myself.

"I recommend not going that far in again," Marek said.

I gave him a look that I said I didn't appreciate the humor in his statement.

"Now, do it with James." He said.

"But he isn't a vampire," I protested.

"Try," Marek said patiently.

I looked at James, and he smiled, but he looked nervous. I didn't blame him. Being a test subject for my power couldn't be a fun thing. I pushed into James, and instead of seeing a lake, I found tendrils of smoke. The smoke danced around and skittered away from me when I tried to go closer.

James made a noise, and I pulled back a little. When I did, I found a shimmer that I had missed before. It was almost clear with a hint of gray. It was like the smoke I saw but more substantial. When I dipped below the surface, I saw his power. It wasn't as vast as Marek, but he had a great deal of his own. It resembled Marek so much I wondered if James was even human.

Testing the theory, I dug into my own power and found a lake there as well, but mine was crystal blue. When I dipped below the surface, I found swirling colors of gold, red, and orange mixing within the blue. The size was much larger than James, just about equal to Marek.

I gasped when I realized it. No wonder they wanted to protect me. If I could harness all that power within me, I would be as powerful as Marek.

I pushed my senses out to my neighbors and even farther, searching for their power. The mundane humans all had a small pond within them but lacked anything underneath. Their colors were all the same, but none of them matched James. I started to feel dizzy, so I pulled back.

"You aren't entirely human, are you?" I blurted out to James.

His face went blank, and he said, "Why do you say that?"

"Your power looks different than other humans and even different than mine," I said.

He looked at Marek. Marek nodded, encouraging him to answer.

"My father was a vampire," He admitted.

My eyes widened in surprise. James looked ashamed, and he wouldn't meet my eyes.

"Is that even possible?" I asked.

"It's rare. After a vampire is turned, they retain some human traits for a time. That includes fertility for males. If that vampire has sex with a human woman, she can get pregnant. The result is a dhampir." James said.

He said dhampir like dam-peer. It was a term I had heard before but never thought it was possible. The literature on the subject made it seem like dhampirs were crazy mindless killing machines. That description didn't fit James at all.

"So, your father was a vampire," I said, testing the words as I spoke them.

"That explains a few things," I said, recalling times when he had moved faster than a human could or was stronger than a human could be.

James looked at me like I might blow up at any minute. There was a tiny bubble of panic that I couldn't deny, but I held it together. I lived in a world of the supernatural now. It wasn't any worse than my werewolf ex-boyfriend. I wondered how many other boyfriends I had that were not entirely human.

"How far were you able to search?" Marek asked quietly.

"I stopped after looking a few blocks out. They were all human." I said.

He smiled and said, "A valuable skill."

I smiled back at Marek. Knowing who was near and how powerful they were could come in very handy. If I found a vampire, maybe I could get away before they got too close.

"Keep practicing. You need to stay vigilant and trust your guard. Going forward, James will be your near guard, and a team will handle the perimeter. Do not go anywhere without him or the team. James knows what to do." He said, then stood.

He moved toward the door as if he was going to leave.

"Where are you going?" I asked, upset that he was leaving again so soon.

"I'll be where I am most needed." He said, then nodded to James and left.

It shouldn't have bothered me. Marek wasn't someone I needed near me. In fact, he often made me feel like I was a freak. He lacked humor, and he treated me like I was too easily broken.

"What is that supposed to mean?" I asked James.

"It means," James said, coming over to me and wrapping his arms around me, "that you and I are on our own again for now."

I could feel Marek outside. He couldn't just walk away like that. James and Marek had been with me since before I learned to use my powers. I felt safer when they were both near me.

"We'll be fine without him," James said, pulling me back to him.

"I'm sorry," I said, feeling my bond with Marek pull as he started driving away from the house.

He had just returned and then was gone before I was ready for it. I held back the panic and tried to focus on James instead. He was here with me, and he was actually looking happy about it. I focused on the brightness in his eyes and the sensual line of his lips. I ran my fingers along his jawline.

"Ember," James started, but I stopped him with a finger on his lips.

He shook his head, pulling my hand away.

"Don't try to distract me Ember, we need to talk through this." He said.

I closed my eyes and took a deep breath. Talking about Marek walking out without so much as a word of comfort was not appealing. The fact that I shouldn't be surprised weighed heavily on me.

"I don't want to talk about it," I said, stepping away from James and sitting on the couch.

"You are drawn to him," He said.

Just hearing him say it made tears come to my eyes. I didn't want to be drawn to Marek, but somehow over the past week, we had become close. So close that I didn't want to admit how much I wanted him.

I nodded reluctantly. It hurt to admit it.

"I don't want to be," I said.

"I know," He said, sitting down next to me. "I understand."

"Do you? Because I'm not sure that I do." I said.

"Vampires can be magnetic, and their power addictive. There is nothing you can do to change it, but with practice, you can learn to resist it. I'll teach you how." He said.

"That would be amazing if it's true," I said and looking into his eyes.

"It's true," He said, smiling.

"Then teach me how to block a vampire," I said.

We spent the rest of the evening honing my skills. I wasn't sure it would work, but it was better than not being prepared at all.

Chapter Eleven

Over the next few days, I spent my time researching Viktor's empire and learning more about supernatural creatures. James hooked me up with his research team, and together we made considerable headway on figuring out where my sister might be. I wasn't able to find her using my Sight, which was becoming more frustrating by the day. James assured me Viktor wouldn't have hurt her, but it was hard to believe.

For the first time in a week, I was alone or what passed as alone these days. I could feel the Guardian team around me, but thankfully couldn't see any of them. James had to go into his office, and he would join me later. I took my frustration outside to my patio. Sitting there in the evenings was something I missed, and it brought a piece of normalcy to my otherwise crazy life these days.

I tried not to think of all the things I had lost recently, but thoughts of my sister and Nikko kept plaguing my conscious mind. My reality had changed so significantly that I had to define a new normal for myself. The weeks had been hard, but I was learning to deal with them.

I heard a car and turned my head to see a red Porsche coming down the street. The driver pulled up along the curb and stopped. Nikko stepped out of the car and smiled at me. I shook my head. Why was he here?

He was in jeans and a t-shirt so he must have just come from the gym. He was the only man I knew who could make casual clothing look like it just came off a designer's catwalk. His dark hair was brushed back from his face and was a little longer than he usually wore it. As he walked toward me, I couldn't help but notice how good he looked. It was like those jeans were made to show off his powerful legs and slim waist. He could take a woman's breath away; he had always been able to take mine away.

He hesitated for a moment, but when I didn't move, he walked right up to the low fence that surrounded my patio. My heart started racing, and I rubbed at my chest as if that would make it stop. Could he hear it pounding?

"Hi Em," he said hesitantly like he was trying not to spook me.

"Nikko," I said breathlessly.

"Are you okay?" He asked.

A quick laugh, more of an escape of air came out of me. These days I didn't even know what okay was.

"You're kidding, right?" I said.

He winced. His face looked pained, but it cleared quickly.

"May I?" He asked, gesturing to the chair next to me.

I thought for a moment then nodded my head. He slowly entered the patio and moved to sit in one of the chairs. I sat with him.

"I miss you," He said, looking into my eyes.

What I saw stabbed at my heart. This is a man I love...loved. Not quite a man anymore now that I know he is a werewolf and also a cheater. That word isn't quite right, but it's all my brain can come up with.

"It's been hard for me too," I offered a small smile, but it quickly faded.

The pain was still raw, but I tried to push it away.

"I'm sorry, I was an asshole the other day at the office. I don't know why. I just know that I'm sorry. I'm sorry for everything." he said, and the pain and hurt showed on his face, tears gathered in his eyes.

"I know," I said and grabbed his hand.

At my touch, he closed his eyes, and a few tears fell silently down his cheeks. I tried to connect with him, but nothing happened. I could feel his pain without the link because I had it too. My own tears gathered and fell, watching him silently weep.

"I love you, but I can't trust you," I said softly, squeezing his hand.

He winced at the words but nodded his head that he understood.

"I know," He said and let go of my hand.

I looked away and half expected to see a Guardian standing across the street in the trees. It's where they usually hang out. I could feel one close to the building but hidden.

"Both our lives have changed dramatically, and in ways, we never thought could happen," I said.

"I can't live without you. I know I can't ask for everything to be the same, but I want you in my life. I don't know how to live without you." Nikko said.

The pain in his eyes hurt to look at, and I almost told him what he wanted to hear.

"I want you in my life too, but I don't know how to do that. When I'm hurting, I go to you or Sam, but this time you were the one that hurt me." I said with tears in my eyes.

Nikko squeezed my hand.

"I hate that I'm the one that hurt you more than anything else. If it was some other guy, I would kick his ass, but I can't kick my own ass." He said, angry at himself.

I laughed at what he said, and he looked at me like I was cruel.

I held up my hands, "The mental image of you trying to kick your own ass is hilarious. You have to admit."

He realized what he said and smiled, allowing himself a small laugh too.

"Thank you," He said, looking serious again.

"For what?" I didn't know.

"For talking to me. You didn't have to." He said.

"I know," I said, and I almost leaned into him.

His vulnerability was playing my heartstrings, but I held myself back. I had decided to move on, and I couldn't let myself fall back into what was comfortable, ignoring the issues.

"I should go. I'm sure your Guardian is foaming at the mouth right now." He said and stood to leave.

I stopped him and hugged him. I couldn't help myself. I loved this man regardless of the hurt he caused me. I couldn't stand to see him in this much pain and not do something about it.

He squeezed me tight, and I thought I heard him crying. In fact, I knew he was crying by the wetness I felt on my shoulder. I relaxed into him and took a deep breath of the man I loved so much it hurt. My love had changed, though. This was no longer the man I could trust without hesitation. I had to be on guard with him, and not leading him on would be important.

"I need you to understand something, Nikko," I said and pulled out of his embrace. "We are not in a relationship anymore, which means you can't just show up like this again. I need you to ask permission to see me next time. Can you do that?" I asked.

He looked down but nodded his head.

"Say it," I said softly.

He looked into my eyes, "I understand and will ask permission to see you next time. I'm sorry..." he turned to go, but I stopped him.

"Hey, it's okay," I said, then let go.

He nodded, but I could tell he was still crying. My heart broke again, watching him walk away. He was my best friend, and it hurt to let myself feel his loss, but it was necessary. I couldn't let him past my guard anymore.

"You are too kind to him," Marek said, stepping out from the shadows.

I didn't think he would let me be so close to Nikko without being there to supervise. I knew Nikko still had Guardians, too, which meant that Marek would be aware of his movements. I had felt him there but hadn't acknowledged him.

"He's already hurting I don't need to add to it by being cruel. I don't have it in me." I said, looking back at Marek.

He was in his usual black leather jacket and dark jeans. The darkness of the night softened the edges of his face and made him look more handsome.

"You ignore your own safety for his feelings." He sneered.

"No, for mine," I said and turned away from him.

Before I knew what was happening, he had dragged me inside then he grabbed my arms. The look on his face was intense.

"Do not gamble with your life. You have been training and have improved, but you are not yet ready to handle a werewolf on your own." He was shaking, and his fingers were bruising my arms.

"You're hurting me," I whispered.

He winced and dropped his hands but didn't back up. The bond between us came to life, and I gasped at the feeling. It was intimate, and as he brushed against my mind, it ignited my desire to be closer to him. I stepped into him and lifted my hands up to his chest. When I touched him, I felt every part of him.

The link between us was stronger than it ever had been. I grabbed onto it out of instinct, and Marek growled, but it was a sound of pleasure. It was almost a purr, and I loved how it felt so much I pulled harder on the bond. In an instant, Marek's lips pressed against my neck, and his tongue found my pulse.

As the vein jumped against his tongue, I could feel his desire to bite me, and I wanted him to do it. I wanted him to sink his teeth into me and pull my blood into his body making. I pressed my hand on the back of his head and pulled him closer. His teeth scratched my skin.

"I cannot resist your commands much longer, Ember. If you do not stop, I will bite you." Marek warned me.

The words made sense, but I couldn't stop pulling him closer, trying to push his fangs into my skin. I needed him to bite me more than I needed air to breathe.

"Bite," I demanded and pulled as hard as I could on the bond.

His teeth sunk into my flesh a moment later, and I moaned in pleasure. Every pull of my blood into his body had an answering tug between my legs. He drank greedily and the pleasure built with every swallow. I could feel our bond growing and take over. The feeling was so intense it was all I could think about. I didn't want this feeling to end.

I felt Marek pull away, and he locked eyes with me. He was breathing hard, and his eyes were dilated. He cradled my face in his hands. He was shaking.

"*Milaya moya*, a mating bond cannot be unmade. Do not push me to do something you do not want." He said.

I could feel the desire coming from him and his hesitance because he wasn't sure I knew what I was doing. My brain wasn't so clouded that I didn't understand it, but I also didn't care.

"I want it," I said.

"Your desire is clear, but you will be walking away from everything in your human life. Can you live with that decision? Could your friends, your family?" He asked.

My head cleared enough to think straight, and I wondered if I really wanted the bond or if I just wanted the feeling. Maybe it was the same thing...

"Do you want it?" I asked, knowing the answer but needing to hear it.

His eyes burned with the intensity of his emotions. He wanted it more than anything.

"You know I do." He said through clenched teeth.

What he didn't say was that he didn't want it right now. He didn't think I was ready to commit my life to him, and that was the reality of the situation. I would have to leave everything behind to be his. I fought the pleasure of the bond long enough to decide.

"I don't want to force it just because it feels so good. I'm probably not ready for the consequences." I said, letting go of the bond.

Marek visibly relaxed then pulled me into his arms. He was glad I hadn't forced him, but he longed for the day it would happen. It wasn't just my power that Marek wanted. He wanted me.

"You knew I may not be able to stop, but you did it anyway." He said, stroking my back.

"I did," I said.

"Why?" He asked, pulling back so he could look at me.

"You know why," I said.

"No, I can feel what you are feeling, but it does not explain it." He said.

I thought about it for a moment before responding.

"When we connect, it isn't like anything I've ever felt. It is more intimate than sex, and I want it more each time I feel it. You've been blocking me, and I hate how that feels more than anything. I needed to feel you." I admitted.

"And the blood exchange?" He asked, going still as if afraid of what I might say.

My body throbbed, remembering the feeling I got when he took my blood, and when I took his. It was near orgasmic just thinking about it.

"I don't want to like it, but I do," I admitted.

"There is nothing to be ashamed of, Ember. You are drinking pure power when you take my blood, and you are feeling my pleasure when I take yours." He said.

"Why do I think I hear a but coming?" I said.

"We can exchange blood anytime you want, I give my blood to you freely, but you cannot wrap the bond around us, or it will become something more. I have said it before, but I will remind you again that you do not want to tie yourself to me permanently without thinking it through. If we were mated, you would be mine, and no one else could have you." He said.

"I think it will happen," I said.

He thought for a moment, then asked, "Is that the vision you had?"

"That must be what it was. There isn't another explanation for it." I admitted.

"How did you feel in your vision?" He asked, hesitantly.

"Happier than I have ever been in my life," I admitted.

He smiled and pulled out his pocketknife. He put it to his neck and made a small incision. His blood bubbled up into a small dome.

"Drink," He said, pulling me into him.

I latched on like an addict and downed the magical concoction that spoke to my soul. I could feel the bond snapping with energy, and I longed to grab it and pull it tighter to me.

"Resist it," Marek said, knowing what I wanted to do.

I didn't grab the bond. Instead, I sucked harder on his neck, making more of his blood flow into my mouth. His body became rigid, and I could feel his pleasure.

"You are mine with or without a bond." He said into my mind.

The bond surged with energy having been fed with our blood. It felt extraordinary, and for the first time, I could see tendrils of the dark vampire energy mixing into my power. It both excited me and terrified me.

The wound on his neck started to close, and I forced myself to pull away. I felt a drop of blood on my lower lip and ran my tongue over it, not wanting to waste it. Marek stared at my tongue as it moved across my mouth, and I knew he wanted to kiss me.

I leaned into him and that was all the invitation he needed. He pressed his lips against mine, and the familiar velvety feel of them had me kissing him back with twice the intensity. He responded in kind with a thrust of his tongue into my mouth. He crushed me into his chest, and I was lost in the pleasure of him.

I dragged my tongue against one of his fangs, drawing blood, and he gasped in pleasure as he sucked it down. He returned the favor, and I sucked his blood down, feeling the ecstasy of his kiss combined with his blood. I wanted more than just his tongue inside me, and that's when I realized that I really did want him, not only the blood.

Nikko had my brain tied up in knots, but when I was with Marek, it all dropped away. It wasn't just Marek's power or the pleasure of his blood. He was the strongest person I had ever known, and I was drawn to that strength.

I could feel the bulge in his pants pressing into my stomach, and I wanted to climb his body so that it pushed into just the right spot between my legs. I wondered if all of him would feel like velvet. I was already melting from his kiss and wanted to know what sex would be like with him.

He pulled back, and I gasped for breath feeling lightheaded.

Marek traced my jaw with a finger and whispered, "I can read your every desire then match it without you ever saying a word."

"And what is it that I desire?" I asked, looking into his blue eyes.

"You wish to drown the pain by taking me to your bed." He said softly.

The words stung and tears filled my eyes.

"You're an asshole," I snarled.

"Your emotions are still raw from Nikko. Now is not the time to jump into another's bed," he said, then leaned in and kissed me.

It was a softer, much gentler kiss. It promised love and caring, not just sex and lust. That kiss was everything I desired and more.

"Tell me this isn't a lesson," I said, hoping this wasn't one of his torture Ember sessions.

"It is not a lesson," He assured me.

"You are the perfect man," I said, leaning my head against his chest.

"I am not a man," He reminded me.

I smiled, but a tear trailed down my cheek. I had to get my love life in order. Marek was right, I couldn't use him to drown the hurt. Throwing myself at every attractive male in my sight was reckless. I had to get my head straight and worry more about my sister and less about my love life.

He kissed the tears away and wiped the wetness from my face.

"When you are ready," He said.

I nodded.

He went out the patio door and disappeared. He didn't go far; I could still feel him outside. He was waiting for James to get back before he left.

"Shit," I said under my breath.

I'm going to have to tell James.

Chapter Twelve

The delicious aroma of coffee filled my lungs as I watched a barista prepare drinks. It is a smell that speaks to me all day long, not just in the mornings. James stood next to me as I ordered a vanilla latte for me and a mocha for him. He came into the office with me this morning to finish up some of our research and accompany me while I reviewed a project Bob Manetti requested me to review.

Bob called last night to make me an offer to return to work. Instead of coming back to full-time, I compromised and agreed to do piece work for him. It was a perfect arrangement that let me choose which projects I committed to and which ones to pass up. I would retain an office at the firm but also have access to work remotely. It would keep my bank account from going empty and still let me prioritize finding Natalie.

Since I was still under Guardian protection and because Marek made it clear not to go anywhere without James, James and I came in together. People in the office were starting the think he was my assistant, which made me giggle. Needless to say, it didn't make him happy at all.

James selected a table near the counter and sat while I stood near the pick-up area, waiting for our coffee. I was feeling impatient this morning. I wouldn't be able to sit for long. Something was bothering me, but I couldn't put my finger on it. It was an allusive flutter pinging around in my brain. I expected a vision, but one hadn't come.

I also wasn't in a hurry to sit down with James to chat. Up to this point, I had avoided telling James about what happened with

Marek, and I was hoping to prolong it even further. I was starting to agree with Marek about how I was using him and James to avoid my feelings.

While I waited, I pulled up the summary that Bob emailed me of the project on my phone. As I scrolled through, a man walked over and stood next to me. I looked up and met the sparkling green eyes of a middle-aged man. He had dark hair with a slight grey at the temples. He smiled when our eyes met, and I smiled back.

"Hi, do you work in this building?" the man asked.

I looked up to see he was speaking to me, and I replied, "Yes, I work at the law firm on the 5th floor. You?"

"I have business here and thought I'd grab some coffee." He said vaguely.

I gave him a polite smile then looked away, but he kept talking to me.

"Is that your boyfriend?" He asked, pointing toward James.

"Uh, no, not really," I answered.

I fidgeted, hoping James was paying attention in case this guy was a creeper. I looked over at James, but he wasn't looking at us.

"Does not really mean you are single?" He asked and smiled.

He had a charming smile. I thought he might be flirting with me, so I matched his smile.

"Um, I guess so. Why do you ask?" I said.

"I'm just curious." He said.

He smiled again, and it felt forced this time.

"Who are you meeting?" I asked, curious if he was a client of the firm or if he was going to one of the other businesses.

"Right now, I'm meeting you. I'm Asher, by the way. What's your name?" He asked, reaching his hand out to me.

I froze. What were the chances this was the guy Marek had mentioned? Asher looked at me, expectantly.

"Sorry, I'm Ember. Nice to meet you." I said and reached out to shake his hand.

That was a mistake. When I touched Asher, I felt a rush of power move up my arm and into my chest. It made my lungs feel like hardened steel. It quickly became hard to breathe. I tried to push back but only succeeded in delaying the process for a moment.

"You're Guardian isn't very good, is he?" Asher whispered, smiling an evil grin.

Not only was he holding me immobile somehow, but he was also crushing my hand in his. I tried not to buckle under the weight of the spell he had on me, but it was taking all my effort.

"Release me," I bit through clenched teeth.

"But we've only just met, and you have something my client needs." He said and pushed more power into me.

He pushed me into a chair. Then my body froze in place as his power flowed over me. It was like being turned to stone. I couldn't turn my head to see where James was or if anyone was looking at us.

"Don't worry, Ember, my employer doesn't want you dead, or you wouldn't be breathing. Now tell me, what makes you so special?" Asher said, pulling my hand into his.

If someone saw us, they would probably assume he was my boyfriend holding my hand while talking. Of course, if they looked hard enough, they would see the terror in my eyes.

"I don't know what you are talking about." I bit out defiantly.

"Oh, come now, you have a full Elite Guardian team trailing you plus this guy." He motioned toward where James was sitting. Not that I could see him.

"The Council doesn't waste resources on powerless creatures. I can feel the vast amount of power you have, so be a good girl and tell me exactly what you can do." He insisted.

I held my tongue, not giving him anything. That only pissed him off.

"Don't make me hurt you," Asher said. "I might enjoy it."

The look on his face made it clear that he could back up the threat, but I didn't think it would be wise to give him what he wanted, either. I decided to hedge a bit and see how far I could push it.

"I can do something," I offered.

"Well, that is a start," Asher said distractedly. "Now, don't go anywhere, my dear. I have to take care of your Guardian. He is trying to interrupt."

He let go of my hand, and I instantly felt relief but still couldn't move. I heard a scuffle behind me, but I couldn't see a thing. From what I could tell, no one in the cafe had any idea what was going on either. Asher must have been able to make people not see things. I thought that was unique to vampires, but apparently not.

"Now, where were we?" Asher said, grabbing my hand again.

A stabbing pain hit me as he touched me, and if I were able to take a deep breath, it would have forced me to gasp. As it were, I took in as much air as possible and squinted my eyes at the pain. Tears welled up but didn't fall.

I tried to reach out to James but couldn't find even a thread of him to connect. I hoped he was okay. If not, I was on my own. Although with him likely immobilized like me, I was on my own anyway.

"What can you do, Ember?" Asher asked.

The barista called my name, and Asher left again to grab the drinks I ordered. Asher spoke to the lady briefly. While he was occupied, I tried to link with Marek.

"*Ember?*" Marek responded.

"*Help, we need help!*" I said frantically.

"*I knew I felt something. Where are you?*" Marek asked.

"*Coffee shop in my office building. Asher is here. I don't know what he did to James.*" I said.

"*Can you run?*" he asked.

"*No, I can't move. He has me immobilized,*" I said.

"*I am on my way. Do anything you need to do to stay alive, anything.*" Marek said.

"*Hurry,*" I said, then dropped the connection.

I could feel the tears falling down my cheeks, and that's when Asher walked back over to me. He set the drinks on the table as if they were for us.

"What were you doing? I could feel something." Asher said.

I shook my head, refusing to speak. He didn't look amused.

"Tell me, or I will make you speak." Asher threatened.

I could feel a throbbing start moving up my arm from his hand. It got more intense the longer I kept quiet. The pain grew into sharp stabs of electricity that grew in intensity every second. I held out as long as I could. It felt like minutes but was probably closer to seconds. It wasn't long before it was more than I could bear.

"Okay," I squeaked.

The pain died down enough for me to take a huge breath. Asher pulled me to my feet and tucked me under his arm. He started walking us out of the coffee shop at a slow pace. As we moved out the door, I finally got a good look at James, and what I saw scared me. He was sitting very still, but his eyes darted around the room. He was frozen in place, unable to follow me.

I pushed my senses out to find the Guardian team that should be outside. Marek put a larger team on the perimeter to back us up in case Asher showed. I felt them, but none of them were moving either. Asher must have taken them out too.

"Tell me what you were just doing," Asher said.

"I was looking for the Guardian team," I admitted.

It was a small truth, and I was having a hard time concentrating. I hadn't intended to tell Asher anything.

"That wasn't very nice, Ember. We were having a polite conversation, and you had to break my trust." He said, looking indignant.

"I'm sorry," I said, apologizing.

He pulled me faster toward the building exit. It was hard to walk, but he managed to tug me along with him somehow. I thought frantically to come up with something to do. Marek said to do anything, so I focused on Asher and tried to set him on fire.

His clothing started to smoke before he lifted his sleeve and tapped on a tattoo. It looked like a chain holding a vessel at the end, like a priest's incense burner they use in churches. It flashed gold, and then my fire fizzled out before even singeing him. My shock turned to fear.

Asher grabbed my arm, "That was interesting. You are lucky my clothing didn't catch. I can't stand it when my clothing gets ruined."

His eyes were glowing with the same golden light that had flashed from his tattoo. He stared at me, and I took the chance to take a peek at his power. What I found surprised me. He didn't have much, if any at all of his own. He was human but not powerful by himself. The power he was using had to be coming from whatever he did to the tattoo.

"What else can you do? There has to be something." He insisted.

He pulled me out on the sidewalk, and then I knew I had to figure something else out quickly. The situation was becoming more dire.

"I can't do anything else," I insisted.

He gave me a hard look and dug his fingers harder into my arm. I would have bruises in the shape of his hand for sure.

He dragged me toward an SUV parked along the side of the building. It was in the fire lane, blocking part of the drive. He had it waiting there as a matter of convenience.

"I don't believe you. It doesn't matter, though. I'll make you talk." He said then pulled open the back door of the car.

I estimated it had been about five minutes since I contacted Marek. I had no idea where he was or how long it would take him to get here. I couldn't risk trying to connect with him again while fighting Asher. I had to find a way to distract Asher so I could get away. This was my last chance before I was pushed into the vehicle.

I scanned the area again and found that Nikko was in the building. He was in the elevator, almost to the ground floor. He would help me, and the fact he's a werewolf had to mean he could hold his own.

I tried to freeze Asher with my kinetic power, but he shrugged it off like it was nothing. I looked around, but there wasn't anything that stood out for me to throw at him instead. There were a bunch of windows on the first floor, but that was it. With nothing else to use, I resolved to break the windows. I focused on the ones closest to us and willed them to break. They wobbled slowly at first. Then as they cracked, I pulled the glass shards toward Asher.

Glass flew through the air, some hit me, but mostly they hit Asher as he was pushing me into the car. Asher fell to the ground, and I felt him release me. I jumped out of the car and stood over Asher on the ground.

He started to stand, but before he could move, I kicked him in the kidney two times. He fell to the ground, but I didn't stop. I kicked him a few more times for good measure until I thought he was too hurt to move again. I ran around the car and went in through the broken windows back into the lobby of the building.

Nikko ran out of the elevator and pushed me behind him.

"Run, Ember. Don't stop." He yelled.

As I moved through the lobby, I looked over and saw James running out of the coffee shop. I nodded at him, then proceeded down the back hallway. It led to a back door that James and I had agreed would be a good escape route if it was needed.

As I ran, I heard Nikko yell out in pain, but I didn't stop. I hit the exit door full speed, which bruised my arm. When I burst through the door, I saw Marek's car pulling into the lot. I almost burst into tears with relief.

The tires squealed as he took the turn too fast then he stopped right in front of me. The passenger door flew open, and he yelled for me to get in.

"What about the guys?" I asked as I jumped in and closed the door.

Marek pealed out, not even having to think about what I asked.

"They can take care of themselves." He said, taking another corner too fast.

I gave him a hard look but realized he was right. If a dhampir and a werewolf couldn't hold their own against a human, then there was nothing I could do to help them.

"How did you get away?" Marek asked.

"I shattered the windows and threw the glass at him. It knocked him down. I kicked him a few times before running away. Nikko distracted him from there." I said.

My breathing was still heavy, so it was hard to get the words out, but the farther we got from the office, the easier it was to get air into my lungs. I focused on calming down. Marek still drove too fast, but I didn't care. I wanted to be as far away as possible.

"Asher took down your team and the one assigned to Nikko," Marek said.

"How did he know?" I asked.

"He had to know an elite team would be on you, but he must have seen the others when he arrived. I called Nikko when I couldn't reach any of the team members." He said.

"He jumped right into the fray. He didn't even hesitate." I said, feeling both proud and thankful.

Marek grabbed my hand and said, "Are you hurt?"

"I don't think so. Maybe a scratch or two from the glass, but nothing else." I said.

He took a deep breath, and I knew he was searching for blood. He wasn't sure if I knew whether I had a more significant injury. I couldn't feel anything at that moment.

"I'm fine, Marek," I said, squeezing his hand.

He held on a little too tight to my hand as he drove. I liked that he did it. Something about it felt good.

"Did you reveal Viktor's claim on you?" Marek asked tentatively.

"No," I said.

I saw the instant relief on his face, and it hit me how big of a deal that was. I resolved never to use that letter.

"Good." He said.

"Where are we going?" I asked, not recognizing where we were headed.

"Council headquarters. It is the safest place in the city. The Egyptian should not be able to reach you there." He said.

I wondered what it would be like to finally see the Council. I hoped they were welcoming.

Chapter Thirteen

I screamed as the doctor set my broken arm. Note to self. Don't run full speed through an emergency exit door using your forearm as a battering ram. It only ends in pain. Marek knew I was injured before I did and had taken me directly to the medical wing of The Council headquarters.

He was currently staring at the handprint shaped bruises on my arms.

"I got away from him," I said, trying to sound like I had done something right.

"You did," He admitted.

It didn't do anything to remove the concerned look on his face. His lips were smashed together in a thin line, and he wouldn't look me in the eyes other than to check them for injury. I had several cuts up and down my arms, and there were enough cuts on my face from the flying glass to make it seem like I had taken the brunt of the blow.

We hadn't heard from James or Nikko yet, but Marek assured me an emergency response team had been deployed to the scene. They would have arrived within minutes of me leaving and should be reporting back at any moment. I wasn't able to connect to either man (even though I had tried) to see if they were hurt, so I had to wait for news to get back to Marek.

Marek ran his hand up my arm as the bruises started to fade. I looked up at him then and saw a small smile on his face. He was happy I had taken blood from him yesterday. If I hadn't, I probably would have been hurt worse today and required blood now.

My skin pebbled into goosebumps as he trailed his fingers over my shoulder and onto my neck. He moved to sit next to me on the bed and slipped his hand up to my jaw. There was a long cut running along the bone there. Marek bit into his thumb, drawing a bead of blood to the surface. He smoothed it across the cut, and I felt it heal almost instantly.

He repeated the process over every cut he could find. He had to bite into his thumb several times to bring the blood to the surface again and again, but eventually, he healed every injury. I watched him while he did it, and each one made me shiver a little. I loved how it felt when his blood healed me, and it made me wonder why I could feel the magic now when I hadn't before.

When he finished, he wiped off the blood with a damp cloth and finally met my eyes. What I saw there took my breath away. He was content that I was okay, but there was more to it than that.

"You..." I started, but he interrupted me.

"No, not here." He said and leaned in to press a soft kiss on my lips.

He moved so fast I almost didn't think it happened, but then I felt a wetness on my lips. When I ran my tongue over it, I tasted his blood. It exploded with power as I swallowed it.

My broken arm flared with pain, then just as suddenly it didn't hurt at all. The lethargy I had felt from fighting Asher's hold on me lifted slightly too. Marek had healed all my remaining wounds with nothing but a smear of blood. I couldn't stop staring at him.

I kicked the door open to our bond, letting him feel everything I was feeling at that moment. His eyes brightened as if a light had backlit them, turning his ordinarily deep blue eyes to more of an ice blue.

His power flared, and I felt it call to me. The small taste of his blood wasn't enough for me, I wanted to drink from him and feel all his power wrap around me.

"Am I interrupting anything?" James asked, walking through the doorway.

I felt my cheeks flush, but Marek didn't move, he kept staring at me.

"I will be back," He said into my mind.

I nodded my understanding, and he stood up. He pulled James into the hall for a few minutes, then I felt him leave. He was going to check with the team to see what happened after he rushed me away from the scene. James walked back into the room.

"Are you okay?" I asked James looking for any injuries.

"I got patched up on the ride here. I had bruises mostly," James said, coming over to sit in the chair next to the bed.

"How bad was it?" I asked, cringing.

"Not as bad as it could have been. I don't want to think about what would have happened if Nikko hadn't gotten there when he did. Are you okay?" James said, looking me over.

"I broke my arm, but it's healed now," I said, moving my hand and finding no pain remaining.

"He's good at that," James said. I assumed he was referring to Marek.

"Vampire blood is a handy first aid kit when you need it. Where is Nikko? Is he okay?" I asked.

"Nikko was hurt worse than me. If you want, I can take you to him." James said.

"Yes, please," I said, jumping off the bed.

I followed James down the hall. There were several rooms like the one I had been in along the corridor. Further down, we passed through a security door that led to rooms in the ICU. My heart jumped in my chest at seeing Nikko was in the ICU.

We arrived at his room, where Nikko was surrounded by nurses and beeping machines. To the protest of several nurses, I walked right into his room. He had a bandage on his head just over his left eye. One of his arms was wrapped and bound against his chest. He looked like hell.

"He's unconscious but healing," James said and motioned me over to the chair next to the bed.

I sat down and grabbed Nikko's hand on the arm that wasn't bandaged, which was one of the few places he didn't look hurt. I couldn't believe how messed up he was. I instantly felt terrible for leaving him there.

James told me he would be down the hall if I needed him and left me alone with Nikko. As he left, he instructed the nurses to work around me if they needed something, and they backed off at his order.

It was several hours before Nikko woke. I had dozed off a bit from sitting still for so long and startled awake when Nikko spoke.

"This feels familiar," Nikko said.

"Hey, how are you feeling?" I asked, sitting up.

A nurse hurried in and started taking vitals. I glared at her, but she was done quickly then left.

"Better than I should. Are you okay?" He asked, looking for injuries.

"Just a few scrapes and bumps, all healed now," I assured him.

"Good," He relaxed into the pillow.

"Thank you, Nikko. If you hadn't been there, I'm not sure what would have happened." I said.

He took a deep breath that looked pained. I didn't want to know how bad the injuries were before now. I assumed he had already received every treatment possible to this point, and yet he still looked like death warmed over.

"I was surprised when Marek called, but I'm glad he did," He smiled.

His skin looked pale, and his smile didn't have the same warmth it usually did. It tugged at my heart to see him hurting.

"I was glad you were there until I saw how bad you were hurt," I grimaced.

"If it hadn't been me, then it could have been you," Nikko said softly.

"What can I do for you? Do you need anything? I can get a nurse back in here," I offered.

"You holding my hand is doing more for me than anything a nurse could do." He smiled.

I squeezed his hand and smiled back. He didn't look good, but he was going to be okay. My anxiety lowered with every breath he took. I sat with him for a while but knew he was trying to stay awake for me.

"I don't want to keep you awake. I should let you rest," I said, leaning down and kissing Nikko softly on the forehead. "I'll check on you later."

"Love you, Em," He said and fell back asleep as soon as his eyes closed.

"I know," I said softly and left the room.

Marek was waiting for me just down the hall.

"I am told he has responded well to treatments and will fully recover within a day or two." He said.

"I wanted to stay, but I was keeping him awake. He needs sleep to heal." I said.

"You could use some rest yourself," Marek suggested.

"I'm fine," I said, knowing I looked like crap.

"Yes, you look fine." He said with a small smile to soften the bluntness of his statement.

I laughed. I knew I had been in rough shape, but hearing Marek point it out was suddenly hilarious. I was exhausted even though I had been healed of most of the wounds I received.

Marek pulled me back down the hall to the room I had been in and told me to lay down. There was no point arguing with him. He pulled a blanket up over me then sat in the chair next to the bed. When my body relaxed into sleep, I fell into a dream.

Natalie was lying in a large bed with red silk sheets covered with velvet and cashmere blankets. She looked peaceful lying there, cuddled under the covers. The headboard was covered in gold leaf, and the walls were paneled in mahogany. It looked like a mansion.

She looked clean and comfortable, which was much better than the last time I saw her. It actually looked like she was being taken care of now instead of abused. It made me feel better to see her like that even if I was still angry at her being taken away.

Natalie stirred at the sound of a door opening. She didn't wake, but someone did enter the room. I saw a shadow fall over the bed covers, then a hand appeared. It was a man's hand, and he moved to stroke my sister's face. At first, I thought it was Viktor, but then the arm came into view. As his sleeve pushed up, I saw his forearm was tattooed with familiar runes.

Asher Sanz was in the room with my sister, but it didn't make sense. She should be with Viktor, and Asher should be with the Guardians. Asher stroked her forehead and moved a few stray hairs off her face. He pulled the covers up tight around her then left the room. She remained asleep, but as I looked closer, I realized she looked pale. She must be ill.

The vision started to shatter, but I tried to maintain contact. I had to see more to know what was going on. I felt hands on me, and the vision cleared completely.

"What is it, Em? What's wrong?" James asked.

He was pulling me closer and trying to comfort me. I was still in the bed Marek had put me in. I could feel him at the other end of the complex. He had left James to look over me.

"He has her," I said through tears.

"Who has who?" He asked, confused.

"Asher has my sister. I don't know how or why, but he has her." I said, feeling my body shake.

James sat back in shock, and I could feel Marek's concern as he felt my pain.

"Are you sure?" James asked.

"I saw her with him," I said, feeling scared.

James didn't say anything. He looked like he wanted to pull me into a hug, but he was holding back. Then the reason walked through the door.

"What is wrong?" Marek asked.

Marek's presence filled the room. It was like all the available light focused on him. James moved so Marek could take his place next to me.

"Asher has Natalie," I said to Marek.

"When did this happen?" He asked, wanting to find out any detail that would help him find Asher.

"I don't know. It must have been before he came for me today. She looked different, better actually, but I think Nat isn't well." I said.

"He could be working for Viktor," James suggested.

"It's possible, but I'm not sure," I said.

Every time I had seen her with Viktor, she was dirty and disheveled looking. This time she was clean as if she was freshly showered and put to bed to be kept comfortable. Viktor wasn't caring and certainly hadn't shown any sign of it in the past.

"James, put a team on it and monitor their progress," Marek said.

James nodded that he understood and pulled out his phone as he stepped into the hallway. I assumed he was going to have the research team and whoever else track Natalie down. This time I was glad because I knew they were good, and I didn't want to leave Nikko to go running around town searching for mansions. The Guardian teams were better qualified for this search.

To me, Marek said, "James will take care of it, but for now, you need to prepare for a council meeting. They want you and Nikko there for the incident debrief."

"What does that mean exactly?" I asked, confused.

"They want to hear your version of events, and alternatively, they want to know if you are as good as I say you are." He answered.

I smiled at him, was he complimenting me to the higher-ups?

"I'm sure I look really intimidating from this hospital bed," I said sarcastically.

"Hold that thought," Marek said, taking a step back from the bed.

I was confused until I heard steps coming from the hall.

A man about Marek's height with similar musculature entered the room. He was dressed in a three-piece suit that looked out of place in a hospital but lovely on him. It was tailored perfectly and sat well on his lean frame. His purple tie stood out against the dark gray of the suit, but it didn't detract at all from the overall look.

The two men nodded at each other, and I looked at Marek, trying to figure out who this guy was, but he didn't give me anything. The man walked in and sat on the chair next to the bed and leaned back. He looked at me as if he was waiting for something. I raised my eyebrows at Marek, wondering what was happening.

"From what I understand, you are our new Seer, is that correct?" The man said to me but looked at Marek.

"Sebastian, let me introduce you. This is Ember Summers." Marek said, gesturing toward me and bowing slightly to the man.

"Yes, yes, what an interesting specimen." He said, eyeing me up and down.

I became self-conscious and didn't like the way he was looking at me. It was like I was merchandise for sale. Marek gave me a look that said to ignore it. Instead, I dipped my mind into his pool of power to see what this guy had. It felt similar to Marek. There was a darkness that said he was a vampire, but his power level was almost half of what Marek had.

"Ember, you can address him as Grand Master. Sabastian was recently elected the head of The Council of Guardians. He and I are old friends." He said.

"It's nice to meet you, Grand Master," I said, reaching out to shake his hand.

I had read about the protocol for vampires, but there was no guidance on how to act with a Grand Master outside of the Council's meeting, let alone in a hospital room. He outranked Marek in the organization but not in power.

I gave Marek a quizzical look, and he brushed it aside with a slight wave of his hand. I felt a surge of power, and just as quickly, it disappeared. It had come from the Grand Master.

"You surprise me, Master Volkov. I did not think you would take such a keen interest in this one." He said it casually, but Marek wasn't happy about it.

"You forget yourself, Sabastian. Has the Grand Master title gone to your head?" Marek said it calmly, but I could feel the power he put into those words.

Marek wasn't taking any shit from this guy, regardless of his title. It was also interesting to learn Marek's full name. I guessed Master Volkov meant his surname was Volkov.

"My apologies," Sabastian said, bowing to Marek.

I noticed his bow was lower than what Marek had given him, and that was significant. Marek outranked him even if Sabastian did lead The Council of Guardians.

"Forgive me for asking Grand Master, but to what do I owe the pleasure of your visit?" I asked, remembering to use all the flowery language due to a master vampire.

"Ah, yes. I suppose I do look out of place." He laughed, patting his suit. "I had to meet the Seer who bested the Egyptian. Sanz took down an Elite Guardian team within minutes, but he couldn't beat you!"

"I assure you I didn't do it alone," I said, looking up at Marek.

If Marek hadn't been there, I might not have gotten away so easily.

"Indeed. Well, you two make a good team." Sabastian smirked.

He stood and clapped Marek on the back, "She is a beauty and powerful too. I'll see you both later."

The Grand Master winked at me then left. Marek looked like he was about to laugh.

"What just happened?" I asked.

"Sabastian likes you," Marek said.

I narrowed my eyes at him, but he didn't elaborate.

"Trust me," was all he said.

Chapter Fourteen

M y first Council meeting had begun, and I was the subject matter. I sat between James and Nikko while Marek stood near the leadership team. There were five people, a few vampires, and a few humans leading the Council. Sabastian sat in the middle, and Marek hovered near the end. It was hard to tell if Marek was a ruling member or if he was with them because he led the Guardians.

My Elite Guardian team was sitting to our left, and they were being chewed out by Marek. I felt horrible for them. I wouldn't want to be the target of his anger, but when it came to me, he seemed to get even angrier. They had just finished their report, and Marek was fuming.

"Where is he now?" Marek said.

"We don't know his exact whereabouts, Master," said one of the team members.

"Let me get this straight. First, you were taken out, leaving the asset in imminent danger. Then when Ms. Summers freed you from the spell that was holding you down, you subdued him, had him in the transport van, but when you arrived at detainment, he was gone. You have no video, data, or personal observations of any kind telling you when he got away or where." Marek said.

His tone was so condescending that every member of the team had their heads down, including me. I felt like it was partly my fault. I could have fought Asher and made sure he was taken out instead of running away. I wondered what might have happened if I had stayed. With my powers, I should have been able to hold him down until back up arrived.

"*Do not blame yourself, Ember,*" Marek said in my mind.

"*I had him Marek, but I ran away,*" I said, looking up at him.

"*Not accurate, the team failed you, and they deserve to feel it. You could have been killed.*" He snapped back.

I raised my hands in surrender. The others were looking between us, trying to figure out what was happening. They didn't know we could speak mind to mind. The Grand Master had a small smile on his face, but no one else was looking at him. James looked pained, and Nikko had his eyes squinted as if narrowing his eyes would allow him to see what was happening.

I looked back at Marek. He realized others had noticed our conversation, and his face shut down. All expression was wiped away, and his blank face emerged.

"Guardian Johnson, what have you done to recover the Egyptian?" Marek asked.

"All available teams have been deployed along the route and surrounding areas. I have the loft Asher was spotted at being watched, and special ops are in place should he show. We will have him soon, Master." The man named Johnson replied.

"See to it personally, Johnson. However, your team is to stay out of the field until each member has had their performance reviewed by me." Marek said.

"Yes, Master," Johnson said head bowed.

"Team dismissed," Marek said.

The team stood immediately and left the room without a word. Their discipline was evident, and I couldn't help but think they didn't deserve such harsh treatment. I tried to shake that thought as Marek laid into James next.

James explained his version of events as Marek looked at him sternly. James had felt a presence and tried to raise the perimeter guard only to not be able to reach them. As he started to alert me, Asher Sanz put a spell on him to immobilize him. James shook off the hold, the Egyptian had on him two times, but each time he was recaptured.

Marek acknowledged that my account of the events corroborated the one James was giving and asked Nikko to weigh in. They each told their story up to the point where I fled out the back door of the office building. I perked up, curious to hear what had happened.

"As soon as Ember was out of sight, Sanz was up and moving, so I engaged him," Nikko said. "He hit me with some kind of stunning spell before throwing me through a wall. James pulled me out of the rubble, and we both went after the guy. I got in a few good strikes, as did James. I went down a few more times and was knocked out."

"That's when I was able to corner the Egyptian and take him down. The backup team arrived shortly after that and helped me bind Sanz for transport." James said. "He went quietly once subdued."

"Guardian Leigh, the next time you take down a target like Sanz, I suggest you stay with the prisoner until they are in their cage. Although I recognize that in this case, the choice was a difficult one given the injuries Mr. Manetti sustained, his status as an asset, and his connection to Ms. Summers." Marek said.

James bowed his head in acknowledgment. I looked at him and smiled, I knew he had helped Nikko, but I didn't realize he had chosen to stay with him instead of seeing Asher to containment. He knew I would be devastated if anything happened to Nikko.

"Thank you, Master, I will heed your command," James responded.

"You are dismissed. Please show Mr. Manetti back to his room. The Council has other matters to discuss with Ms. Summers." Marek said.

I smiled at James and Nikko as they left. They had fought for me, and I was grateful.

The Grand Master addressed me after the others had left. The matter of Viktor's mating claim on me was to be debated. Marek had prepared me for it, but I still wasn't happy to be discussing it.

"Ms. Summers, we are all glad to see you safe and sound. I understand there is a matter you wish to address the Council about, is that correct?" Sabastian said.

"Yes, Grand Master, Viktor Ivanov has made a claim on me that I wish to block. He has no bond with me, and I made no consent to become his mate. I request that the Council set aside his claim and recognize my independence." I said, hoping I covered everything Marek had told me to.

The council members looked at each other as if my request was distasteful. Marek had explained that it was unusual but that if I wanted to be rid of the claim, I would have to fight for myself. He wouldn't be able to step in other than to corroborate events.

"Ms. Summers, this request is highly unusual. Master Ivanov is a vampire of esteem and has the means to offer you significant wealth should you make your bond with him permanent." Said a councilwoman with blond hair.

"I understand the offer and respectfully repeat my request to be freed from him. We have no bond." I said.

"Master Volkov, what say you to this request? There are protocols in place for vampire mates." Said a councilman with black hair at the far end of the table.

"Indeed, we do Master Hartman, but, in this case, I detected no bond between Ms. Summers and Master Ivanov. Therefore, my orders have been to treat her as we do all those not claimed." He said, bowing slightly.

"Surely, a bond exists, or she would not have been claimed." The blond spoke again.

"If I may," The Grand Master said, "I met with Ms. Summers before our council convened, and I did not detect a bond between her and Master Ivanov."

I watched Sabastian, he had danced around the fact that Marek and I had a bond. Maybe ours wasn't a mating bond, but surely, he could sense it.

"I feel deliberation is required on the matter Grand Master." The blond conceded.

"Very well. Master Volkov, I request your presence in our deliberations. Ms. Summers can retire to the residence building, and we will summon her once a decision has been made." Sabastian said.

"I appreciate the invitation. I will remain," Marek said.

Marek turned and said in my mind, *"Go to James, he will take you to my room. Wait for me there."*

"Ms. Summers, you are dismissed until a decision is made." The Grand Master said with a smile.

I inclined my head to him, caught Marek's eye briefly then walked out. From what Marek had said to me before, having him in the deliberation would be a good sign. He was certain Sabastian would allow him to remain if it happened. What surprised me was that the Grand Master had invited him to stay.

I nodded my thanks and then walked out of the room to find James. I trusted Marek to plead my case. If he couldn't make it happen, it wasn't going to go my way. He knew vampire law, so if he thought this had a chance, I had to believe him.

I walked down the corridor, hoping to spot James along the way. The building felt more like a mansion than an office building. When Marek first told me we were going to the Council headquarters, I had imagined a typical corporate office. This was more like a compound.

The hallway I walked down led from the medical wing to the offices and back to the residential areas. There were training facilities, including a full gym, exercise machines, free weights, and what Marek said was a complete tactical training course and obstacle course. It sounded like a fun place to spend time.

I turned a corner and found James sitting on a bench. His head was in his hands.

"Hey, you," I said, stepping closer to him.

He looked up and forced a smile.

"Are they done in there already?" He asked.

"No, they sent me away so they could chat. Marek said to have you show me to his room." I said.

"I figured. It's this way," He said, motioning toward a hall I hadn't seen yet.

I followed James through a doorway that opened up into an area with stairs and elevators. He stopped in front of the elevators and hit the button to go up.

"Did the meeting go alright for you? It's hard for me to tell since I don't have any experience with these things." I asked.

"Yes, I fully expected Marek to ride my ass for losing the Egyptian, but he didn't. I'm sure he will say more in private." He said, rubbing his hand over his face.

He looked tired, and I realized that not only had he fought a crazy powerful guy today, but he also had expended his own power to heal Nikko. Then he had to make a report in front of all his bosses. It had to be hard.

"You look tired. Do you get to go home soon?" I asked, concerned.

He gave me a look and shook his head.

"What does that mean?" I asked.

"Ember, I don't get time off. I'm still your near guard until Marek relieves me." He said.

"Even in here? I would have thought I didn't need a guard here." I said, confused.

"There is no chance Marek would leave you unguarded for a moment with Sanz on the loose. He could be anywhere, even here." He said.

The elevator arrived, and we got on. James hit the button for the top floor. I raised my eyebrows at him, and he laughed.

"Marek is one of the highest-ranking members of The Council. What he calls a room is actually one of the penthouses. He acts modest, but he lives well." James said.

"Do you have a residence here?" I asked.

"If I have to be here overnight, I stay in the barracks. Guardians have their own space near the workout facilities. It's more convenient if we have to go out on a call in the middle of the night." He said.

The elevator stopped at the top floor, and James led me over to two doors. He entered a code into a keypad on the door on the left, and the door opened. He held the door for me, and I walked in. I wasn't prepared for what I saw.

The entryway flooring was white marble, and the walls were a deep turquoise color. Gold framed paintings lined the wall, and an ornate table sat a few feet past the door. The table had a crystal bowl and a gold lamp with a black shade. It was stunning and didn't feel like Marek at all.

"The living room is straight ahead, and the kitchen is connected. Are you hungry?" James asked.

"I could eat," I said.

The living room had dark hardwood floors and high ceilings. The furniture was modern in style but looked comfortable. The living room connected to the kitchen, which was light and bright. It had more marble, but this time on the countertops. It was stunning.

"When Marek said room, I pictured a tiny room like in the clinic downstairs," I said.

"He doesn't consider it his own. Marek travels a lot and is rarely home." James said.

I followed James into the kitchen and sat at the large island. He started pulling food out of the refrigerator and heating things up. It looked like several meals' worth of leftovers except it was too organized.

"Why does a vampire have food in his fridge?" I asked, confused.

James laughed, "Because he knew you were going to be here. He had the chef prepare some food for you. All you have to do is heat it up."

"It sounds like he went to a lot of trouble," I said, wrinkling my eyebrows.

"With as many people as are here every day, there is always food around. If you want something and don't see it in the fridge, you can call down to catering and have it brought up. Just tell them you are in Master Volkov's penthouse." James said.

"It sounds peculiar to hear him called Master Volkov. I didn't even know his last name until today. Yours too." I said.

"Everything is more formal here. Marek doesn't demand a title in the field in case someone overhears. That would be hard to explain away." James said, smiling.

He assembled a plate of roasted chicken and potatoes then added a soft roll on the side. He set it in front of me, and my mouth started to water. It looked delicious.

James made a plate for himself and sat next to me. He got us both a beer, and we dug in. I had eaten my food so fast that it was almost gone before I noticed.

"So, do you like your job?" I asked, and he looked at me funny. "I mean, you get to hang with me and eat dinner. It's got perks, right?"

He grinned at me and shook his head.

"Eating dinner with you is a perk." He admitted.

I smiled back at him and chucked him on the arm. He grabbed

me and threw me over his shoulder. I scream giggled as he ran with me into the living room. He threw me down on the couch and started tickling me. I laughed so hard I couldn't breathe.

James was on his knees focused on tickling me, so when I threw my leg over his shoulder and flipped him off me, he was shocked. He landed on his back on the floor with me on top of him.

"How did you learn to do that?" He asked, marveling at what I had done.

"The internet," I said as I stood up.

I helped him up off the floor, and he stood. Then he stepped in close to me. He didn't look like he was laughing anymore.

"James," I said softly.

I didn't want this to turn into a kissing moment. I had decided that we wouldn't be more than friends, but he and I hadn't spoken about it. It was an awkward moment, but the right time to say something.

"I know," He said and pulled me in for a hug.

He kissed me on the top of the head and suggested we watch a movie. I left him to navigate the multiple remotes and giant tv while I cleaned up dinner. I brought over our drinks just as James started a movie.

I found a blanket on the arm of the couch and pulled it over me. It may be Spring in Colorado, but that didn't mean the weather was getting any warmer. James grabbed another remote and turned on the fireplace. It was cozy and comfortable.

I must have been more tired than I thought because I woke up later, cuddled up to a warm body. I started to panic, thinking it was James until I smelled warm vanilla musk and felt the expansive power of a familiar vampire.

"Hey," I said, looking up at Marek.

He brushed the hair out of my eyes and adjusted his hold on me.

"I need to stop waking up to a different person than I fell asleep

147

with," I said.

He laughed, "You need your rest, it has been a long day."

"What time is it?" I asked, trying to see if the sun was up or not.

"It is about midnight," He answered without looking at a clock.

"You say it is, never it's. You don't like contractions, do you?" I observed yawning.

"No, I do not," He said, smiling.

I grinned back at him. I've heard it said that the more you like someone, the more attractive they become. I would say that is true with Marek. I did not like him at first, but he has grown on me, and the more I like him, the more handsome he looks to me.

"How did the meeting go?" I asked.

His face lost some of its humor as he replied.

"They recognize you do not have a bond with Viktor, but they are reluctant to make a decision. They are unsure if they have the authority to grant what you ask." He said.

"So, their decision is not to decide? That's bullshit." I said, feeling angry.

This group that was self-appointed to protect others were refusing to protect me from a crazy vampire. It was ridiculous.

"They are delaying a decision, yes." He said.

"You look worried," I said, studying his face.

"I am wondering if you have a bond with him that I cannot detect. He must believe he has one," He said, wrinkling his eyebrows in concentration.

I thought about it for a moment and tried to find any piece of Viktor's blood within me. I searched every part of me and dipped into my power to see if anything was resembling him there. I found nothing.

"We don't have a bond. I am sure of it." I said.

Marek looked relieved, but he was still worried. He was the one that convinced me to seek the Council's aid in breaking Viktor's claim.

"That is good," He said, but he was still deep in thought.

"Since the Council won't act, that leaves only one way to break Viktor's claim," I said.

"No, we will find another way." He said.

"Always trying to protect me," I said, putting my hand on his cheek.

"It is my duty," He said.

"The job," I said, upset that was his only reason.

Marek pulled me close and lifted my chin so I would look him in the eyes. What I saw there was different than his words. I should have felt it all, but I hadn't opened up to it.

"Part is the job. The rest is entirely personal." He said.

"Marek," I said.

He brushed a few strands of hair from my face and kissed my forehead. It wasn't what I expected, but it was no less welcome. I yawned and blinked hard to clear my eyes. I wanted to spend more time with Marek, but I was exhausted.

"Come, I will show you to the guest room." He stood and pulled me by the hand down the hallway.

Walking behind him, holding his hand, was surreal. This was the guy that I knew mostly as an asshole, but I trusted him more than anyone I knew. I couldn't explain it, so I just went with it. He was a powerful man, well vampire.

A few doors down, he opened a door and ushered me in. I was surprised by the décor. Instead of the modern cold style of the living room and kitchen, the guest room was warm with traditional touches that I loved. A king-sized bed of dark mahogany took up a large portion of the room. It was covered with a white duvet and blankets in shades of dusty pink and grey. The contrast with the dark wood was stunning.

A white chandelier draped with strings of crystal beads and candle style lights hung from the ceiling. It looked like it belonged in a French boudoir, not a downtown loft. The light created a pattern on the ceiling that was intricate and beautiful. The walls were a soft white with an accent wall of deep navy behind the bed.

"It's gorgeous," I marveled.

"I thought it would suit you," Marek said, smiling.

I wondered if he had it made up for me or if it had been this way before.

I noticed a bag sitting on a high-backed chair that resembled one of mine. When I opened it, I saw it was filled with my clothing and some toiletries. It was everything I needed. I looked at Marek, and he seemed proud to have surprised me.

"I had someone pick up some of your things so you would be more comfortable," Marek said.

"Thank you," I said, smiling at him.

"The room has an on-suite through that door. I will be down the hall if you need anything." He said and turned to leave.

"Marek," I said, and he turned back to me.

"Any word on Natalie?" I asked.

"Not yet, I expect another report by the morning." He said, then left.

I wondered if he was going to bed then realized he was my near guard for the evening. He would be awake and close by if I needed him.

Chapter Fifteen

Marek and James were arguing while I tried to eat my breakfast. The team had found something last night, but the news wasn't good. They thought Natalie was being held in Viktor's coven home, which was not a place they could go in. There wasn't a way to go in to get her without a very public fight.

I shoveled the last few bites of omelet into my mouth and washed it down with a vanilla latte. There are serious perks to living in the compound as a guest. I distantly wondered if I could get a coffee to go.

James was trying to make a point about breaching the north side of Viktor's complex when I interrupted.

"Wouldn't it be easier if Viktor invited me in?" I suggested.

Both men looked at me like I was crazy.

"He already promised to find me when the time was right. I can push the timeline and make him see me now." I said.

"He wouldn't let any of us near you if you did," James said.

"It is not an acceptable risk," Marek added.

"I have a few neat tricks of my own thank you very much. I can take care of myself better than either of you give me credit for." I said.

Marek stared at James for so long I was sure they were talking to each other in their minds. I tried to dip in only to get slapped back by Marek. It made my head hurt, and I rubbed at it until they turned to me.

"It could work," Marek said.

I had to pick my chin up off the floor because Marek was going to let me go in without backup. There had to be a catch, but I didn't see it yet.

"What's the plan?" I asked, trying to hide my giddiness.

I had taken out Asher Sanz, I was confident I'd be able to handle much of what Viktor could throw at me.

James said, "You make contact with him and ask for an audience. Viktor will want to meet you somewhere you will feel safe, but instead, you ask to see his home. If he thinks you are seriously considering mating with him, he might go for it."

"That is a big 'if.' I have made myself clear many times that I want nothing to do with him. Why would he believe me now?" I asked.

Viktor wasn't stupid, deluded yes, but not stupid.

"Use as much truth as possible to sell the idea," James said cryptically.

"Such as?" I asked, not knowing where he was going with this.

"Vampire blood. You have grown a taste for it. He will know that as soon as he is close enough to you to detect our bond. You also want your sister back. If he gives you both, it is a reasonable bargain." Marek said.

"So, if he releases my sister, I'll agree to form a bond with him to see if we can make it work? It's weak, and what's to stop him from taking me as his mate without permission?" I said.

"You will," Marek said with a hint of pain on his face.

It was gone before James noticed, but I saw it and felt it from him. He wasn't happy with it but knew it was our best shot.

"How?" I asked.

Marek looked at me, and I understood. He would teach me, but I wouldn't like it.

"Lessons," was all Marek said.

I pushed my plate away. I felt a little ill at what I was going to have to do to resist Viktor, but if it got my sister back, I was all in. I told Marek that, and we got to work.

James called in a few Guardians to wait outside the apartment in case they were needed. He wanted what was actually happening to remain a secret as much as possible. I appreciated it since when I drank vampire blood, things got personal. I was hoping James would stay outside too, but Marek insisted he stay.

"James has brought you out of it before, and he can get through to me if needed," Marek said as an explanation.

I shook my head and agreed. This was going to suck, but it was going to feel awesome before that. James was going to be in for a show.

"How are we doing this?" I asked, anxious to get this done.

"I will try a psychic attack first. Then we have a blood exchange, and you will try to resist me. Viktor doesn't know what you can do, so I will not tell you what to expect from me. Then you roll me as if I were him and make me do something I wouldn't normally agree to. Do not tell me what it will be until you are sure I am in your thrall. Understood?" He explained.

"Got it," I said nervously.

If I couldn't stop Marek, this was all for nothing. I had to be strong enough so I could get Natalie back. I could do this, I just had to stay focused. Marek wouldn't go easy on me, which would help.

"Block me from your mind," He said, then hit me so hard with a psychic attack that it doubled me over.

He picked and pulled and hit and tried to steal everything in my brain. It was all force, and at first, I couldn't do anything but bare the pain. I remembered some of what James had taught me about blocking vampires, and I took a deep breath and pushed an imaginary wall out from my mind. It started as a tiny bubble keeping my thoughts from Marek first, then it grew.

I felt a tiny bit of relief as the bubble expanded out beyond my head and began to push down my body. Marek's attack grew, and the bubble threatened to pop. I turned it to glass just as it covered my body. That was a mistake.

Marek smirked and shattered the glass. The broken pieces cut just like real glass. I felt every cut as they drew blood. I heard James yelling, but I tuned him out. We weren't stopping, no matter what. I had to learn this the hard way. It was the best way.

Marek paused his attack for a split second. He could smell my blood, and it was calling to him. I used it to my advantage. I took a few steps closer to him, and he took a step back before realizing what he had done. It was too late. I already pushed myself into his mind.

The steel wall stopped me from getting too far, but not before I felt his fear. I copied his wall just as he tried another attack. This time he bounced right off, but he didn't stop. I held the wall up as he hammered at it. It was exhausting, but I pushed all I had into it.

"Don't use up all your energy in one defense, Ember," James said.

I let up slightly and still held the barrier. I wasn't being drained as severely, although it was still taking a lot of energy to maintain. Marek kept up the psychic attack as he stepped forward. I held my ground, but he came closer ever so slowly.

"What are you doing, Marek?" I asked.

He smiled and dropped the attack. I slumped from the sudden release but stayed aware of what he was doing. The lesson was far from over.

"That was good, Ember," Marek said but frowned at all the cuts on my skin.

They were healing but not as quickly as he wanted them to.

"Now, the blood exchange. Come here." He ordered.

He pulled me into him and struck my neck so fast I didn't have a chance to move. To say it hurt would be an understatement. All the times I had let him take blood before it hurt a little but not like this.

I cried out and punched him. It didn't slow him down at all, but it made me feel better. Then Marek turned his bite into the most exquisite silky warmth I had ever felt.

I pulled Marek closer and ran my hands up his body then around his neck. My fingers ruffled through his hair and then back down over his chest. At that moment, I realized I was getting dizzy and remembered that he was still drinking my blood. He usually stopped by now, but this is a lesson, and he wouldn't hold back even if it might kill me.

"Focus, Ember," James said sternly.

I used the panic I felt to pull myself out of the haze Marek had put me under and focus on getting him to stop drinking. I put my hands up to his neck, thumbs right over his larynx, and pushed as hard as I could. I put a little of my power into it, and he immediately stopped drinking and pulled back.

His lips dripped with blood, my blood, and he looked pissed. He tried to talk and realized he couldn't. I had crushed his voice box.

He grabbed me and threw me toward the wall. I used my power to slow myself down and hit with the same speed as if a human had thrown me. It still hurt.

Before I could get up, he wrestled me onto my back and bit my neck again. This time I couldn't move my hands. He had them held above my head, and his legs pinned my legs down as well. I couldn't move him.

The golden warmth filled me again, and I knew what it was this time. It was the mating bond. It felt beautiful, and I couldn't help my body arching under his. I could feel his body responding, too. I had to fight really hard to not want it, not to want him.

I pulled at the thread of our bond. Now that we had shared

blood, I could easily find it even with Marek shutting it down. I pulled tentatively at first and felt the warmth coming from Marek wane. Knowing I had found the right thing, I pulled on it hard. I practically yanked it into me, and he stopped drinking.

"Off my neck vampire," I said softly but infused it with power.

He stopped drinking, and reluctantly let me go. He stood up but kept his eyes on me. He wasn't entirely under my control, so I pulled on the threads again, and his control slipped enough for me to get under it. The snarling look on his face went away, and he started to shake. He was fighting it, but I had him.

"Kneel," I said, infusing my word with power.

Marek continued to stand, although shaking, he still wouldn't move. I second-guessed my command. Maybe making a vampire kneel was too difficult. There wasn't anything more debasing in vampire society than to kneel to someone perceived to be less in power, especially someone who wasn't a vampire.

I wobbled as I stood up and walked toward him, making sure I had a hold of him still. Then I reached out and touched his cheek. Our connection increased with the contact, and I commanded him to kneel again. His teeth ground together, and his hands balled into fists. His knuckles were white from the strain, but his legs began to bend.

He kneeled, but he continued to shake. I had him, but the control was hard to maintain. He was fighting me even though he was on the ground before me.

"Release him, Ember," James said.

I looked at him. I wasn't sure that it was a good idea. I wanted to be far away from Marek when I let him go.

"You passed the test. I will not hurt you." Marek said through gritted teeth.

I took a deep breath and let go. Marek collapsed to the floor, and I went with him. I didn't realize how much effort I was putting into the hold. When I let it go, my body had had enough. I lay gasping for breath on the floor, and Marek laughed. He laughed!

"You're an asshole," I said, groaning.

"You like assholes," He said softly.

I looked at him, and he was smiling. I couldn't help but smile back. Dammit, he was becoming my Kryptonite.

James was there a moment later, helping me to my feet and over to the couch. I fell into it and was thankful this was only a lesson. As much as Marek said he would go all out, I think he held back.

"James, thank you," Marek said, dismissing him.

He bowed and left the apartment. I saw the men and women he had standing by when he opened the door. From what I could tell, he took them with him.

"You could have fought harder," I said to Marek once we were alone.

"Maybe, maybe not," He said, sounding uncertain. "We are evenly matched."

My eyebrows raised in disbelief. A master vampire just admitted that I had an equal amount of power as he had. I didn't take that lightly.

He stopped fighting the bond at that moment and then rushed over to me. Most of the cuts had healed, but I was super tired and finding it harder to stay awake than I should have.

"You used more power than you ever have before, and I took a lot of blood from you." He said, pulling out his knife.

"I just need to sit for a bit," I said, insisting I was okay.

Like usual, he didn't listen to me and pressed the point of his knife into his neck. He crouched down in front of me, kneeling between my legs. The symbolism stood out. He was happy to kneel before me. It made me wonder if I really did force him to kneel.

He pulled me forward and brought my face to his neck. I stopped protesting and leaned down, pressing my lips over the first drop of blood. I swallowed the power and savored the caramel flavor. Marek wrapped his arms around my waist and pulled me in closer to him. My legs wrapped around his body automatically.

After a few swallows, I felt myself perk up. I was more drained, pun intended than I had realized. I needed to pay more attention to what my opponent was doing. Viktor could drain me before I knew what was happening, and if I was dead, so was my sister. I pulled away from Marek, but he didn't move.

I ran my tongue over my bottom lip, cleaning away the last drop of his blood. Marek watched with hunger in his eyes. It wasn't a craving for blood.

"Marek," I whispered.

He pulled me down onto his lap with my legs, straddling him. It was the most intimate we had ever been, and if my breathing was anything to show for it, I was excited. His blood was an aphrodisiac, and I was primed and ready for whatever happened next.

"How do you feel?" He asked.

"Much better," I said, our faces so close our lips were almost touching.

"I do not want you to do this," He said, leaning his forehead against mine.

I closed my eyes and wrapped my arms around him.

"Did you hold back at all earlier?" I asked, referring to the lesson we had just completed.

"No," He said.

I felt a sharp pain in my chest that wasn't my own. He was well and truly afraid for me to face Viktor.

"If I don't do this, I lose my sister, and that isn't an option," I said.

"I know," He said.

"I can do it," I insisted.

He nodded, but it was clear he didn't like it.

A knock at the door interrupted us. Marek sighed. Then he lifted me off his lap and set me back onto the couch as if I didn't weigh a thing. It made my heart rate speed up, and the corner of his mouth lifted. He paused for a moment after he stood, then walked away to answer the door.

The knock on the door was James. He had news.

"A package was delivered for Ember," James said.

He brought the box to the kitchen island and motioned me over. It was a large brown box with a lift-off lid. It was huge.

"Is it safe to open?" I asked, approaching the box.

"It's been checked, and no spells or any other dangers have been found," James assured me.

I lifted the lid and saw a card on top of a gorgeous navy colored gown. The card was addressed to me. I opened it and read it aloud.

Master Julien Le Veneur requests your presence to honor his daughter, Sasha Le Veneur coming into society at Nine O'clock this evening.

Your presence is expected in formal attire enclosed.

* One guest is permitted

"Shit!" James exclaimed.

He ran his hands through his hair and looked like something terrible had just happened. The behavior was uncharacteristic of his usual calm.

I looked to Marek for his reaction, and he was the picture of serenity. His emotions were conflicted. He was afraid and yet accepting.

"Why am I being invited to a teenager's coming out party, and why are you so upset about it?" I said, looking first at James and then at Marek.

"This is no teenager's party, Ember. It is the presentation of Master Le Veneur's newest vampire." Marek said in a tone that had me feeling scolded.

"Why am I invited to a vampire party?" I asked.

"Julien is honoring you with the invitation, and you will attend," Marek said, ignoring James.

Marek pulled his cell phone out of his pocket and spoke in Russian to the person who answered. It sounded like he was mostly barking orders. Master vampires were prone to superiority complexes from what I could tell. It was a side effect of a society that honored those with a lot of power above all others.

"Okay, who is my plus one?" I asked, hoping it was Marek.

"I will assign a Guardian of proper rank to accompany you," Marek said.

I looked at James. I would have assumed he would be the one to accompany me if Marek wasn't going to do that job.

"Dhampir's aren't accepted at vampire events. We are the vampire's dirty secret, not something worth an invitation." James said.

He looked upset, but his words made sense.

"Why can't you come?" I asked Marek.

"I cannot be your chaperone," Marek said, holding up his hands when he saw I was about to protest. "I expect I will be attending in my capacity with The Council of Guardians. I attend most new family announcements."

"Will this be a room filled entirely with vampires?" I asked.

Both James and Marek nodded yes, and my stomach dropped. Navigating the protocols and social norms of a vampire gathering was going to be a significant challenge.

I moved to the couch and sat down hard. The weight of what I was about to walk into had hit me. I would be the only prey within a group of predators. It was madness.

"Ember, you will be an honored guest. There is little danger." Marek said.

I looked at him and saw his confidence, but underneath there was a sense of discomfort. He wasn't as sure as he wanted me to think he was, and that was what had me scared. If the most powerful vampire I had ever heard of was frightened, I should be too.

"I'm going to need a few things to go with that dress," I announced.

Chapter Sixteen

My stomach flipped a few times as my companion and I approached the mansion. It was a large estate in the Belcaro neighborhood of Denver surrounded by a high brick wall and even higher trees that created a private space within the city. The Tudor home was massive and looking at it all lit up took my breath away. It wasn't my personal style preference, but it did impress none the less.

The front door was flanked by vines that grew up the height of the structure, softening the brick and making it feel welcoming. I went up the stairs, noticing the guards stationed on either side of the door looked past me as if they didn't find me worth their notice.

Marek had to be insane to trust no harm would come to me while I was here. This coven was loyal to Viktor and had to be in on his plans. Of course, Marek sent one of his best bodyguards to accompany me to the party, so his confidence may have been mostly bluff.

My guard was a high-status vampire and a trusted bodyguard, protecting key members of The Council. He looked as normal as I imagined a vampire could be. His blonde hair was trimmed short above his ears, and his face was pleasing if a little ordinary. I supposed he would blend in well in a crowd if it weren't for his expensive suit.

Caden motioned me forward, where I stepped into the entry vestibule. The ceiling was painted gold, although it could have been real gold, I certainly wouldn't know the difference. I expected there would be someone to take my wrap but quickly

EMBER'S SHADOW - INTO THE DARKNESS

remembered that this was a vampire party, so no one else would have the need to wear a jacket.

Caden tugged me forward then motioned to a bench where a maid waited. He helped me remove my fur wrap and handed it off to her. She curtsied and opened a door that looked hidden until she tapped it. She hung up my shawl as Caden led me further into the house.

A spiral staircase took up the center of the room with several doorways leading to other parts of the home. Based on the amount of noise coming from straight ahead, it was clear that was where we were supposed to go. I didn't wait for Caden to follow. I just walked forward with confidence.

One of the tips Marek had given me for tonight was to exude confidence and not let anyone push me around. My power would be apparent to any vampire in the room, and anyone else would figure it out in short order. If I let anyone think I was below them, it would make this night more difficult to survive.

I walked forward and entered a large room with gleaming wooden floors and an intricate coffered ceiling. When I stepped through the doorway, every eye in the room turned my direction.

Caden caught up to me at that moment and put out his arm. I slipped my hand around his elbow and allowed him to lead me further into the room. At his appearance, several of the interested vampires turned their heads back to their own companions. The ones who continued to look, stared at me like I was the most interesting thing they had ever seen.

"You are stunningly beautiful milaya moya," Marek said in my mind.

I turned to see him standing casually against the far wall. I tried to keep the smile off my face, but I must have failed because he frowned slightly. I worked to make my face blank and looked away. Caden was looking at me when I turned around. He smiled and inclined his head toward a woman who was standing to his right.

She was tall with long black hair and emerald eyes. She wore a dress that matched her eyes. She smiled at me when our eyes met, and I instantly liked her. I matched her smile then looked at Caden.

"Ember, if I may introduce you. This is my sire Sabrina Thorn, master of her coven." Caden said.

"It is a pleasure," I smiled. Sabrina inclined her head to me, acknowledging my rank.

"You have made a name for yourself in a short time Madame Summers. Finding you on the arm of my son is a welcome surprise." Sabrina said with a sly smile.

Her power crackled over my skin, but it didn't affect me the way that Marek's power did. Maybe it was because she was female, but I think it was because she wasn't as powerful. She had more than most of the vampires in the room but nowhere near as powerful as me.

"Sabrina is a master vampire with a large coven. Be careful what you say to her." Marek broadcasted into my head.

I resisted the urge to roll my eyes at Marek. I appreciated the information but didn't need the warning.

"Thank you, madame. I find your son very pleasing." I stated politely.

The fact that Caden was part of her family made me nervous. Marek had assured me he was someone we could trust, but I wondered how far that trust would go if tested. Would he protect me over her?

Caden smirked and said, "She is following protocol well, don't you think mother?"

"I wouldn't tease her, Caden. She has more power than most of the vampires in this room combined." Sabrina said, touching his arm.

She curtsied to me before stepping away. Her emerald skirt flared out and rustled pleasantly when she moved. The curtsy was another nod to my rank, and it shocked me enough that I was struck dumb for a moment.

"Shall we mingle?" Caden said, and I nodded.

He led me through the room, introducing me as we went. Each person bowed or curtsied to me or both of us when we moved on. The ranking system was evident, and somehow, I was above all we had met.

We turned to the next group we would meet, and I found that I recognized one of the vampires that stood before me. We hadn't met before, but I had seen him. He was slightly taller than Marek, who stood near him, and his long blonde hair fell just below his shoulders. He was handsome as most vampires were, but he was clearly important based on how others kneeled or bowed before him.

Marek's eyes found mine as Caden and I stopped before their group. He inclined his head slightly to me, showing me to be his equal. The group before him all bowed, including the striking blonde next to him.

"May I present Julien Le Veneur, our host and master of his coven," Caden said with a bow.

I started to curtsy, but Julien took my hand and bowed before me, placing a kiss to my knuckles. It shocked me so much that I didn't know what to do for a moment. Master Le Veneur felt similar in power to me and being a coven master should have tipped his rank higher than mine.

"Your shock is evident, Madame, but your honor is deserved. I can assure you that I do not debase myself without cause." Julien said, smiling.

His voice held a slight French accent that was beautiful. If my romantic interests weren't pulled in another direction, I would be very interested in this man. He was well dressed and looked

NICHOLE M. BRIDGES

like he was born to it.

"Then, I thank you, sir. And I compliment you on your beautiful home. I have not seen its equal." I said, smiling back at him.

"And you honor me," Julien said, bowing again. "Your words have not done her justice, Master Volkov. She is a wonder."

Marek smiled at Julien. I felt the pride coming from him and a touch of joy.

"That she is," Marek agreed.

The smile on his face brought a smile to my lips as well.

"She has delighted everyone she has met this evening," Caden added.

"You are all too kind," I said, giving Caden a look for laying it on too thick.

"If you will permit me, Madame, I would ask the honor to escort you for the remainder of your introductions," Julien said with bowed head.

Marek inclined his head, indicating his approval. I didn't need it.

"I graciously accept Master Le Veneur," I said.

"Please, call me Julien." He said, reaching out his hand to me.

"Very well, Julien," I said, taking his hand.

He led me away from Marek and Caden, much like Caden had led me around the room before him with my hand on the crook of his elbow.

"I must say that the way you speak my name delights me. Do you speak French?" Julien asked.

"I am sad to say I do not. I wish I did." I said.

"I'm sure you will in time. Your pronunciation is *presque parfaite*, nearly perfect." He said as we walked.

"Merci," I said, remembering the French way of saying thank you.

Julien laughed and said, "You continue to surprise me, Madame.

166

I had not anticipated your wit, and your beauty shines in this gown."

He motioned to the gift he had given me with my invitation.

"I owe that to you. It fits perfectly. How did you know my size?" I asked curious to know more about this man, well vampire.

"My sire shared a great many things with me, including your size." He said, but he didn't seem pleased.

"And did he ask you to invite me?" I ventured hesitantly.

"You know Viktor does not ask, but it matters not. I am glad to have you on my arm. Every vampire in this room wishes to have the honor. Don't you see the envious eyes?" He motioned with his hand to the others.

What I saw surprised me. Every person who wasn't already engaged in a conversation had their eyes on me. Marek would be displeased that I had been so ignorant.

"I'm sure some of the admiration is for you. They are here to meet your daughter, are they not?" I asked.

"Indeed, but as with any vampire function, this is an opportunity to be seen and impress those above one's rank. If you allow me to continue, I shall do just that." Julien said, smiling.

I inclined my head to him and let him lead me on. He smiled and turned me to see who he wanted to introduce me to next. My breath caught as my eyes landed on the vampire he intended me to see.

"Sire, you honor me with your presence," Julien said, bowing to his maker.

"Julien," Viktor nodded to his son.

"*Votre intention,*" Julien bowed, motioning toward me.

I could only guess what he was saying, but I was sure it was something I did not like.

"*Mon destiné à,*" Viktor said, bowing to me.

That I understood. With his words, the room went quiet. Every ear in the building was awaiting my reply.

"Are you speaking French to try to confuse me, Viktor?" I said, trying to sound amused.

"Would you prefer Russian *moye prednaznacheniye*?" Viktor said with one eyebrow raised.

"French is more pleasing to the ear, but the words you speak I suspect are not accurate," I said, turning to walk away.

He reached out and grabbed my hand, attempting to pull me back. I turned back around so quickly that several people gasped at how quickly I moved.

"Touch me again without my permission Viktor, and I will not be so polite," I said, raising my power to push him back and make him let go.

He surprised me by stepping back on his own and raising his hands in surrender. His eyes still held mine, but his physical being had retreated.

"Take care, or you will start a fight right here," Marek said in my mind.

I fought not to turn and look at him. Instead, I looked at those that were standing nearest to Viktor. I was disappointed not to find my sister among them.

"She is not here," Viktor said as if I hadn't already known.

"Why?" I asked him, staring at him expectantly.

"She is the guest of another this evening," He said, grinding his teeth together at the end.

I stepped closer to him, and I could swear that he almost flinched.

"Who?" I asked insistently.

"I believe you already know." He said, looking sad.

I nodded but dared not say the name. Every vampire in this room would be upset by it if I did.

Julien stood by me as if waiting for me to take his arm. I decided the confrontation with Viktor had to wait. I took Julien's arm and motioned him forward. I wasn't going to give Viktor any more of my time. I would find him later or after the party.

After a few steps, Julien spoke, "You deny my sire at your own peril."

"He is a misogynistic dinosaur from the past. In this day and age, one asks a lady for her hand, he does not take it without permission." I said, daring him to contradict me.

"I can see why he likes you," Julien smiled.

I looked up at him and saw that he was genuinely amused.

"I insulted your sire, and you are happy about it?" I said softly.

"Did you say anything that wasn't true?" Julien asked, leaning into me.

I narrowed my eyes at him but found that he was genuine.

"I think I like you, Julien," I said with a small smile.

All eyes were on us as we walked. I hadn't realized it until that moment.

"*Retour à la fête!*" Julien said to his guests.

They all immediately resumed what they were doing and stopped staring at us. Julien clearly held power in this room, and if I was going to be around this group of vampires, I needed to learn French. I probably needed to learn Russian too.

"Are we friends, Madame Summers?" Julien asked.

"That depends. Why are you asking?" I asked.

Julien quickly led me through a doorway and around a corner. The area was empty of vampires making it seem private. He turned me to face him.

"Marek is a friend of mine and someone I respect. He hasn't bonded anyone in centuries. When you stepped before me tonight, I knew instantly you shared a bond with him." Julien said.

"Explain to me how that makes us friends, Julien," I said.

"It doesn't, but I guarantee you I'm not the only one that noticed your connection to Marek. As a friend, I will stand with him if anyone tries to take advantage of that knowledge as I would with you. Given the conversation you just had with Viktor, you are going to need a friend." Julien said.

"I can use more friends," I admitted.

"You don't make anything easy, do you? I'm offering you my friendship. Do you accept?" He asked.

I thought for a moment and was going to reach out to Marek until I felt him behind me.

"He is trustworthy," Marek whispered into my ear.

I shivered at the feel of his breath on my skin and his hands touching my bare shoulders. I kept myself from leaning back into his body. It wasn't a good idea to broadcast our connection.

"Then I accept," I told Julien.

"Wonderful!" He exclaimed and pulled me in for a hug.

I could feel my vampire bristling behind me, so when Julien let go, I stepped back into Marek. His hands went back to my shoulders, and I felt his lips touch against my neck. It happened so quickly, though; I wasn't sure that Julien even noticed.

"I am going to go get my daughter. Will you be the first to meet her?" He asked me.

"Of course," I said, feeling honored.

"Good, stay here. I'll bring Sasha down." Julien said then rushed off.

Marek turned me around and pressed me into the wall, looking around to be sure we were alone.

"Are we alone?" Marek asked.

I scanned the area and found everyone was in the main room. I told him so.

"You denied Viktor publicly. He will not let that go." He said, worried.

"I think he needs my help," I said.

"What do you mean?" He responded.

"He doesn't have Nat. He said she is a guest of someone I met recently. That can only mean that Asher took her from Viktor." I said.

"And you believe him?" He said.

"It didn't feel like manipulation, but I can't be sure," I said.

"Stay near to Caden or me. Julien will help you, but only if it doesn't go directly against his sire." Marek said.

"Good to know," I said, feeling scared.

He moved closer to me.

"*Milaya moya*, I have wanted to touch you since you walked through the door. The thought of you wearing a dress given to you by another vampire has been driving me insane." He said, stroking the bare skin of my shoulders and neck.

If he was going for a distraction, it worked. I couldn't think of anything but the feel of his fingertips sliding along my neck and down over my shoulders. Then down my arms and up again. My entire body was tingling.

He leaned in like he was going to kiss me, but I ducked out of the way. He looked upset.

"Don't you dare mess up my lipstick. Every woman in this house is flawless. I can't compete if my lipstick gets smeared." I said.

He smiled and said, "Every eye has been unable to look anywhere, but at you, since you arrived. And you worry about your lipstick."

"That doesn't help me, Marek," I said, feeling self-conscious.

He smiled and pulled my hand to his lips. He kissed my palm, and my thoughts quickly shifted from nerves to desire. His lips might be magic because he was the only one that had ever kissed me there and certainly the only one that could put me in a haze of sexual desire with one kiss.

"Are we interrupting?" Julien asked with a smirk.

"Shit Julien, you scared me," I admitted then wished I hadn't.

The woman next to Julien stifled a laugh. She had long dark hair styled in thick waves trailing down her back. Her dress was beautiful black silk with spaghetti straps that skimmed her body in a flattering way. She was gorgeous.

"New love is a beautiful thing," She said.

Marek gave her a look, and her face dropped instantly.

"I meant no offense Master Volkov," She said, looking at the ground.

I looked between the vampires and realized no one was going to tell her it was okay.

"It's no big deal. Ignore him. You must be Sasha. I'm Ember." I said, smiling.

She looked at Julien and Marek before responding to me.

"I'm pleased to meet you, Madame Summers," She said, clearly taking the formal thing seriously and adding in a low bow to top it off.

"We are all friends here. Call me, Ember." I said, walking over to her and pulling her hand into mine.

She squeezed my hand, and I thought she was glad to have someone treat her like a human.

"In private only," Julien mentioned.

I rolled my eyes at him, and Sasha laughed. She covered her mouth, but it was too late. I laughed with her. She was my kind of people.

"Shall we?" Marek said, reaching for me.

I took his arm, and we walked ahead of Julien and Sasha. All eyes turned our way when we stepped into the main room. It was clear to everyone that we were walking in with the guest of honor, and they craned their heads to see her behind us.

When Julien stepped through the doorway, a servant rang a bell. Sasha looked terrified, but when she saw me, I smiled back at her, and she relaxed. I gave her a thumbs-up, and she laughed. It made her look more beautiful to see her with a big smile.

Julien gave me a look but ended up smiling when he saw Sasha's reaction. It was clear that if she was happy, he would be happy. If I was a sinister character, I could use that to my advantage. He's lucky that I'm not.

He turned to the crowd and addressed them.

"Ladies and gentlemen, may I present my newest daughter, Sasha," Julien said, and the crowd erupted in applause.

Everyone crowded in to introduce themselves to her. She looked nervous but was doing really well, considering how many vampires were giving her attention. I'm not sure I could have handled it any better.

Marek tensed suddenly beside me. I checked on his mood and felt concern coming from him. He pulled us away from the crowd. We headed toward a door that opened up to the back yard. Whatever he was upset about clearly involved me, or we wouldn't be leaving.

"What's going on?" I asked as soon as we were outside.

"My team spotted the Egyptian nearby. I need you to see if you can track him." He said.

"Shit," I stage whispered.

This was not expected, but if I could find him, maybe we can find Nat too.

I concentrated on the area and felt each person, vampire, and other supernaturals. As I looked out further, I found a human and a vampire a few blocks over, moving quickly toward the mansion.

"I have a vampire and a human moving this way," I said.

"Is the human, Sanz?" Marek asked.

I concentrated harder on the human trying to find the well of power within. It was familiar.

"Yes, it's him. Why is he with a vampire?" I asked.

Marek pulled out his phone and typed so fast I couldn't see what he wrote. Then he went still. Marek was probably communicating with the on-site Guardian team. He had explained that they had a bond that he could use for when technology took too long or was unavailable.

"Where is he exactly?" Marek asked.

I pushed the location through our bond, it was easier than trying to explain. A huge perk of having a connection with him.

"We need to warn Julien," I said.

He was the host of this shindig. He deserved to know shit was going to get real.

"Go inside and see if you can bring him out here. If you see Caden grab him too. He hasn't responded to my text." Marek said.

I half ran, half wobbled on my high heels back to the main room. I didn't see Caden but found Julien stuck within a group of well-wishers. He looked like he was enjoying it, but I was going to have to rain on his parade.

When I walked further into the room, someone grabbed me, pulling me over next to a large flower arrangement. When I looked over, I saw it was Viktor.

"What the hell? Didn't I warn you about touching me without permission? That includes grabbing me and yanking me around Viktor." I said.

"Your sister is near, and I'm afraid you are going to be very angry with me." He said.

"More upset than I already am?" I said, yanking my elbow out of his hand.

"Yes," He said and actually looked remorseful.

"Jesus Viktor, what did you do?" I asked.

"You will find out in a moment. I assume you have a Guardian team here, correct?" He asked.

"Yes, of course," I said, feeling like he was asking stupid questions.

"Good, we are going to need them." He said.

"We?" I asked incredulously.

"Yes, we. Natalie's captor is a powerful man of which I'm sure you are aware." He stated.

I thought for a moment and wondered if he was sincere. If he was, the enemy of my enemy was my friend and all that.

"Shit, can you tell Julien without anyone hearing?" I asked.

He nodded his head.

"Good, do it. I need to find Caden. You go out back and tell Marek what you just told me." I said.

Viktor bowed to me then left to go out the back door.

"Incoming Marek. I sent Viktor to you. He says Nat is nearby, and he wants to help...I think." I told him through the bond.

"Viktor?" He asked, just as confused as I was.

"I know. I'm going to see if I can find Caden." I said, then pushed into the crowd of the room.

I didn't see Caden among the crowd, but I did see his sire. Sabrina looked cozy next to a handsome vampire I hadn't seen before. I decided I had to chance her anger for interrupting them. I needed Caden more.

As I walked toward her, she caught my eye and smiled. She leaned into the vampire next to her and whispered something. They both laughed. I hoped it wasn't about me.

"The topic of the night approaches," Sabrina said as I stepped up to her.

"I hope not," I said, cringing slightly.

She laughed, "You have out staged the guest of honor, poor dear, but why wouldn't you? I'm so glad you came to talk to me."

"I was hoping you might know where Caden is. I seem to have misplaced him." I said, hoping it sounded benign.

"Let's see," she paused for a moment. "He is on his way over."

She motioned to the other side of the room, and I saw Caden making a beeline for me. I looked at the vampire standing next to Sabrina and tried to look interested as he spoke.

"Madame Summers, I'm Nicholas Blake. It is very nice to meet you." He said.

"He is a member of Julien's coven and a specialist on the bounty hunting side of their business," Sabrina added.

He could come in handy in a fight most likely. I hoped there were more like him at this party.

Caden took my arm at that moment, and I made my apologies for having to step away.

"Did you get Marek's message?" I asked.

He nodded, "And the subsequent messages threatening me for letting you out of my sight."

I laughed, "He can be overprotective sometimes."

Caden just looked at me. It was clear he didn't see the humor in my statement.

"He was with you at the time," He said.

"That is a losing argument," I said, smirking.

I knew precisely what Marek was like, and I didn't feel sorry for Caden. He had to know Marek better than I did.

Julien found us as we were about to go into the back yard.

"Tell me this isn't as serious as Viktor is making it out to be," Julien said to me.

"I'm afraid it might be. Come on," I said, stepping outside.

I stopped short when I saw Marek, and the two vampires ran into me. I didn't think that was possible.

"What are you doing?" I said, running over to Marek.

Marek had Viktor by the neck and was holding him up so that his feet didn't touch the ground. At the sound of my voice, Marek turned to look at me. He was pissed off, and I could only imagine what Viktor had said to cause this.

"Since he can't talk, he is telling me it was to save her," Julien announced.

"He was wrong to do it," Marek said through clenched teeth.

"What is going on, guys?" I asked, confused.

Marek dropped Viktor, and he crumpled to the ground grabbing at his neck. I could see a purple mark in the shape of Marek's hand.

"As you requested, I filled him in on the circumstances, and he was not happy to hear it," Viktor said.

"Clearly," I said like he was the biggest idiot in the vicinity.

He probably was given his proclivity for acting in his own interests.

"The team is in place, Master," Caden said to Marek.

"Good, we are going to need every one of them in addition to any able body willing to jump into the fray," Marek said, and my eyes went wide.

Julien nodded to Marek and left faster than I could track. My guess was he was going to rally his own troops and see to Sasha. At least I hoped he was going to make sure she would be protected. For a new vampire, she is powerful, but she could also be a target given her lack of experience.

"You want to fill me in on what Viktor said to you that made you strangle him?" I asked Marek.

"No, I do not." He said truthfully.

"What did you do?" I said to Viktor, grabbing him from the

ground.

I pushed him up against the exterior of the house, holding him tight with my power.

"I saved her life!" He exclaimed but didn't elaborate.

"Natalie?" I asked, and Viktor nodded. "How?"

"I do not want to tell you," He pouted like a child.

"Spill it, Viktor!" I yelled.

Then I felt Asher Sanz step into the yard. He held a vampire by the arm, and she was struggling, trying to get away. I couldn't get a good look at her.

"Well shit," Viktor said.

I was so surprised at his use of a curse word that I dropped him. He fell to the ground in an inelegant heap. He looked up at me as if he was begging for his life. A surge of dread filled my body as I took another look at the vampire Asher was holding.

"Natalie?" I asked with a croaking voice.

No, no, no, no, no, this couldn't be true.

"Ember, help me. This guy is insane!" Natalie yelled.

Asher punched her in the face, and she reacted with uncontrolled anger. Her face no longer looked human. She was suddenly a monster.

I took a step back, and her eyes locked on mine. She snarled, and Asher let her go. She was on me within a second, but both Caden and Marek were there too. They stopped her just before she could take a bite out of my neck.

"Viktor, after I kill Asher, I am coming after you," I promised.

His face turned white, and he nodded.

Guardians poured into the back yard and surrounded Asher.

"Ember, a little help here," Marek said, struggling with my sister.

My jaw dropped as my sister landed an elbow into Caden's nose, knocking him out cold. He fell to the ground, unmoving. Marek lost his grip on her a moment later, and she launched herself at me.

"Natalie!" I yelled as she ran toward me.

Chapter Seventeen

All hell broke loose as soon as my sister came after me. Guardians jumped out from the trees and ran after Asher or tried to take down my sister. A Guardian I didn't know grabbed Natalie and started to yank her head as if he was going to break her neck. I seized him with my kinetic power and made him let go of her.

"She lives, asshole!" I yelled at him.

When I thought he understood, I slowly let him go. He stepped away, letting my sister loose in the process. She hesitated for a moment, thinking she might go after the Guardian then thought better of it and turned to me.

Blood was running down her face from where Asher had broken her nose. It seemed to be what was fueling her rage, but I was no expert on newly turned vampires. What I did know was that I was the only human close to her, and her instincts were telling her that she needed blood.

Viktor stepped in and tried to hold her while yelling for her to gain control. It would have been comical if it wasn't so scary. Natalie finally had the upper hand on Viktor, but she had to become a crazed vampire to get there.

Natalie threw Viktor into the wall, dislodging several bricks where he crashed. I hoped Julien didn't get upset about that and rethink his offer of making me a friend of the coven. Satisfied that Viktor was down for the moment, Natalie turned back to me. As she leaped forward, I grabbed her with my kinetic power and stopped her mid-step. She looked like a crazed Barbie doll about to jump into her Malibu dream car.

I resisted the urge to laugh because, really, this was insane. My sister was boring and cute and deserved the white picket fence and 2.5 kids in the suburbs. That would never be available to her now.

Marek stepped up next to me and asked, "What do you want to do with her?"

"I can hold her for a while, but not forever," I said.

"Let her go, and I'll grab her. I can take her down without hurting her." He said.

"I can help," Viktor piped up in the conversation.

"You are the reason she is here, Viktor. I think you've done enough." I said, seething with anger.

"Let her go *milaya moya*. You can trust me." Marek said.

I could trust him. I spared a look for Viktor, who looked like he had a broken arm. It made me feel better.

"I'll let her go when you are ready. Viktor, stay out of the way and let Marek handle this." I said.

Viktor took a few steps back, giving Marek plenty of room to work with. Marek bit into his wrist then nodded to me. I didn't like what he was planning, but I followed his lead after giving him a look letting him know I wasn't happy about it.

I released Natalie, and Marek subdued her by putting his bleeding wrist in her face. She latched on like a hungry puppy. While she drank, he took a pair of cuffs out of his suit jacket and restrained her.

"Viktor, talk to her. Order her to submit." Marek said while pulling out his cell phone.

Viktor leaned down and started talking to Natalie while Marek spoke on his phone. He put his phone away, and a Guardian came running around the corner of the building.

"This is Natalie Summers. Take her to the complex and put her on ice. This is her maker; he will come with you and assist. Under no circumstances is she to be harmed." Marek said.

The Guardian confirmed her orders and took control of Natalie. Viktor seemed to be helping.

"Viktor, if you lose her or if she is harmed, I will kill you," I said, making it clear he needed to stay in line.

"Do not worry, Ember. She is my daughter; I would do anything for her." Viktor said and started soothing Natalie so that she would release Marek's wrist.

It was the kindest I had ever seen him be with her. Apparently, he liked vampires much more than humans because he had never been kind to her before he turned her.

When Natalie released Marek's wrist, she looked at me, but it was as if she didn't recognize anything she was seeing.

"Guardian Lopez will take good care of her and will not let Viktor do anything circumspect. She knows him." Marek assured me.

Lopez nodded to me and raised an eyebrow to Viktor. She clearly knew he wasn't trustworthy.

"Thank you," I said.

"Asher just took down another Guardian. We need to go," Marek said, pulling me away from my sister.

She was out of it but appeared to be in good hands, so I followed Marek.

We walked into a tornado of activity centered around Asher Sanz. A team of Guardians surrounded him, and random vampires who must have been part of Julien's coven were sprinkled around the yard fighting alongside them. It didn't look like they were making any headway.

When I got closer, I saw James directing the team. Having fought Asher before, he was an excellent choice to lead the fight.

Marek stayed next to me and pulled Caden over to cover my

right flank. I'd rather have James in that position, but it occurred to me that with Marek guarding me, he was left to lead the team. I didn't realize he was that high in rank, but it made sense. Marek seemed to trust him more than anyone else.

Asher noticed me as we closed in on his position. He blasted a few Guardians with what looked like lightning then stepped toward me. Marek stepped forward, and so did Caden. They were the wall between Asher and me.

"Finally, you come out to play Ember," Asher smiled.

"I couldn't let everyone else have all the fun," I yelled, jumping into the fray.

To my surprise, the Guardians and Julien's vampires made space for me to step in. Marek and Caden stayed glued to my side as I moved forward, but they didn't hold me back. I spared a glance at Marek, and he inclined his head, giving me the lead.

James settled in near Caden on my right, and I felt as prepared as I was going to be for this fight.

I told the team to give me more space. I didn't want to accidentally burn up an ally with my fire. As I moved forward, Asher focused solely on me, but his eyes darted from side to side as if he was looking for something.

"What's the matter, Asher, lose someone?" I yelled, hinting about my sister.

He narrowed his eyes at me but didn't reply. Natalie had been a distraction to keep us busy while he worked his magic. I saw several items on the ground surrounding him and realized they were part of his arsenal.

Asher threw what looked like stones toward a group of vampires that were clustered near the far wall. The rocks exploded into silver spikes, several of them finding homes in the nearby vampires. Their screams told me the myths about vampires and silver were true.

Asher bent to pick up a small jar and made a move to throw it, but I caught him before he could. He was frozen in place but holding him was a struggle.

"Nobody likes a party crasher Asher. Why are you here?" I asked as perspiration formed on my forehead.

This guy was super strong and about to break out of my hold. I had to distract him with talk while I figured out my next move. The vampires circled around him now that he was immobile, but I couldn't warn them that I was about to lose him. I told Marek with our bond. He nodded and moved out while James slipped into his spot on my left side.

"Are you speaking with that vampire telepathically? My, my, you are valuable." Asher said, smiling.

He had started to move his arm, and I couldn't hold him back any longer. I released him, and Marek crashed into him a moment later. Unfortunately, the bottle Asher held shattered, and the contents poured over Marek with a little on Asher as well. They both screamed in pain, but Marek was hit harder than Asher.

I felt Marek's pain for a second before he shut down our bond. I lost my breath at that moment. The pain was excruciating. I watched as Marek writhed in the grass, and my anger boiled to the surface. It didn't have far to travel after seeing my sister as a vampire and having Asher attacking everyone.

I ran toward Asher and pulled him away from Marek. If I did anything with them so close together, I risked hitting Marek too.

Asher rolled away and got back on his feet. I had to ignore Marek then even though it pained me to do so. I wanted to wipe off that crap so it would stop burning him.

"I've got him," James said and kneeled down with Marek.

That left me and Caden and a bunch of vampires who didn't know me. I felt a whip of air hit me, and a tall blonde vampire stepped up to where James had been.

"Nice timing, got any cool tricks?" I asked.

"A few," Julien said, winking at me.

I focused on Asher and saw a line of burned flesh mark his left cheek along with splotches on his arms and chest. At least he got something of his own spell.

"Come with me quietly, Ember, and I'll promise not to harm anyone else," Asher said.

"How about you come quietly with us instead, and we promise not to harm you?" I countered, smiling.

"Tempting but no," Asher answered, then flung more magic.

Whatever it was, it didn't hit me because Julien lifted his hands and a wall of air formed to block it. There was a little smoke and then a poof, and the spell dissipated.

"That was neat," I said to Julien, and he just smiled back.

Asher's brow furrowed briefly, but that didn't stop him. He rolled up his sleeve and found the rune he wanted. He began to chant, but instead of letting him finish, I set him on fire.

He stopped his chant and touched another rune to put out the flames. The moment his fingers left his arm, I tried to freeze him again. I was able to slow him down but couldn't hold him. He was going to break free and finish that spell.

Just when I thought Caden was a useless statue beside me, he ran forward to engage Asher. James stepped up beside me to take his place. He grabbed my hand and squeezed.

I assumed that meant Marek was okay. I could feel Marek was further away now but couldn't get a good read on how he was doing. I had to trust that James took care of him.

Caden got in a few good hits and knocked Asher to the ground. I ran in and pushed Asher back with my kinetic power. He actually sunk through the grass and into the dirt below.

"Impressive," Julien smirked.

I shot Julien a smile, but in my distraction, Asher escaped our hold and struck Caden so hard he flew through the fence. Then he shot into the air and turned on me. Julien put up a force field of air in front of me, but it wasn't enough to stop Asher's magic.

My bones started to ache, the pain increasing slowly. I froze Asher in place, but it didn't matter, the pain just kept coming. It felt like every bone in my body was about to crack. I fell to the ground, and when I hit, the pain increased again. I couldn't stop the screams from coming after that.

"Ember!" I heard James yell, but I couldn't see him.

I was consumed in pain, and with every breath, it grew stronger. I knew Marek had been hurt, but he was the only one that would be able to hear me if I reached out. I opened our connection and felt his pain immediately. It was followed by his fear and anger. I tried to think words, but I failed. The pain was too intense.

Someone grabbed me, and I screamed when the movement ratcheted up the intensity of the pain. I reached out with my senses, looking for Asher. I had to take him down in the hope that it would end this pain.

I found him right in front of me, and I concentrated on making him burn. I focused with enough intensity to burn his body to ash. I heard screams and hoped none of them were our team.

Some of the pain receded enough that I could open my eyes. Arms etched with chemical burns surrounded me, and I realized it was Marek who had come to me. I wanted to turn and make sure he was okay, but I couldn't do that until I was convinced that Asher was dead or out of commission.

Asher was working on the flames and gaining headway in putting them out. I stood with help from Marek and focused on holding Asher's hands out to his sides with my kinetic power while making the fire burn brighter. He screamed when he felt the flame licking up his torso and into his face. I poured more of my energy into those flames, making them turn blue. It looked awesome if you ignored the fact that a man was burning alive.

"Let him go *milaya moya*," Marek whispered.

"No, he will kill me. I can feel it." I said.

"We need him alive," he insisted.

Asher fell to the ground, and I fell with him. I could feel something running down my face, but when I moved to wipe it away, the pain intensified.

"Let go now, it is a death curse," Marek said urgently.

I wondered what a death curse was, and my distraction allowed the flames to die down a bit and turn to a normal yellow and red. The pain in my body lessened. Maybe he was right...I let the fire go but kept hold of Asher kinetically.

"Take her," Marek ordered someone.

I tried to protest until I saw who had stepped in. James looked a little worse for wear, but compared to Marek, he was practically injury-free.

"Hey there, badass. Let me help you." James said.

He helped me limp over to a garden bench where he sat me down. It hurt to do it, but it felt better than standing. My left leg wasn't working right, and I suspected it was broken.

James started inspecting me for injuries and found so many he pulled out his phone and asked for an ambulance. I stared at where Asher was smoldering and was shocked to see him move. Marek pulled him off the burned ground and cuffed him. The Guardian team stepped in and finished subduing Asher.

Marek looked like hell. Half his face was burnt, but I could already see parts of it healing. Most people wouldn't notice he was limping, but since I was used to seeing him glide around like he was on ice skates, it was noticeable to me.

He looked up and caught my eye. One tear slipped out of my eye, and it pissed me off. I didn't want to cry. I tried to move to wipe it away only to realize one or both of my arms must be broken.

A second later, Marek was there, wiping the tear away for me. Seeing him up close was worse. He looked like acid had been

187

poured over him, and I guess that is precisely what had happened. I didn't know what Asher's spell was meant to do, but clearly, maim was part of the effect he was going for.

"Jesus Marek," I said, looking at every place the acid spell had hit him.

"I will heal," He assured me.

"You need blood," I said, leaning forward.

"You need blood more than I do," Marek said and pulled out his knife.

"I don't want to hurt you," I said, shaking my head.

"Declining my blood in public will hurt me more," Marek said in my mind.

"Okay," I said, giving in.

More vampires were walking around outside now that the skirmish was over. Vampire society was built on strength, and a vampire's offering of blood should not be refused.

He cut a deep gash in his wrist, and blood began to pour out of it. Several heads turned our way, but I ignored them.

"I need your help. I think my arms are broken." I said.

The look on Marek's face was of pure anger. I knew he was thinking of killing Asher himself, but he held back. His duty was a rising force in his decision making if what I could tell from our bond was any indication.

Marek sat down beside me and cradled me while holding his wrist to my lips. I latched on right away and started feeling some of the pain go away with each swallow. After a few minutes, I could tell the pain was consuming him, and I pulled back. He wasn't happy about it, but he didn't make me drink any more.

Marek was still holding me when James showed up with paramedics and a stretcher. He tested lifting me, and when I didn't cry out in pain, he moved me over to the stretcher. It hurt but tried to keep it hidden. There were too many people milling around to witness my weakness, so I sucked it up.

"Are you riding with Ember? One of us needs to ride with Asher," James said.

"I'll go with Asher. You help them heal her." Marek said.

Marek looked at me, and I smiled to let him know it was okay for him to leave. He was the head of the Guardians. It was his duty to ensure a dangerous man like Asher made it to lock up. He escaped once before; Marek would be sure it didn't happen again.

Chapter Eighteen

I opened my eyes to a familiar ceiling and the beeping of hospital monitors. The ambulance ride was rough even after having Marek's blood and James' healing treatments. When the doctors took a look at me, they found I had hundreds of microfractures in most of my bones. It was worse in my arms and legs. They were shocked I had been able to walk and thanked James for making me come in on a stretcher.

It could have been much worse if Marek hadn't talked me out of burning Asher alive. Asher had a death curse of some kind that partially triggered when I turned up the heat on the flames. Marek's quick thinking saved me because it would have killed me in a slow, excruciatingly painful way otherwise.

I chanced moving an arm and didn't feel any pain, so I tested my foot. When that didn't hurt, I rolled over onto my side. It hurt a bit but not more than being sore.

"Hey there. How are you feeling?" James asked.

"A little sore still but much better than I was," I said.

"Good, we were worried." He said.

"How's my sister?" I asked, hoping she made it here.

"She is fine as long as we keep humans away from her. New vampires need time to learn control. She is too new to be able to do it yet." He said.

I tried not to dwell on the fact that my sister was now a vampire. The implications were severe for her life and my family. I couldn't think of a way to explain her condition to the family, so I put it out of my mind.

"How is everyone else?" I asked, thinking of Marek and all the Guardians who had been taken down.

"Mostly fine. A few will need some time to heal. No fatalities." He said.

"Good," I said and sunk back into the bed.

It was exhausting to use my powers, and I had almost literally burned myself out. If Marek hadn't been there to stop me, I would most likely be dead now.

"Marek has been interrogating Asher all night," He added.

"He what?" I asked, sitting up.

"Ow, that hurt," I said, feeling the pain of moving.

"You didn't think he would put him in a cell then walk away, did you?" James asked.

"No, but he was hurt really bad. Did he find anything out?" I asked.

"No, and he will keep at it until he has the answers he wants," James said.

I wondered how long it would be before Asher caved if he caved more likely. A vampire can last a lot longer than a human, but Marek was severely burned in the fight. He would need blood to heal and time to rest. As much as I wanted answers to who hired Asher, I wasn't sure Marek should keep at it.

"Show me where they are," I told James sitting back up.

"No, no, no. You are staying here." He said, pushing me back into the bed.

"James, I can move you with my mind," I said flatly.

"Please stay here?" He said, changing tactics.

"Not going to happen," I said, swinging my legs over the side of the bed.

"Shit," James said and slumped forward.

I patted him on the back, "I can track Marek without you, but it would be easier if you just showed me where he is. Besides, if I collapse on the way, you can carry me."

James groaned then stood up. "I'll show you."

I beamed a smile up at him, and he just shook his head. I caught a hint of a smile as he turned away.

He led me down the hall and into a small chamber outside the hospital wing. There was a guard and a large metal door that more closely resembled a vault. I recognized the Guardian as Johnson, whose team was overcome by Asher the last time we faced him.

"Why is she here?" Johnson asked James.

"You can speak directly to me. I'm capable of answering for myself." I said slightly miffed at his lack of acknowledgment and assumption that James was in charge of me.

"I apologize, Ms. Summers," He said.

My eyebrow quirked up. I was used to the title the vampires had given me and expected to be called madame.

"Madame Summers is here to help with the interrogation. I'm sure Marek is aware she is here and would not want you to prevent her entry." James stepped in and said.

My lips formed a slight smile even though I was trying to keep the emotion off my face. I felt Marek approaching, and I hoped he wouldn't protest.

"I was given strict instructions not to let anyone in. I'm sorry." He said, but he didn't look sorry.

"I would stop talking now, Luke," James recommended.

James must have noticed that my fists were balled up, and my nostrils were flaring. James is a smart man.

My anger fizzled when the vault door creaked and began to open. I could feel Marek on the other side, and he wasn't happy. I couldn't tell if he was upset with me or the situation. Unfortunately, I was about to find out the hard way.

His eyes met mine when the door swung open. He looked better, but it was clear he hadn't fed or had any time to rest. Half his face showed clear signs of the burns, and his clothing was in tatters where the acid had eaten through.

Viktor walked in behind him, and James had to grab me before I went after him. Viktor gave me a smug look, and before I knew what I was doing, I had slammed him into the wall.

"Ember," Marek said sternly.

"He made my sister a vampire," I said to Marek, and he raised an eyebrow but didn't say anything.

"I saved her life," Viktor said in his defense.

"You are full of shit, Viktor," I said with venom in my voice.

"Hear him out," Marek said.

I gave him a withering look, but he just tilted his head as if challenging me to make him butt out.

"Fine, how?" I asked Viktor.

"Put me down first," Viktor said.

I huffed out a big breath and let him go. I didn't put him down, I dumped him on his ass.

"You may regret that," Viktor said.

"Spit it out, Viktor. I'm in no mood to be respectful to a vampire that not only kidnapped my sister but tried to kill me." I said.

He bent at the waist in a tiny bow. It was more than I ever expected from him. Every interaction I had ever had with him was arrogance and disdain. I didn't think he was capable of showing respect.

"We had an incident at the compound in Phoenix that left your sister critically injured. As I alluded to in the letter, a third party who is interested in you infiltrated the building and got to your sister. By the time I arrived, she was near death with no way to revive her but bring her into this life. Shortly after we arrived back in Denver, we ran into Asher Sanz, and he took dear Natalie away." Viktor said deadpan as if it were true.

I laughed, "That is quite the story Viktor. Why lie?"

"It is true," He insisted.

I looked at Marek and then at James. They both looked convinced, which confused the hell out of me. Viktor was not a trustworthy character.

"How are you convinced by his story?" I asked them both.

"I spoke to your sister. She confirmed it all." Marek said.

Viktor was looking smug, but I didn't buy it.

"Keep grinning Viktor, and I'll be happy to start a barbeque with you as the kindling," I said, threatening him.

"Ember, there is no need for that," Marek said, scolding me.

I took a deep breath. Marek was frustrated with me. He was probably upset that I interrupted his interrogation as well.

"Fine," I said.

I ran my hands over my face and pulled my hair back. It didn't help clear my head at all.

"Come with me," Marek said.

He grabbed my hand and pulled me past the vault door. I noticed everyone else stayed behind. I wondered if we were going to see Asher, but I didn't ask. Marek wanted me away from the others for a reason, I was sure.

He led me through a few corridors and then into an area with several metal doors. They were reinforced but had a residential look to the exterior. I expected to see Asher when he opened one of the doors, but instead, it was a living room with what looked like a bedroom off one of the walls. I sensed a vampire coming out of the bedroom and was shocked to see my sister.

"Em!" She yelled and ran over to me.

Marek stopped her before she got to me.

"I'm okay, Master Volkov." She said to Marek.

"Natalie," I said on a sob.

It seemed like it had been forever since I saw her looking like herself. She was very different now but still my sister.

Marek let her go, and Natalie walked over slowly, eyeing him. He nodded, and then she flung her arms around me. She pulled me in a little too hard, so I backed her off with my power. She gasped.

"What was that?" She marveled.

"I have a few tricks that I didn't have before," I said, smiling.

"No way! What can you do?" She asked.

I laughed and moved with her to the small couch. Marek shadowed our movements. He didn't trust my sister enough to give more space. New vampires were dangerous. She had proven that last night.

I told her the whole story. Marek stood quietly and watched Natalie while we talked. About thirty minutes into our conversation, Marek interrupted. It was time to go. Natalie's feeding was due, and he didn't want me anywhere near her when that happened.

I left promising Nat that I would visit every day. Marek appeared to dislike that idea, but no one was going to keep me from my sister now that I had her back. She wasn't the same, but she was still my sister.

Marek led me back out of the maze that was part dungeon, partly secured housing. He explained that when new vampires had trouble adjusting, the Council provided the locked down housing so that they could learn in safety. I was glad for it because the alternative was my sister set loose on the general public. That could mean dead humans, and I knew she wouldn't be able to live with that.

"You should still be in the hospital," Marek commented.

"You should feed and rest so you can heal," I replied.

"I do not need blood," He said.

Vampire or human, all men are stubborn and don't like to admit when they are wrong. I could see Marek was struggling, but I didn't want to point it out. Vampires detested weakness, and their excellent hearing combined with our current location meant I had to be careful. So, I let his comment go.

To my surprise, Marek led me to the elevators for the residents. I thought for sure he would try to make me go back to the hospital wing. Although I wouldn't admit it to him, I was still hurting, and all I wanted to do was lie down.

He hit the button for a floor I hadn't been on before, and I looked at him, confused. I had fully expected to be going up to his penthouse. He ignored me, but I thought he was actually trying to hide the pain from me too. We were both beat up from the fight with Asher.

The elevator stopped at the second-highest floor, and I followed Marek out. He pulled out a key card and opened a door on the west side of the building. It looked nearly identical to Marek's penthouse except that the style was more rustic and a bit more traditional. It was a warm and cozy feeling.

"Where are we, Marek?" I finally asked.

"This is your suite," He said and handed me the key card.

I walked over to the windows and saw the same view I had seen from his apartment.

"Is this directly below your penthouse?" I asked.

"Yes," He said.

I walked back to him, and he didn't move. He just stared at me.

"Why am I here, Marek? Asher is locked up, and Viktor is occupied. I could go home." I said.

"I would like you to stay here until you are fully healed." He said.

I was exhausted, but I didn't want to say that. I wanted Marek to stop trying to protect me when I didn't need protection.

"Ember, please," He said and stepped closer to me.

"Fine," I said and stepped away to further explore the apartment.

I ended up standing in front of the living room window again, staring at the gorgeous view of the mountains. It was so beautiful and peaceful that it held me as if I were in a spell.

Marek walked up behind me and put his hands on my arms. He stroked up and down until I leaned back into him.

"Are you going to stand until you fall down?" Marek asked softly.

"I'm too tired to decide what to do," I admitted.

He scooped me into his arms, and I didn't fight him. I slide my arms around his neck as he took me down the hall past a guest bedroom and into the master bedroom. I didn't get a good look at it admittedly. I could barely keep my eyes open.

Marek set me down on the bed and started pulling off my shoes. I was wearing medical scrubs. The gorgeous dress from last night had been destroyed in the fight. Then after I got to the hospital, the nurses brought me these scrubs and some sensible shoes. They were an ugly shade of green, but at least they were comfortable.

"Do you want a bath?" Marek asked.

"Yes, but I'd probably drown from falling asleep in the tub," I said.

Marek smiled at me then pulled back the covers so I could scoot in. I laid down, and the mattress felt like heaven. It was so comfortable.

I looked up at Marek and said, "Are you going upstairs to rest?"

"No," He said.

"Are you going to go back to torturing Asher?" I asked.

"Interrogate," He corrected.

"Right. Wouldn't it go better after you had some rest?" I asked, hoping it didn't make him mad.

"I am fine," He said.

"Of course, you are," I said, holding back from pushing him any more than I already had.

He was a centuries-old master vampire, if he couldn't take care of himself, he wouldn't have made it this far in life. I had to stop trying.

"James said you refused blood when the doctor wanted you to take more. Why?" He asked me.

"I don't want the blood of some random vampire," I said.

It made me feel nauseous at the thought of having an unknown vampire's blood inside me.

"It was an intravenous medical procedure, not a direct feeding." He said.

"And what if I suddenly start connecting to a random vampire and talking to him from miles away?" I said.

"That would not happen," Marek assured me.

"Uh, huh," I said, not believing him.

My life these days was nothing but weird things happening, and I didn't want to be tied to another vampire. I preferred to not be linked to any vampire, but if I had to pick one, I liked the one sitting next to me the best.

He leaned over and kissed me on the forehead. When he pulled back, he had a smile on his face. He looked very handsome when he smiled like that. I couldn't help but stare up at him and want him to kiss me properly.

"What are you thinking?" He asked.

"Don't you already know?" I said.

"I cannot read your mind. I can only hear when you broadcast to me." He said.

"That's a bummer. It was a doozy." I said, smiling.

He laughed, and my body decided it would be an excellent time to throb in a sensitive area that eliminated my ability to think. I was already in a bed, so it wasn't that much of a leap to want him in it with me. Marek raised an eyebrow, and I squirmed. It was one thing to be attracted to him, it was something else entirely to have him know about it every time it happened.

"Madame Summers, I believe you are aroused," Marek said, grinning.

"What's this madame stuff?" I said otherwise, ignoring his comment.

I tried to roll onto my side, and a sharp pain stopped me abruptly. Marek stopped me from moving and tried to find the pain. His nimble fingers traced my ribs until he found the one that was still broken. The doctor had mentioned that without an additional dose of vampire blood, the remainder of the fractures would take time to heal. I had hoped he meant hours not as slow as an average human heals.

"I can feel the break," Marek said, looking severe.

"A side effect of being human is we take longer to heal. Pushing on it doesn't help the pain, Marek." I said, pulling his hand off of me.

I swallowed the pain and rolled back over. Laying on my back helped incrementally. I just needed to be able to breathe, and sleep would do the rest. I told Marek as much, but he didn't agree. It wasn't surprising.

"Take my blood." He said.

"I'll be fine," I said, panting slightly through the pain.

"Why refuse?" He asked, confused.

"I'm tired, Marek. Can we have this discussion another time?" I asked.

"I will call in a healer instead." He offered.

"I just want to sleep," I told him.

His lips pressed into a hard line. He wasn't happy with me. He nodded and stood up to leave. He lingered at the door for a moment then walked away.

Chapter Nineteen

I woke in the middle of the night, having been startled by a noise. I jumped out of bed and immediately regretted not taking more blood when Marek offered. The pain in my ribs made it hard to breathe, but I didn't let it slow me down. There was a vampire in the apartment who wasn't Marek, and I was still on edge from our battle with Asher.

You really can't sneak up on a vampire, so I didn't bother. I walked down the hall, ready to use my power if I needed it. It was dark, but the faint glow from the windows helped me see the outline of a man sitting on the couch.

"What are you doing here?" I asked, flipping on the lights.

"Sorry, Madame Summers. I didn't mean to wake you." Caden said, shielding his eyes from the light.

"Don't most vampires move silently?" I asked, sitting next to him.

"I didn't realize the front door would slam." He said.

He looked apologetic, but I was confused about why he was here. I assumed either Marek or James would be around.

"You got the short straw, then, huh?" I asked.

"Marek doesn't trust anyone else with you other than James," Caden said.

"Why is that?" I asked.

"I think you know," He said, giving me a look like I was dense.

"I'm actually surprised anyone would be here at all. With Asher locked up and Victor otherwise engaged, I don't see the point." I said.

Caden regarded me for a moment before he spoke, "You are a high-level asset. You will always have protection from the Council."

"Are you saying I'll have a bodyguard forever? I don't like the sound of that." I said.

My mind was spinning with how intrusive it would be to have someone around all the time. Although I have managed to make the James and Marek show work so far, I didn't want to be tied to the hip with them for the rest of my life.

"You will have our protection for as long as Marek deems it necessary or for whenever you request it. It isn't as bad as you think. Most of the time, you won't even know someone is there. We are trained to blend in." He assured me.

"I don't see that as the benefit you think it is," I said.

"It won't be a burden, really." He assured me.

He laid his hand on mine and squeezed. It was reassuring, and he seemed like he would be a good friend.

I moved to stand up and felt a sharp pain in my side again. That rib wasn't healing like I expected it to.

"What's wrong?" Caden asked, moving to inspect my injury.

"It's a cracked rib," I said, trying to breathe shallow so as not to anger the bone.

"I'll call for the doctor," He said and pulled out his phone before I could protest.

I had to admit the pain was growing worse like it wasn't healing at all. I had ingested a large quantity of Marek's blood and that combined with the other healing treatments should have been enough.

While I sat as still as possible, Caden told the doctor what was happening. The look on his face didn't make me feel any better. Something was wrong, and I had a feeling I was the center of the issue.

I felt a tug on the bond and knew Marek was on his way up to the apartment. He had sensed my pain even though I had been blocking it from him. I must have slipped.

"What did the doctor say?" I asked when Caden put his phone down.

"He said to keep you still until he gets here," He said.

"That sounds like a good plan because if I move, the pain gets a lot worse," I said through gritted teeth.

Caden helped me lay down on the couch and find a position that didn't jab me with more pain than I could stand. As I lay there, the pain increased and felt hot too. I didn't think this was a normal broken rib situation.

Marek arrived within seconds of me lying down, and the look on his face told me this was a serious situation. His lack of stoicism made me panic.

"What is it?" I asked him.

"You are blocking me. Let it through. I must know what you are feeling." He said, kneeling next to me.

I thought about fighting him on it but gave up because it was too exhausting to keep blocking him. When I let it all go, he bent over and grabbed his side like he was the one hurt. The look of shock on Caden's face brought my panic to a head.

"What is it?" I gasped.

Neither of them answered me either because they didn't know or couldn't bear to tell me. A knock at the door saved them from further grilling.

The doctor had arrived and hurried to my side. Marek and Caden looked on sternly as the doctor examined me. When he moved his hand to my side, he confirmed what I had suspected.

"This is more than a broken bone." He said, looking at me and then Marek.

"Explain," Marek said.

"Someone laid a spell, and while some of the pain she is feeling is from the broken rib, the rest is from the spell. It is keeping her rib from healing and spreading out into the nearby tissues and bones." He said.

"How do we remove it?" Marek asked, looking tense.

"We need to move her to the hospital. I need to do more tests and see if we can isolate the spell so we can create a counter spell to reverse it." He said, looking concerned.

"You said not to move her," Caden said.

All three men were looking sternly at each other.

"I'll be fine," I said as I tried to sit up.

They all jumped to stop me, and if I hadn't been in so much pain, I would have laughed. The sight of them all jumping was comical.

"I'll have my team here in a few minutes. Just lay still for now." The doctor said then walked off to talk into his phone.

Marek knelt next to me again and took my hand. His face was back to its usual stoic blankness.

"I'll be fine," I said again as if that would make it all better.

"Did you feel this last night? Has it been festering since then?" He asked.

"I don't know anything about spells, Marek. How could I have known about this?" I said.

"It has to be Asher. He is the only magic user you have been near. It could be a side effect of or part of the death curse." He said.

He walked off, lost in thought, and grabbed the doctor. They were buried in conversation when the medical team arrived. Marek pulled Caden to the side then Caden rushed out of the room.

Furniture was moved so the stretcher could be brought closer to the couch.

The doctor came over to give me instructions before they started moving me. His team was going to lift me using their power instead of doing a physical lift. That would minimize the pain and move me quicker than they otherwise would be able to do. The key here was to get me to the hospital without aggravating the spell.

To my delight, James walked through the door before they got started. The doctor clapped him on the back and motioned to me. James walked over.

"Hey, you. Keeping us on our toes again, huh?" He asked, smiling.

His smile was a welcome sight among all the stern faces in the room.

"Not by...choice," I said, feeling the pain more when I talked.

"Well, you have me now. What more could you want?" James said, smiling.

I tried to smile. It must have been more of a grimace because his face fell.

"I'm fine," I said unconvincingly.

"Stay still and focus on me. We are going to move you. Don't panic when you can't move. That is all part of the process. Ready?" He asked, looking into my eyes.

I nodded, then winced. The pain was growing, and I was not looking forward to being wheeled over bumps on a stretcher.

The team lined up next to the couch and on the other side of the stretcher. James moved too but stayed in sight. With one word from the doctor, I felt pressure all over my body, and then I floated into the air. It was like being put into a vice of air and lifted around.

I moved through the air slowly until I was over the stretcher. The team dropped me down gently, and I didn't feel a thing. The pressure released, and then James was there holding my hand.

"You okay?" He asked.

"Yeah," I said, closing my eyes.

"The doctor is going to give you a sedative to get you downstairs. Are you okay with that?" He asked.

"Will I lose consciousness?" I asked.

I didn't want to be left unaware. It was one thing to pass out from the pain, but to be medically put out wasn't something I wanted.

James looked to the doctor, and he came over.

"You may fall asleep, but with all the vampire blood you have in your system, it won't last longer than it takes to get you downstairs." The doctor assured me.

I agreed, and the doctor directed one of the nurses to get an IV going while they strapped me onto the stretcher. They didn't attach the straps that would typically go over my middle so as not to aggravate my side. Once I was secure, the nurse gave me the sedative.

James held my hand as they rolled me toward the door. I felt the sedative kick in, but the pain was still there. I just didn't care as much about it.

I felt heat coming down my arm from James and realized he was sending his healing power into me as we moved. I smiled up at him, then my eyes started to droop, and I fell asleep.

I fell into a vision where I heard screaming and saw Asher Sanz chained to a wall bleeding from several wounds. His arms were stretched out in a straight line, and his skin was covered with what looked like plaster. It must have been to keep him from touching those runes he has tattooed all over him. His stomach was smeared with plaster, and more wounds gaped and bled along the surface. He was in rough shape.

Marek was in the room with him, and Asher was giving him a death stare. If Asher could kill Marek with his eyes, it would have happened right then. It was clear the torture portion of the interrogation had begun.

"Tell me about your death curse. How is it counteracted?" Marek said.

"It wouldn't be much of a curse if it could be counteracted," Asher replied.

Marek struck him in the face, and blood sprayed against the wall and across his right arm. He looked up and smiled.

"Were you supposed to kill her?" Marek snarled.

Asher looked confused, "What are you talking about?"

"Your death curse is going to kill her! She triggered it when she burned you." Marek yelled.

"That was not intentional," Asher said, furrowing his brow.

He appeared to be deep in thought for a moment then looked up.

"She isn't dead already?" He asked, looking suspicious.

"No, she lives," Marek said.

"I don't understand. My death curse would have killed her instantly. And there is no counter curse. Are you sure the spell has my signature?" Asher asked.

Marek went still, "You were the only magic user near her to have laid the spell. I felt it myself when she triggered your death curse."

"I may be powerful, but if she isn't dead, then she beat my curse already," Asher said.

"Who hired you?" Marek asked.

"I don't reveal my clients, Marek. You know that better than anyone." Asher said.

That was an interesting tidbit. I filed that away for later.

Marek hit him again, and more blood poured out of his mouth. It dribbled down his chin and onto his chest. It made my stomach queasy.

A sudden jolt woke me, and the pain in my side became unbearable. I cried out, unable to hold it back. Tears poured from my eyes, falling down my cheeks.

"Shhhh, it will be okay," James said, holding my hand.

I opened my eyes to see him sitting next to me. I was in an ICU bed with nurses running around moving tubes and drawing blood. I was hooked up to an IV of blood.

"Whose blood is that?" I asked, reaching to pull the tube out.

James stopped me before I could do anything.

"That is keeping you alive. Don't pull it out." He said, chastising me.

"Explain," I said.

James told me the doctor was able to see the spell, and it had attached itself to my DNA. Vampire blood was the one thing that could hold the enchantment back for now, but it was only effective at keeping it back. There was no progress toward removing the spell.

"How long was I out?" I asked.

I grabbed for the IV again. Whatever was in there with the blood was making my arm itch.

"About 15 minutes," James responded.

I thought about my vision while I was asleep and all the events of the past few days. This didn't feel like something Asher did. It was more personal.

"Asher didn't do this," I said.

"How do you know?" James asked, confused.

"He told Marek, and I think he is telling the truth. A death curse would have killed me immediately. This happened long after I fought Asher, and I have an overwhelming need to get that vampire blood out of my body." I said, gritting my teeth.

"I can think of only one vampire who wouldn't want you having someone else's blood and who would do something like this," James said.

"Exactly. What is our newfound friend up to right now? I think he should be the one in interrogation with Marek, not Asher." I said.

James went silent for a moment, and then I heard Marek coming down the hall. He wasn't happy, and I almost felt sorry for the one responsible.

Marek entered the room and ordered everyone out except for James. He came over to me and took my hand.

"How are you doing?" He asked.

I looked at him like he was an idiot. He knew exactly how I felt because I was too weak to block him.

"Where is Viktor?" I asked.

His eyes narrowed, but he answered, "With your sister."

"You need to bring him here now," I said.

"We think he knows what is going on," James added.

"Not just knows but is responsible." I corrected James.

Marek looked at James. James nodded and left the room.

"What just happened?" I asked.

"If I go get Viktor, I will kill him." He said then sat in the chair next to me.

"What are you thinking?" He asked.

"I think Viktor hired Asher when he couldn't get to me himself. He also had Asher prep a little something that Viktor could use if he needed to. I saw your torture session with Asher. I believe he was truthful when he said the death curse would have killed me instantly. He also seemed to know more than he would say." I said.

"Did you see anything that showed you Viktor is involved?" He asked.

"No, that's why I want him here. I think he will out himself to save me." I said.

"Why don't you think he wants you dead?" Marek asked.

"Because he wants me bound to him more than he wants me dead. He has been playing nice to get closer to me and get us all to drop our guard around him." I said.

My arm was itching, and my stomach felt queasy looking at the vampire blood in my IV. I knew it was related to whatever Viktor did to me, but I couldn't prove it yet.

"Leave the IV alone," Marek said, pulling my hand away from the tube.

"I don't want it," I said, fighting him.

"It is what is keeping you alive," He said more forcefully.

"It's hurting me," I said, feeling the liquid starting to burn.

I felt movement down the hall and recognized Viktor's signature aura. Marek was distracted by it, so I took the opportunity to pull the IV from my arm.

"Ember, no!" Marek yelled and grabbed my arms.

He yelled for a nurse, and one can running. She pushed Marek out of the way and grabbed some gauze to staunch the blood seeping out of my arm.

"I don't want it. It's burning me." I said through gritted teeth.

At that moment, Viktor walked through the door and saw me fighting them. He smiled, and I knew he was responsible. Why else would he be pleased by me refusing the blood of another vampire?

"Tell me you know what is going on, Viktor. She just refused the only thing keeping her alive." Marek snarled.

"Now, now, Marek. You don't have to get so testy. I'm sure Ember knows what she needs, and I'm happy to give her whatever she wants." Viktor said, smiling still.

"What did you do to me?" I asked, then snarled at the nurse when she tried to insert a new IV.

The nurse scrambled back, holding up her arms in surrender.

Marek told her to leave, and she did.

"My dear, I believe you know what you need. Why else would you call me here?" Viktor said, stepping closer.

As he got closer to the bed, I felt it. An overwhelming desire to drink his blood overcame me, and I sat up in the bed. The pain dampened as he got near, and I was suddenly afraid of what I might have to do.

"You couldn't get me to do it voluntarily, so you pushed the issue by putting a spell on me. Let me guess, to keep me from dying, I need to drink your blood?" I asked.

"It's what you want, Ember. I can't deny you what you desire." Viktor said, but he didn't admit anything.

Marek was fuming.

"What did you do to her?" Marek asked.

It looked like he could barely restrain himself from going after Viktor.

"I just pushed her a little," Viktor said, stepping up next to me.

I could smell him now. He had a mix of evergreen and citrus about him. It reminded me of the wine he gave me once before. The wine I knew he spiked with his blood.

"Will this take the spell off of me?" I asked.

"No, Ember. We will find another way," Marek insisted.

James and Marek both looked stricken, but I knew what I had to do. I laid back down with more pain than I thought possible. I looked at Viktor.

"Yes, ingest enough of my blood to form a bond, and the spell will be satisfied," Viktor said

"You will not leave this room alive, Viktor," Marek said with such venom that I was shocked.

"She is but a plaything for you, an object of your sexual desire. I will make her my queen! She deserves nothing less." Viktor yelled at Marek.

"I've got this," I told Marek. In his mind, I said, *"We practiced this, and you said I could do it. Trust me."*

He looked at me with raw pain and vulnerability that made my heart hurt. Having another vampire's blood was going to crush him, but it was what we practiced. Viktor didn't know I could roll a master vampire. If we were to create a bond, it was going to be on my terms. I would make Viktor my bitch.

"Let's do this before the pain makes me pass out," I said for effect.

"Yes, my darling," Viktor said and sat on the edge of the bed.

He lifted my wrist to his lips and tilted his head, asking for permission.

"Just a sip, enough for the bond only," I said.

He struck without hesitation and took a large mouthful of my blood. Unlike when Marek drank from me, I didn't feel a thing. He swallowed then reached out his arms for me to come to him.

"You have to come down here, I can't sit up again," I said, patting the bed next to me.

Viktor was going to have to either kneel or lay down beside me. I wanted to take from his neck to make sure I got enough blood.

Viktor laid next to me, and I was closer to him than I ever wanted to be.

"Do you have a knife?" I asked him.

He pulled a pearl-handled blade from his pocket and opened it. He handed it to me then moved his head to the side so I could reach him easier.

If I could have taken a deep breath, I would have. Instead, I steadied my breathing and plunged the knife into Viktor's neck. It felt good to stab him, and I made sure to dig the knife around to cause more blood to flow. He winced but didn't say a word.

His blood pooled and then started dripping. I didn't have to force myself to do it. My body decided his blood was what I needed without my permission. I latched onto the flow and swallowed the first drops. The pain in my side subsided a bit, and I knew this would work.

Still gripping the knife, I pulled Viktor in closer and sucked hard on his vein. He moaned as I drank his blood mouthful after mouthful. I could feel his emotions rising to the surface of my mind the more I drank. He wrapped his arms around me and pulled me closer so that his entire body was pressed into mine.

As I felt the bond start to form between us, I also felt my bond with Marek dulling. Tears formed as the final strings that bound us pulled and finally split. I heard him call out. It was painful for him to feel it. Viktor let out a small laugh. He must have felt it too.

I wrapped a leg around Viktor so he could feel me closer and get his guard to drop completely. He pulled me into his body and rolled to his back with me on top of him. I straddled his hips and bit into his neck to get the blood flowing faster. I could feel the rush of the bond and of Viktor's power. It was a heady mix of ancient wisdom and power.

He was older than Marek but also infinitely crueler. I could see his real character now that we were so close to the bond. It was just seconds away from forming, and I felt him pool his power so that he could make me his. The rush was pleasurable but lacked the bliss that I had with Marek. I fought to keep that thought to myself.

Right before Viktor took control of the bond, I reached out and grabbed it from him. Viktor gasped when I took it from him. I used his surprise to my advantage and pulled ob the bond harder than I ever had with Marek. I wanted no mistake that Viktor was mine to control. He cried out when I took control and I felt the bond snap into place.

I pushed the knife I still had in my hand to his throat and pulled my lips away. As I licked the remaining drops of his blood away, his eyes followed my tongue with longing. I could feel the press of his erection between my legs, and I was glad for all the clothing between us.

I didn't anticipate feeling anything for Viktor, but the bond allowed me to feel his emotions. He wanted me something awful. The sexual tension ratcheted up too high, and I had to stop myself from grinding into the hard bulge in his pants.

I didn't feel anything in my side anymore, so I risked my next move.

"Get up, Viktor," I said, moving off of him.

"What for my darling? I believe I am right where you want me." He said, grinning.

I brushed away a wave of desire. Then I pulled on the bond again, this time making him bend to my will. Viktor cried out in pain and grabbed his head.

"I said, get up!" I pushed power into the command.

Viktor still struggled, but he did as I said. He stood next to the bed, shaking.

"Now, on your knees," I said.

I didn't need the knife anymore, so I lowered it and stood up beside Viktor. He fought me a little more, but another push of power had him on his knees.

"That's a good doggy," I said, smiling.

Marek gave me a look like I was pushing it. He was probably right.

"What are you doing, Ember?" Viktor asked.

It wasn't easy for him. He had to speak through gritted teeth. His body trembled as he looked up at me.

"You wanted a bond Viktor but what you don't understand is that I'm the more powerful party here. You are mine." I said and pushed more power.

He winced and fell forward. He was on hands and knees when two members of the Council leadership walked into the room. I looked at Marek, and a small smile formed on his lips. He must have called them as witnesses.

"Now Viktor, I want you to tell me everything you have done to me, including what you did to my sister. Start from the beginning and don't leave anything out." I said.

I pushed more power into the command, and Viktor sang his little heart out. It turned out he pulled my sister into his scheme so he could get an introduction to me. He had bonded her to him so that he could control her and get into my life without suspicion. He had indeed hired Asher Sanz and used him as a distraction so he could put a spell on me during the battle. The only thing he didn't know was who the third party was that attacked his crew in Phoenix.

By the time he was done telling me what he had done, the Council leaders had him in shackles, and several guards were at the ready to take him away. He looked up at me with awe.

"You are the most powerful creature on this planet. I was right to go after a bond with you. I can feel your strength." Viktor said, smiling.

"Not for long, Viktor. This isn't going to be permanent." I said, smiling down on him.

He frowned then looked at Marek. Viktor moved faster than I could track, but the guards caught him before he could do anything. Marek walked up to him and punched him in the face.

"That is for forcing the woman I love to take your blood," He said and motioned the guards to take him away.

My jaw was on the floor when Marek turned to me. He moved like a gust of wind and was suddenly in front of me. He pushed my chin up and smiled while looking into my eyes.

A shuffle of feet told me the onlookers all left the room with Viktor.

"You love me?" I asked.

Marek pulled me into his arms. It was weird to not be able to feel his emotions. It was like a piece of me was missing.

"How do you feel?" He asked.

He ran his hands over my side then back up my body. His fingers slid over my neck and into my hair. I couldn't think clearly with him touching me.

"Ember, how do you feel?" He repeated.

"You love me?" I asked again.

He held me close and said softly, "I do."

"Now tell me that letting you drink another vampire's blood healed you, or I will lose my mind." He said.

"It worked," I said, reassuring him.

"Good because watching you drink from another vampire was the worst thing that has ever happened to me in this long life." He said.

I was shocked speechless. When Marek moved to walk away, I couldn't move.

"Ember?" He said, concerned.

"I...I," the words wouldn't come out of my mouth.

He smiled and pulled me into his arms again.

"Shall I carry you, or do you think you can walk?" he asked.

The smile on his lips was sweet and tentative, like he wasn't sure how I felt. I realized then that he didn't know how I felt. Our bond was broken. It brought tears to my eyes.

"What is wrong *milaya moya*?" He asked.

"The bond..." I couldn't bring myself to say it.

"I know," He said softly and brushed the tears away.

Not having Marek's feelings merged with mine was a physical pain. It was worse than I had imagined it would be. I pulled myself together. It wouldn't be permanent, or at least I didn't think it would be. I had to distract myself from it.

"What does it mean when you say *milaya moya*?" I asked.

"It is what a man calls his beloved, it translates roughly to my sweet." He said.

"Oh," I said, a little disappointed.

I thought maybe he was telling me he loved me all along.

"I can call you *lyubov moya* if you prefer." He said.

"And what does that mean?" I asked.

"My love," He said.

I smiled and shook my head, "no, the first one is what you've always called me. I like it when you say it."

He smiled and leaned his forehead into mine. My heart was racing, and I didn't know what to do.

"Have you healed?" Marek asked.

His hands ran down my arms until his fingers entwined with mine. We stood there looking into each other's eyes for a moment. I had to do an inventory of pain and found nothing.

"I think so," I said, finally taking a deep breath.

"Good," he said.

"Can we get out of here? People are standing in the hall listening to us." I said.

Marek nodded and walked toward the doorway. He narrowed his eyes as he exited the room. The people who were in the hallway scattered like roaches when the lights turn on.

Marek reached out to me so he could hold my hand. My stomach fluttered as I accepted it. We were in public holding hands after Marek had declared his love for me. The social repercussions in vampire society were concerning. I wasn't sure I fully understood the consequences.

I was almost glad he couldn't feel my emotions as we walked to the elevators. My mind was racing with thoughts. I was still freaking out about having to bind myself to Viktor and then the revelation Marek made immediately after threw me for a loop. I had no idea what I was supposed to say to him.

I decided to ignore what had happened and think of something else as we stepped into the elevator. There was more to take care of now that Viktor had admitted, with witnesses, what he had done to my sister and me. What I couldn't change at the moment was his blood in my body.

"How do I get Viktor's blood out of me?" I asked, feeling panicked.

My arms itched, and my stomach hurt. I could feel Viktor's blood weighing me down. Having to block him was exhausting.

"It will be alright," Marek insisted.

"Easy for you to say. You don't feel him trying to pick his way through the bond into your mind." I said.

"You are stronger than he is. Order him to stop." Marek said matter of fact.

"I rather break the bond," I said, leaning against the elevator wall.

"One so new will be harder to break," Marek said, but the look in his eye was hopeful.

"What do you recommend we do?" I asked.

He smiled a wicked smile, and I knew what he was thinking. I walked right into that one. I rolled my eyes at him.

The elevator dinged, and we walked out toward my temporary apartment. I needed to get home, take care of bills, and figure out if I was going to go back to work at the law firm. It probably wasn't in Marek's plan for me to move back home. I had a feeling he was going to insist I stay or have a Guardian 24/7 no matter what I wanted.

Chapter Twenty

We walked into the apartment, and Marek offered to draw me a bath. I agreed. I was anxious to get out of the scrubs and into some comfy pajamas. I had been up most of the night, and the pain had taken its toll.

I gathered my clothes while Marek drew the bath. He was acting differently, sweeter. Marek wasn't sweet, so it was disconcerting.

I brushed my hair until Marek called that the bath was ready. It smelled like vanilla and warmth when I walked into the bathroom. I stripped down and got into the tub. I moaned as the hot water covered my sore muscles.

Marek was standing by the door with a smirk on his face. I had stripped naked in front of him, not even realizing what I had done. I felt a blush on my cheeks and hid it by turning my head away.

"How does it feel?" Marek asked from next to the tub.

I jumped and chastised myself for not paying attention. This is a vampire.

"My muscles thank you. It feels great." I said, forcing a smile.

"Can I get you anything?" He asked, sitting on the edge of the tub.

"No, I just want to soak for a while," I said.

He could see all of me if he wanted to, but he maintained eye contact with me instead. James had done the same thing with me before. It must be a Guardian thing.

He got up to leave, but I grabbed his hand. He turned back to me, face blank.

"We need to talk," I said.

He laughed, "I was wondering when you would get to that."

He sat down on the floor next to the tub, so we were eye to eye. He pulled my hand into his placing his other hand over it. It was another sweet thing that I thought was out of character. I stared at our hands entwined, and he raised them, kissing my palm. He kept his eyes on me the entire time, and he must have liked what he saw.

My body flooded with warmth at his kiss. It was such a random place to kiss someone, but it filled my body with desire for him. He knew what it did to me. With a vampire's sense of smell, how could he not?

"Thanks for clouding my head, so I can't think," I said sarcastically.

"My pleasure," he said and kissed my palm again.

"Marek," I said sternly.

He just smiled.

"This bond with Viktor feels like a disease. How long do I have to wait to break it?" I asked.

"I do not know for sure, but I do not think it wise to remove it too quickly. I need to know the parameters of the spell first." He said, looking pained.

"And Viktor needs to tell us that information. This is never-ending." I said, sinking further into the water.

"My team is speaking with him now. If they are unsuccessful, you can use the bond to force him." He said.

"I can do that now," I said, opening the bond.

Viktor felt a wave of pleasure as I opened the bond. It was revolting to have his feelings invade me. I felt Marek grab my hand, and the nausea died down. I looked up at him and smiled. He was my rock.

"Please tell me you are not naked with that vampire in the room." Viktor snarled into my mind.

"Why? Does that bother you, Viktor?" I replied.

"You are mine. Marek should not be allowed in your presence." He snapped.

"Wrong Viktor. You are mine and will do as I say, or I break the bond in the most uncomfortable way possible for you." I said.

Viktor cringed but didn't say a word. I ordered him to cooperate with the Guardians. He fought me, but in the end, he relented. I saw him in a room with James and Caden. His sudden lack of resistance shocked them. I saw James pull out his phone, and then Marek's pocket vibrated.

"Are you controlling him?" Marek asked me.

I nodded yes, and he confirmed with James. I saw James smile then put away his phone. He told Caden that Viktor would now cooperate with them, and Caden grinned.

I blocked Viktor out and concentrated on Marek instead. I felt a flicker of his emotions and gasped. He looked at me, concerned.

"I felt you for a moment," I said.

"How? The bond broke." He said, looking confused.

"I don't think it did. Maybe the vampire bond is mostly broken, but there is still something there, a shadow. It is drowning under the other bond, but when I pull on it, I can still feel it." I said, marveling at it.

I looked up at Marek and saw a small smile on his face. For him, it was a lot of emotion.

"How do relationships work with vampires?" I asked.

His face shut down into his standard blank form.

"How do you mean?" He asked.

"Do you date, or how does that work?" I asked.

"Are you asking if we go to the movies?" He asked, holding back a laugh.

"Yes and no. All I've read and heard about is claiming a mate. How do you know when you have found your mate? It's a permanent position, is it not?" I asked.

"That is complicated." He answered.

"I'm knee-deep in vampire politics and relationships. I need to know." I said.

"Very well," He said. "I will have Caden fill you in."

"Why not you?" I asked, frowning.

"Because you are naked and wet, and I cannot think of anything else right now." He answered deadpan.

I smiled wide, and I was sure it looked wicked too. His eyes were smoky, and I felt a trickle of desire coming from him. I sat up onto my knees and slipped my hands up to his chest.

"You have too many clothes on," I said, leaning in to kiss him.

He kissed me back and pulled my wet body against his. I could feel the water soaking into his shirt. I moved his jacket off his shoulders, and he let it drop to the floor. He wrapped his arms back around me and kissed me deeply.

He pricked his tongue on a fang and slid it into my mouth. The caramel taste hit me, and fire poured through my body instantly. I yanked at his shirt until he took it off. Moments later, he was naked and in the bath with me.

Water splashed over the sides of the tub as he jumped in and settled in with me. His skin was soft under my hands, and his muscles rippled with strength. My heart raced as he kissed my neck and trailed his tongue along my jaw. I pulled him closer and wrapped a leg around his.

"Is this better *milaya moya*?" Marek said.

"Much better," I whispered into his ear.

"Are you warm enough?" he asked.

"You set my heart afire. I couldn't be cold when you're near me."

I said.

"What else do you feel, *lyubov moya*?" He said softly.

I pulled on the tiny thread of our bond that was simmering in the background. Staring into Marek's bright blue eyes helped me find it. It was a dark warmth I had fallen into many times and a place I wanted to live in forever.

"Can you feel it?" I asked, pulling on the shadow I saw within me.

He closed his eyes and rested his forehead against mine.

"I long to feel you within me, to make you mine." He said.

He stroked my cheek then caught his thumb on my lower lip. I knew what I wanted. I had wanted it all along, and I'd let him talk me out of it before.

"Make me yours, Marek," I said.

Marek kissed me while he ran a hand down my back. I shivered as his fingers walked a path down my body and over my hip. He deepened the kiss, plunging his tongue into my mouth. I danced my tongue around his then accidentally nicked my tongue on his fang. He sucked harder, pulling more blood from the wound.

I tasted his blood, and my body reacted to it. Heat pooled in my abdomen, and my heart sped up. His blood gave me power, but this time it also gave me better access to our almost closed bond. I felt his love and desire trickling through. I pushed my own feelings toward him, and he reacted.

"I felt that," He marveled.

"I told you it didn't break," I said.

"I should listen better," He said.

"Oh, I've known that for a long time now," I laughed.

"Yes, I am sure you have." He said, smiling.

"You say, I am, never I'm. Would it kill you to use a contraction?" I asked, laying kisses along his jawline.

"Probably," He said.

I felt his smile and a wave of happiness. It surprised me how much feeling his emotions made me happy. As much as I resisted the thought of bonding with a vampire, this vampire was worth it. He brought me a strength I hadn't known I needed, and he grounded me when I wasn't capable of doing it myself. Add in mutual respect, and we had the basis for a good relationship.

Marek reached down and pulled my leg up over his hip then slid his hand between my thighs. I threw my head back at his touch, and he moved his mouth to my neck. He dragged his teeth along the tender flesh, and my body felt like it would combust. Heat filled me, and Marek was my only thought.

His pulse synced with mine, and we moved together. Every touch, every caress, every kiss brought us closer, and when he moved to push into me, it was all I could do to not use my power to help. As he pushed himself between my legs, his teeth pierced my neck. I cried out with pleasure. The dual sensation was the most exquisite feeling I had ever felt in my life.

He withdrew his fangs after only a small sip of my blood, but the effect was lasting. I pushed my pelvis into his, and his responding thrust had me panting. Somehow, he was able to hold me still within the slippery tub and move like an expert lover. Given his age, I figured he was an expert.

He rocked into me while holding me close, using the waves of the water to his advantage. I looked into his eyes and pushed the bond open further. His love poured through, and his eyes widened. He felt me and what he was doing to me. I leaned forward and captured his lips. I lost myself in their velvety softness and ran my hands over his body.

We fit well together, and his lean musculature felt glorious under my fingers. His biceps hardened as he braced against the tub, and his thighs rippled with strength as he moved inside me. I let my hands wander over his body and finally settled on his ass. A perfectly formed mound that felt soft over the muscle.

Marek moved a hand between us and brushed his fingers over

my nub in time with his thrusts. He quickly had me melting with pleasure. The heat built between my legs until I was so close to release my body tensed. Marek's body was nearly there with me. I broke from a kiss and leaned into his neck. I wanted to bite him and taste his blood as we came together.

My blunt teeth weren't likely to break the skin, but my overwhelming desire to bite him won out. I closed my teeth over his skin and felt Marek's body respond. He thrust harder into me, and we both came. Our pleasure overflowing the confines of the tub and pushing out into the surrounding rooms. I felt the power between us beyond our emotions rise and expand.

A wave of power exploded as our bodies gave out their last pulses of pleasure. I felt the shockwave expand, and I hoped it wasn't felt by everyone in the building. I looked at Marek with wide eyes. He appeared just as confused.

"What was that?" I asked.

"Besides the obvious?" Marek said, quirking an eyebrow.

"Stop," I said, snuggling into him.

"I felt it too." He admitted.

"What was it?" I asked cringing, thinking I must have done something.

I didn't think either of us had meant for it to happen, but I could be wrong. What if I did something without knowing it?

"I think it was a power merge," Marek said. The expression on his face was one of wonder.

"What is that?" I asked hesitantly. I wasn't sure I actually wanted to know.

"It has been known to happen mostly with mated vampires, but there are documented cases of other supernatural creatures and humans with paranormal abilities being able to do it." He said.

He stroked my cheek lovingly and kissed me. I kissed him back and reveled in the feel of our bond being back in place. A bubble of panic came to the surface at the thought of us, forming a mating bond by accident.

"It sounds an awful lot like a mating bond," I said, feeling uneasy.

"Our power merging means that we are well matched. It is not a mating bond, but it can be felt by those who can sense it." He said.

His stoic face was back even though I could feel his happiness. He was pleased about the power merge, but I wasn't so sure it was a good thing if others could sense it. It sounded too much like a mating bond, and that suddenly scared me.

A knock sounded at the front door, and I groaned. Interruptions were the new normal. I shouldn't have thought we would be left alone, especially after that blast of power. A girl could hope, though.

"I will see what it is," Marek said and sped away.

He left his clothing behind. I hoped whoever was at the door wouldn't be shocked by his nakedness.

I slipped into a robe that was hanging from the bathroom door and heard Marek talking to someone. I searched to see if I could tell who it was and realized it was James. I hurried out to find Marek and James standing in the living room looking concerned.

"What's wrong?" I asked, walking over to Marek.

Thankfully Marek had grabbed a towel on his way to the door. They looked an odd pair with James fully clothed and Marek in only a towel. I would have laughed if it wasn't so awkward. It was apparent the two of us had been naked, given we were both wet and barely covered.

"James felt the wave of power as did the whole compound. He came to see if we knew what it was and if you were okay." Marek said.

I sat down hard on the sofa.

"Everyone felt it?" I asked, looking nervously at James.

"I was hoping the two of you knew what it was. I was in the cell with Viktor at the time, and he went insane the moment it hit. We had to tranquilize him." James said, looking at me, expectantly.

I checked on Viktor by opening the link. He was still there but not as clearly as before. He wasn't conscious, just as James had said.

"I can still feel the link with him, but it's muted," I said, looking at Marek.

Marek's face was blank, but I could feel thoughts swirling around in his head. He was not happy that I could still link with Viktor. He did not want Viktor linked to me in any way, and it created what I thought felt like jealousy.

"I think I know what it was James but humor me for a moment. Does Ember's power feel different to you now?" Marek asked.

James scrunched up his face like he was concentrating. After a moment, his eyes went wide, and he looked at Marek, nodding his head.

"You two want to loop me in?" I asked.

"It is what I thought," Marek said, turning to me. "Scan my power, then scan yours and tell me what you see."

I did as he asked. I looked into Marek and found the lake that was his power. It was glossy black like always, but when I dipped down into it, I saw colors swirling in the black that hadn't been there before. I looked at my power and found shadows in the lake that weren't there before. When I dipped down into the lake, tendrils of black that hadn't been there before were swirled within the color that was mine.

"We each have a touch of the other's power. When you said our powers merged, I didn't really grasp what that meant. I can see clear as day that I have swirls of your power, and you have mine." I said, confused.

227

I looked up at James and wished he wasn't there. I didn't want to talk about this in front of him.

"James, please check in with all the Guardian teams. Report back to me if any of them experienced anything unusual." Marek said.

James nodded and said, "And the situation with Viktor?"

"We will be down shortly to deal with it. Thank you, James." Marek said, dismissing him.

James nodded to acknowledge it and left.

"Do you think we will ever get to be alone for an entire night without being interrupted?" I asked.

Marek sat down next to me and pulled me into his arms.

"When we are here, no. My team is accustomed to having access to me 24/7. Most of what we handle is emergencies, so they cannot wait." He said.

I hadn't thought about what a relationship would be like with him. I assumed, however naively, that once the threat to me was gone, I would return home and to work. My life going back to normal.

"Then we should go to my place, and you can accidentally misplace your phone all night," I said, leaning in to kiss him softly on the lips.

He chuckled softly and pulled me tight against him.

"That does sound nice," he said, kissing a trail down my jaw and onto my neck.

I shivered at the feel of his velvety lips gliding along my skin. He moved me onto his lap, and I sat there with my knees on either side of him. I could feel the bulge under his towel and knew what he wanted without even checking the bond.

I lifted an eyebrow and let him feel what I could feel. He smiled and pushed the robe off my shoulders and down my arms. I untied the waist, and he pulled the material away so that I was sitting there naked. He looked at me, and I felt a blush on my cheeks. He was admiring me like I was the most beautiful woman in the world. It was hard to see myself that way.

I wrapped my arms around Marek's neck and pulled him in for a kiss. As my tongue found him, he used his vampire speed to remove his towel. He grabbed my hips and pulled me in line with his hard length. He held me there, waiting for the right moment. As our mouths found a rhythm and the heat built between us, he guided his length into me.

The feeling of him sliding in place, combined with how Marek felt through the bond, made me gasp. I held still for a moment, just feeling the sensations together. It was almost more than I could handle. Our connection was stronger than before, and it was like feeling in 3D instead of 2D. Every feeling I had rebounded to me as Marek experienced it too.

I ground my hips into him, and he answered it with a thrust of his own. I almost had an orgasm from that one move. I was overwhelmed by the feelings and the newness of being naked with Marek. I threw my head back and ground my hips again. Marek took my nipple into his warm mouth and nibbled until I cried out.

He took that moment to flip me onto my back and settle in between my legs. He kept our bodies connected when he moved and then pushed into me several times in quick succession. The heat built between us, and it wasn't long before both of us were ready for release.

The intensity of the feedback through the bond heightened every touch and thrust of his body against mine. My natural desire to pull the bond closer wasn't there. Our connection was as open and raw, and like nothing, I had ever felt before. It was glorious.

We both found our release at the same moment, and he collapsed next to me on the couch. I could feel his heart beating hard in time with my own. We looked into each other's eyes, and

I knew right then and there that I never wanted to be apart from him. We fit together too well, and it felt so right.

"I love you," I said to him.

He smiled a huge genuine smile that made him look like the most handsome man on the planet. With his dark hair, blue eyes, and flawless skin, how could anyone not think he was gorgeous? It was a marvel I hadn't seen it straight away when I first met him.

"Is that the sex talking or are you serious?" he asked playfully.

"I'm serious, but the sex may have helped loosen my tongue," I said, feeling embarrassed for telling a man I loved him after sex. It was so cliché.

"I'll remember that for future reference," He said, smiling.

"You do that," I said, smiling with him.

He held me for a few minutes before I felt him getting anxious.

"We should go down to the detention center and check on Viktor." He said, kissing me softly.

"Your argument is weakened by the fact we are naked, and your kisses are melting any spark of motivation I could have," I said.

"I will give you two options for what comes next. One, I throw you in the cold bathwater. Or two, you take a quick hot shower with me, and then we go down to check on Viktor. Your choice." He said.

It may have appeared that he was joking about throwing me in cold bathwater, but I knew Marek. He was serious.

"I'll take option two," I said, groaning as he pulled me up off the couch.

He dropped a sweet kiss on my lips before he smacked my ass and told me to get moving. Bossy vampire.

Chapter Twenty-One

I convinced Marek to take a quick detour before seeing Viktor, which is why Natalie was crying in my arms with deep racking sobs that tore my heart out. It was for the best to have Viktor locked away, but the unintended consequence was that my sister was left alone without anyone to guide her. She had made progress up to this point, but she could backslide if no one stepped up to take care of her.

The Council of Guardians helped in situations like these, so the Grand Master sent Caden to evaluate Natalie and see what the best course of action would be. If I could get Natalie to calm down, he would test her to see where she was in her progress.

I looked at Caden apologetically, and he motioned for me to get up.

"Nat honey, I need you to calm down so Caden can talk with you. Can you do that for me?" I asked, but she didn't respond.

"Natalie Summers let the human go now," Caden said in such a commanding tone, I almost jumped backward myself.

Natalie startled and let me go. She was still crying, but she was finally paying attention.

"Madame Summers, if you would please step back from Natalie," Caden said in a much softer and respectful tone.

I took a few steps back toward Marek, who was standing by the door. Natalie lunged at me and tried to grab me again. I was about to stop her with my power, but Caden appeared between us so quickly I didn't have to.

"Stop!" Caden commanded Nat, and she obeyed.

She looked like she was having a hard time controlling herself, but she stayed put none the less.

"I wasn't going to hurt her. She is my sister." Natalie said through renewed sobs.

"Pull yourself together, Natalie. A heightened emotional state leads to reckless behavior, and no matter your intention, you will hurt someone." Caden said.

He was being firm with her and telling the truth. While I would prefer he was more delicate, I understood the danger of a rogue vampire. They were ruled by their impulses and learning to control them was how they were able to function in society.

"I understand," Natalie said.

Caden turned to me and said, "Madame, would you please leave the room for the remainder of the tests? She is walking a thin line of control, and I rather not have you near when she snaps."

"Sure. Will you share your report with me when it is complete?" I asked.

"Yes, madame, I will give you and Master Volkov the same findings I deliver to the Grand Master," Caden said.

Marek opened the door for me, and I hesitated only to give Natalie a quick thumbs up and a smile. I would have preferred a hug, but it was clear to me too that she was having a hard time controlling herself.

Marek lead the way back to the detention wing and toward Viktor's cell. I wasn't thrilled to be seeing him, but the Guardians were struggling to keep him calm, so I had to help.

We arrived in the high-security wing of the holding cells and found James waiting for us. He gave me a warm smile.

"I'll take you in. I have to warn you it is going to be hard to see Viktor like this. You are used to him in all his pompous glory, but he has fallen pretty far." James said.

I looked at Marek, and he gave me a sad smile. I wasn't going to like this one bit.

James led me down the now familiar corridor of detention cells. We passed where I knew Asher Sanz was still being held and found two guards outside the door. It was the only one with exterior guards. He was a handful, so he had guards inside and outside his cell. James or Caden typically were on duty with him, but since Viktor admitted to hiring him, he had been downgraded to a lower threat level.

James stopped at the end of the hall and knocked on the outer door before opening it. He looked at me to be sure I was ready then lead the way inside. I followed him in, and Marek stopped just inside the door.

Viktor was chained to the wall like Asher had been, so that wasn't shocking, but the crazy look in his eyes was new. He strained in his chains even though he looked to be drugged. His movements appeared more human than a vampire should display. When he saw me, he exploded against the chains, and a few rings snapped. The Guardians stepped in quickly and moved to inject him with something.

"No, stop! He will behave." I said, pushing the suggestion through the bond.

Viktor relaxed a bit but still held the chains taught as if he would snap them at any moment. Johnson relaxed a small amount, and a female vampire who I assumed was Murphy stepped back, lowering the syringe in her hand.

"Why did you do it? I cooperated like you ordered." Viktor said, tears threatening to fall.

I realized then that he hadn't just experienced the power surge but must have also felt what had happened before the wave. I had threatened him with something similar, and he thought it was to punish him.

"You did cooperate, and I thank you for that. However, your current behavior is unacceptable." I said sternly.

An essential part of vampire society was the appearance of strength, and if I showed any compassion to Viktor, it would be seen as weakness by him and possibly the guards. He was a miserable mess of emotions and being near him had me feeling the hurt and disappointment within him.

"I do not belong here! I did nothing wrong." Viktor said.

"That remains to be determined, Viktor. You are stuck here until your trial. Either you can do it sedated and chained to a wall or with dignity. It is your choice." I said.

I played on his pride and vanity, hoping it would sway him to behave. I could simply order him to do it with my power, but I rather have him agree to it himself.

"They will not let me see Natalie. I can feel her struggle, but I cannot help her chained to a wall!" He yelled.

He was coming apart at the seams. I'd never seen him so fragile. I stepped forward, and the Guardians all jumped in front of me.

"Step aside," I ordered.

"Please, Madame Summers, the prisoner is walking a fine line of control," Murphy said.

"I am aware of that, thank you. Now step aside." I said, looking at all of them.

James backed off, and the other two did the same. Viktor looked at me, nervously. He remembered how it felt to have me overpower him before. I wasn't sure if he liked it or if it made him angry. It was hard to tell with Viktor.

"I just came from seeing Natalie. She is distraught that you are here and not able to come to her. She is still having a hard time controlling herself." I said, stepping closer.

Viktor would be able to smell her on me. Natalie's tears were still wet on my shoulder.

"You visited her? Good. She loves you. That was very kind of you." Viktor said, looking visibly relaxed.

"I love her, and I wouldn't leave her behind for anything. You know that." I said sternly.

"I do," Viktor said with a sneer.

There was the Viktor I knew.

"You seem to be able to control yourself now. If you behave, I'm sure you will see better treatment from the Guardians." I said.

I snuck a glance at James, and he nodded his head in agreement.

"I don't belong here!" He snarled.

"Yes, you do. When you break the rules, you get punished. That is how it works." I said, pushing a little power into my words.

"Matters of the heart have few rules," He said, sounding defeated.

"Viktor, I have made it clear from the beginning that I have no interest in you. You were my sister's fiancé and an asshole. It was never going to happen." I said.

"You agreed to a blood bond," He said, grasping at straws.

"I agreed to save my life with a blood bond. I did not agree to a relationship with you. You knew I was already bonded to another master vampire. Per vampire law, you should have walked away." I said, stating my point clearly and pushing more power into the words.

He straightened up and said, "We had a bond first."

"No, we did not. You stole my blood and tricked me into drinking yours. A bond never formed between us." I said adamantly.

"Argue all you like; I will not be convicted of the charges," Viktor stated.

"Thankfully, it is not my decision to make. We are, however, stuck with this bond for the time being. Until I break it, you will behave like a civilized being and stop acting like a newly turned vampire unable to control your emotions." I said with power.

I took a page from Caden's book for that speech. I figured if I treated him like an out of control baby, he might respond.

Viktor smiled a wicked grin, "Why have you not broken it already?"

"Don't get your hopes up because we still have a bond between us," I said.

"Oh, I will always have my hopes up as you say. You are a prize beyond price." He said, shooting a look at Marek as if to challenge him.

I sighed and resisted the urge to strangle him. It was classic Viktor, which was good because he was no longer a snarling monster. I could feel Marek seething behind me, but he stayed silent.

"Will you promise me to behave yourself so the next time I visit you look like a respectable vampire instead of a mess? No one would let you see Natalie in this state, and I rather not see it myself." I said.

Viktor perked up at the thought of seeing Natalie. I didn't want to use my sister as a bargaining chip, but he was very motivated by it.

"I agree with that promise. If you continue to visit me and approve, I would like to see, dear Natalie." Viktor said.

"I can agree to visit you if I hear you are behaving like a model prisoner and are not up to any mischief. I cannot make promises about Natalie, but I will speak on your behalf." I agreed.

"Thank you, my darling, I..." Viktor started, but I interrupted.

"No, Viktor. You will address me as Madame or not at all." I corrected him.

"Indeed, I apologize, Madame. I will do as you instruct." Viktor said, bowing his head.

"Good." I said to Viktor then turned to the Guardians, "Please inform me if he does anything besides behave to your exact standards of conduct."

They all nodded agreement, and I stepped toward the door.

Marek stepped out before me and held the door open.

"Thank you, Master," Viktor said through the bond as I walked through the door.

"You're welcome," I said back, shocked at him calling me master. I was sure it was his way of trying to manipulate me.

I felt a swell of affection come through the bond from him. I shut off the flow and walked purposefully behind Marek.

Marek turned when the door closed and raised an eyebrow at me. It was his "I would not have done it that way" look. James followed behind us, clearly wanting to talk to Marek before we left.

"Thank you. I believe Viktor will be more compliant now." James said to me.

"It will benefit Natalie if he can see her. As much as I don't want him anywhere near my sister, she needs her maker right now." I said, and James agreed.

James gave Marek a quick update then left to return to the command center. Marek took my hand and led me down the hall, back toward the residential area. When we were out of sight of everyone and close to the elevators, Marek pushed me into the wall.

"Marek!" I yelped.

He captured my lips with his and kissed me hard, wrapping his arms around me. I softened into his embrace and kissed him back. He was fiercely attracted to me at that moment, but I couldn't place why.

He came up for air a moment later and said, "Watching you give orders was highly arousing."

I laughed and gently pushed him back. "What would your Guardians think if they saw you kissing me in the hall?"

"They would think I had just reformed a bond with the woman I love and could not keep my hands off of her." He said, leaning back into to kiss me again.

"And who was distracting you from your work," I added before kissing back.

"Mmm, indeed." He said and pulled himself together.

"Do you need me anymore today? I'd like to head home and get a few things sorted out." I said.

Marek went a bit stiff and said, "Can you wait until this evening? I have business here today but can take you later."

"I rather go now and get everything sorted. Can you come over after you're done with work?" I asked.

I had thoughts of having him to myself for once and hoped he could make it happen.

"I can and will. I will ask James to escort you to your home as soon as he is sure Viktor has been settled." Marek said, looking more relaxed.

"I'm curious. What will happen with Asher? I saw he is still a guest of the Council." I said as we stopped at the elevator doors.

"He will speak at Viktor's hearing, and the Council will determine if he broke any laws. He will likely be released if Viktor is held responsible." Marek said.

"That is a scary thought," I said, thinking of Asher being released into the world.

"He did a job. He is actually a reasonable man and can be useful. He has his place in society like the rest of us." Marek said.

"Will you ask James to come upstairs when he is ready? I'm going to gather my things and rest for a bit before I go." I said.

Marek agreed and leaned in for a kiss.

"I will see you later. Be safe." He said.

I assured him I would be careful and stepped into the elevator. He watched me until the doors closed. He was still overprotective of me. I imagined that it would never end. As the head of the supernatural protection service, he was pre-wired to prepare for the worst.

Chapter Twenty-Two

I gathered my things from the bedroom then parked myself on the couch to make some calls. I had been out of touch with friends and family, and I was sure they were ready to call out for a search party. Especially my parents since my only updates so far had been texts regarding how I knew where Natalie was but hadn't seen her yet.

I started with the hardest call first.

"Hi, Mom, how are you?" I said when my mother answered the phone.

"Ember, it's about time you checked in. Where is Natalie?" She said.

"I found Nat, and she is still with Viktor. She is going to be out of touch for a while but wanted me to assure you she is okay." I said, feeling my stomach churn with lies.

"Why didn't she call me herself?" She demanded.

"If she were able to call, she would, but she is in the middle of something that is taking up most of her time. I saw her today. She looks good." I said.

"That is very vague. What could possibly keep Natalie so busy she can't make a phone call?" My mother said.

I could imagine her face scrunching up, and her eyes narrowing with anger.

"Viktor has kept her so busy she is having a hard time finding time is all. I was lucky to get in to see her. Give her some time. She will reach out when she can. I'm sure of it." I said, trying to reassure her.

"Tell her she needs to make time for her mother." Mom said.

"I will. I have a few more calls to make but wanted to call you first, so you knew Nat was okay." I said, trying to get off the line.

"Will you be over on Sunday for dinner? You've missed the past couple weeks, and your father wants to see you." She said.

"I should be able to make it work next Sunday. We have some catching up to do." I said.

"That sounds ominous." Mom said.

"Don't worry, I'll fill you in when I see you," I said and hung up with her.

That was not going to be a fun conversation to have in person. She was going to drill me for details I couldn't give. I wondered if Marek would come with me for that dinner.

The thought made me laugh. Although a vampire had come for dinner before, I didn't think it was a good idea to repeat the incident. I needed to come up with a way to tell them about Marek without actually telling them anything about him.

After a few more calls, I had a headache. It seems my life was now a secret that the majority of my friends and family couldn't know about. I didn't realize the impact until speaking with Sam. I wanted to tell her everything but had to keep it light enough not to reveal anything about the Council or the supernatural.

I was wallowing in self-pity when James knocked on the door.

"What's wrong?" He asked when he saw me.

"What isn't wrong, James? My life has become a big secret. All my friends and family can't know what has transpired, which makes talking to them difficult at best." I said.

"Come here," He said, pulling me into a hug.

"How are you still so nice to me after what has happened? I feel like you and I were closer than friends, then I took a drastic detour." I said.

"I admit I didn't see Marek's intentions until it was too late, but I should have. The two of you have been drawn to each other like moths to a flame since you met. There was no other path for you." He said, smiling.

"You are a good friend James," I said.

"Speaking of Marek, he said you want to go home," James said, and his tone told me something wasn't sitting right with him.

"Why is that bad?" I asked.

"You are bonded to a master vampire, and you told him you didn't want to stay here with him. I doubt he's happy about it." He said.

"He didn't say a word about it," I said in defense.

"Not yet," He said.

"Regardless, I need to get home. I have mail, bills, plants to water, you name it, and it's on a list of things I have been ignoring while searching for Nat. I have a life outside of all this." I said, gesturing around the room as if it represented all the paranormal and supernatural happenings.

"I understand, Em. I really do." James said compassionately.

I grabbed my bag and told him I was ready to go. I wasn't going to solve all my problems by talking about them, but it helped to have him to confide in.

He drove me home, and as soon as I stepped into my house, I felt better. It wasn't that the Council apartment wasn't beautiful, because it was, but there is no substitute for home. I threw my bag down by the door and walked out front to check the mail. I returned with a pile of bills and correspondence. As I sorted through it, James sat down at the kitchen table with me.

"Do you mind if I sit with you?" James asked.

"Sure. Are you here until Marek shows up tonight?" I asked.

"More or less. You really don't need a close guard at this time, but since I brought you home, I'd like to stay with you. Otherwise, I'm hanging around outside." He said.

"You can hang out in here with me. In fact, can I pick your brain on vampire culture?" I asked.

"Sure, I'll tell you what I know." He said.

I proceeded to pepper him with questions about vampire society, mating, and everything else I could think of that I hadn't already read about. By the time I was out of questions, it was evening. I learned many things that I probably should have known before entering a relationship with a vampire, but I couldn't reverse what happened. I really didn't want to either.

I felt Marek before he came to the door and told James he had arrived. James went out to him before he came into the house. I assumed he was giving a report since he was acting in his official capacity by hanging out with me today.

As soon as I saw Marek, I had an overwhelming urge to run into his arms. It was partly the bond and partly the fact that I wasn't used to being away from him. We had been near each other every day for weeks, and I had grown accustomed to it.

Marek had a suit jacket draped over an arm. He was wearing a fancy dress shirt and slacks instead of his usual t-shirt and jeans. He looked very handsome.

"You look like you came from a business meeting," I said, walking over and kissing him.

"This is what I wear when I'm not in the field." He said, smiling down at me.

"It's a good look," I said, leaning into him and wagging my eyebrows.

"James mentioned you grilled him about vampires today," Marek said, smirking.

"James is a tattletale, and I didn't grill him. I just asked him some questions. Our power merge and bond have repercussions I need to understand." I said, leading him to the couch and sitting down next to him.

"James is an excellent Guardian, even if his charge challenges his patience." He said, grinning.

"I do not challenge his patience! Wait, are you teasing me?" I asked.

"Maybe." He said and laughed.

I narrowed my eyes at him but smiled because I liked it.

"I've never seen this side of you." I marveled.

"I have been on duty every moment you have known me up until last night." He said.

"So, the first free moment you had, you threw the rulebook out the window?" I said.

"There is no rulebook with you." He said, stroking my cheek tenderly.

I stared into his eyes, enjoying being close to him.

"What are we doing, Marek?" I asked.

"What do you mean?" He asked, confusion pouring through the bond.

"Are we dating? Or vampire married? I'm tied to Viktor, but you and I had a power merge thing happen. Not to mention what Viktor said about someone else that is interested in me. I've learned that it isn't a good thing at all, but we are sitting here like we can have a lovely evening as if we were a normal couple." I said, feeling panicked.

He pulled me closer into his arms and said, "We are not dating or married. You are as close to being my mate as can happen without a mating bond which is infinitely more complicated. I will protect you with my life from anyone that tries to do you harm, and we are sitting here because you wanted to go home."

I looked at him sideways. His last point sounded a little snide.

"Why are you upset?" I asked.

"I am not upset," He said.

"Uh huh," I said skeptically.

"I am disappointed that you chose to leave." He admitted running his hands through his hair.

"Why wouldn't I come home?" I said.

Marek considered what I said for a moment before responding.

"I am a master vampire who has fallen in love for the first time in my life. I have a need, however irrational, to be near you. The hours I spent apart from you today..." He said, standing up and pacing.

"Marek, I feel it too, but I'm sure we will figure out a way to deal with it. Other vampires must be able to handle it." I said.

"They do," He said.

"How?" I asked, waiting for his response.

"They live together. It helps to spend extended periods together if you are going to be apart for any amount of time." He said, turning back to me.

I thought about it, and the idea was actually appealing. I was having the same issues he mentioned. Being far away from him today was difficult, but I imagined having to deal with that every day and it felt unbearable.

"Okay," I said.

"What do you mean, okay?" He asked.

"We should move in together," I said.

His face was blank, and his emotions were unclear. I didn't know if I offended him or made him happy. He started pacing again, which led me to believe he was not pleased.

"Say something," I said.

He looked at me, and a slow smile stretched his lips. He walked over to me and pulled me up to stand in front of him.

"We should live in the penthouse. The security is superior, and it has a larger bathtub than the one you have here." He said.

"The bathtub is point two on your list of reasons for living in the penthouse?" I said, laughing.

"Do you prefer we have a bathtub that cannot fit us both?" He asked, smirking.

I wrapped my arms around his neck and pulled him in for a kiss.

"A two-person bathtub is a vital need indeed," I said, agreeing.

"Good. I can have a team here in the morning to get everything packed up and moved." He said.

"Snap your fingers, and it's done?" I asked.

"Yes," He said entirely serious.

"I keep forgetting that you are a big deal in the Council," I said.

"I am the Head of the Guardians. That means I am in charge of everything." He said.

"Oh, right," I said, dumbfounded.

Marek leaned in and kissed me. He held me close, and it felt good to be in his arms, knowing that we could be together like this any time we wanted. My only concern was the privacy at the penthouse, but I figured we could figure out a way to be alone.

"Now, what shall we do this evening?" He said, looking particularly luscious.

I pulled him close and kissed him, making it clear that all I wanted was him. He responded by lifting me into his arms and walking back toward the bedroom.

I had denied my feelings for him for a while now. I didn't think I was ready to move on from Nikko, but now I knew that Marek was the only one I wanted. He fills my heart with love and being connected to him is indescribable.

His desire burned through the bond as he laid me down on the bed and tucked himself in next to me. He kissed me softly, and I was lost in him when a sudden pain ran through me.

"What is it?" Marek asked.

"It's Viktor, I don't understand," I said, shaking my head.

"What has happened?" He asked.

"Something's wrong, Marek. We have to go." I said, pushing him up.

Viktor's screams filled my head, and I could think of nothing else. It didn't make any sense. He was in a secured facility and should be fine unless he was having another fit. Viktor isn't a weak man. For him to be screaming meant something was very wrong.

Marek followed me as I ran out of the house. I heard him talking behind me, and I assumed he was on the phone. When I got to Marek's car, James was there waiting. He looked spooked, but he pulled open the car door to let me in any way.

"We need to hurry," James said as I slid into the passenger seat.

James slammed the door as soon as I was in and jumped into the backseat as Marek got into the driver's seat. Searing pain filled me as I felt Viktor struggle. I couldn't reach him like I could Marek, but I knew he was fighting for his life.

"James, what do you know?" I asked.

"Something is wrong, I can't get Caden on the phone or anyone else." He said.

"Viktor is freaking out, but I can't tell what's happening. He is hurt. All I can hear is his screaming." I said.

My hands were shaking and my heart pounding. Viktor's fear was flooding through the bond and pulling me into the feeling. I was having a hard time distinguishing his fear from my own.

"Can you feel your sister?" Marek asked as he sped through the streets to get us there as quickly as possible.

"I haven't tried," I said, surprised at myself.

My anger helped me get past Viktor's pain but when I tried to connect to Natalie, I couldn't see her. Since she became a vampire it had been harder to reach her. I looked at Marek and he felt my frustration.

"As her maker, Viktor has a strong bond with her." He said and it was all I needed.

Instead of using my Seer skills alone, I tapped into Viktor trying hard to ignore his pain. As I dug deeper, I found the link between them and used it to see Nat. Her fear hit me harder than Viktor's, but it was also a relief because I knew she was okay.

"She's okay but she's really scared. I can't tell what's happening yet, but we need to hurry." I said out loud so both of them could hear me.

I pushed my way into Viktor's mind and tried talking to him.

"Viktor, pull yourself together. Natalie is in danger. I'm on my way, but I need to know what's happening." I said sternly.

"My dear, if I could get to her, I would." He said strained.

"What the hell happened?" I asked.

"Attacked. They are after dear Natalie. I cannot get to her. I think they have her." He said.

He sounded weak. I could hear his pain and knew he needed blood and a healer immediately. I wasn't sure if we would get there in time.

"Who Viktor?" I asked.

"I do not know but they will not live long after I find them." He said.

"Hang on. We're almost there." I said and broke away from him.

I was breathing hard and holding my stomach. Marek was looking at me more than the road.

"I'm fine, but Viktor isn't. He said they were attacked. They are after Natalie. That's all I got. He's lost a lot of blood, and he's pissed." I said to Marek.

He nodded and ran a red light. The adrenaline was pouring into my bloodstream so fast I couldn't stop shaking. Running red lights was not helping.

"Stay by my side when we arrive. Promise me you will not go anywhere without me or James." Marek said looking at me intensely.

"I promise. I'm not stupid." I said although I felt stupid for not seeing this beforehand.

What good is a Seer who can't predict an attack? Ironically my only consolation was that Natalie is a vampire now and much harder to kill.

Marek drove the car through a garage door and down a tunnel that opened up into a garage area I had never seen before. There were tactical vehicles and SUV's everywhere. He jumped the curb and pulled right up to the door. Essentially blocking it but leaving just enough room for a person to slide through.

I was out of the car and at the door so fast a wave of nausea threatened my stomach.

"Shit Em. How did you do that?" James asked.

I looked at Marek and his shocked expression didn't comfort me.

"No idea. Let's go." I said and ran through the door.

Marek jumped ahead and lead the way. I pushed my thoughts to him and told him where to go. Viktor was out of his cell in one of the hallways. I pushed the image to Marek, and he took us there directly.

I wasn't prepared for what I saw when we arrived. Viktor laid in a large pool of blood. His stomach was torn open and his guts were spilled all over the floor. There was a trail of blood where he had apparently crawled to get to this point.

"Viktor, stop. We'll take it from here." I said running up to him.

Marek stopped me from getting too close and I glared up at him. He moved out of my way reluctantly.

"Do not order me to stop trying to get to my daughter," Viktor said through gritted teeth.

"For Pete's sake, Viktor. You are trailing your insides down the hallway," I said, kneeling down next to him.

He looked up and I could see the pain in his eyes. He cared for her deeply and couldn't stop.

"Fine, but I don't see how you can help," I said and walked quickly ahead of him.

James and Marek fell in step behind me, although I knew they both preferred to lead in case someone came at me. I used my power to find what was ahead and only found injured vampires or dead humans.

When I got to Natalie's door, it was open, and I feared the worst. I rushed in only to find her fighting against two vampires. She was holding her own, but I could tell she was about to fall.

I threw my power at her attackers and grabbed them. They stopped instantly, and I pushed them back into the wall. Their faces were snarling, but their eyes showed fear at being held.

"Unsettling, isn't it? Not being able to move." I said, stepping in front of them.

I spared a glance at Natalie, and Marek held her in his arms. She was shaking but appeared to be uninjured.

James swept through the apartment to ensure no one else was lurking about. He nodded to me then to Marek, curious. I shook off my wonder and refocused on the two vampires.

"Who are you?" I asked.

They both just stared at me.

"If I may?" Marek asked.

I nodded and stepped back a little. James took Natalie into his arms, and Marek moved to the vampires.

"Who sent you?" He asked.

They remained silent, but their eyes darted between Marek and me. It was like they were unsure who to fear the most.

"Answer," I said, sending a little heat into their feet.

They squirmed and then started to scream as smoke began to rise from their shoes.

"Ember," Marek said, and I shut off the heat but pressed them harder into the wall.

Their eyes bulged, and the one on the left started to talk.

"Don't kill us." She said.

"Tell us what we want to know, and I won't light another match," I said, suggesting I was ready to light them up again.

"Who sent you, and why? If you cooperate, we won't take your lives." Marek asked calmly.

He now looked like the most reasonable of the two of us. I guess that meant I was playing bad cop. Fine by me.

"I can't tell you. We were sent to get the vampire and her sister." The female vamp said.

"Why?" Marek asked.

"Our orders were to capture and then wait for instructions." She said.

"Shut up, Trina!" The other vampire yelled.

He wasn't happy she was talking.

"Trina?" I asked the female.

"Yes," She responded.

"You can't tell us who sent you, or you won't tell us?" I asked.

"Can't," She said.

The other vampire went crazy at that. Instead of trying to get us, he decided to move to Trina. He couldn't move while I held him, but I was sure if I let him go, she would be dead.

I looked at Marek and found he was thinking the same thing. We needed to get this guy out of here so Trina would spill more info.

I heard feet pounding in the hallway and turned at the same time as Marek. Maybe I heard him hearing it? He looked surprised again before his face went suddenly blank.

James and Marek moved to the door, and I moved in front of Natalie.

"We are about to have company, Nat. You okay?" I asked her.

She nodded, although she still looked shaken.

"Viktor is hurt," She said, and the pain on her face made my heart hurt.

"I know. I saw him in the hall." I said grimacing.

Familiar faces entered the room at that moment, so I didn't elaborate for Nat how hurt Viktor was. It looked like the cavalry finally arrived.

Caden was covered in blood, and Natalie shrieked when she saw him. I looked at her and then at him. They stared at each other like they needed the other to breathe. I moved out of the way when Caden made a beeline to Nat.

"Are you hurt?" Natalie asked him.

"It isn't my blood," Caden said, looking her over for injuries.

I left her in his capable hands and turned my attention back to our vampire invaders. I looked at the male and felt an urge to give him to Viktor. It made me laugh, and the vampire's eyes widened.

I smiled, and I could see his fear spike before my eyes.

"Stop playing with him," Marek said from behind me.

I jumped. Marek had snuck up on me. I didn't think it was possible with our new bond.

"I was just imagining what Viktor will do to him," I said.

The vampire's Adam's apple bobbed with a gulp, and he looked over my right shoulder toward the door. I could feel Viktor there but didn't think he was a threat given the state he was in.

"Let him go, and you will see it firsthand," Viktor said.

I turned around and saw him standing there, holding his guts in. Natalie gasped, and I almost joined her. I couldn't believe he was standing.

"He is a prisoner, Viktor," Marek said with steel in his voice.

I glared at Marek, but he was right. We needed to learn more from this guy.

"Maybe you can have him after Marek is done with him," I suggested.

Viktor smiled a wicked grin as Marek's face went blank. That was the equivalent of a frown from Marek. I guess he didn't appreciate the humor of the situation, or maybe Viktor's feelings were bleeding through to me.

Guardian Johnson came in then and gave Marek an update. There were groups of vampires like the two we had pinned down throughout the complex. Apparently, there had been a coordinated attack to hit various parts of the complex at the same time.

I went over to Viktor as he slumped against the wall.

"Why are you still standing here?" I asked, trying to push him out of the room.

"I'm not going anywhere." He said, not moving an inch.

"You are literally falling apart," I pointed to his stomach.

Blood oozed between his fingers, and his face was whiter than I thought was possible. He needed blood badly.

"I only need a little blood," He said, glancing at my neck.

"You aren't getting it from me," I said, and I felt Marek perk up.

"How did you get out of your cell anyway?" I asked, realizing it was weird he was wandering about.

"I removed the door," He said as if that explained everything.

"Right, well, you should be in the hospital where a doctor can put you back together and get you some blood. You've lost most of it on the floor." I said, looking down at the puddle growing under his feet.

"I don't seem to be able to move from this spot," Viktor said as his body began to shake.

I grabbed him as he fell both with my hands and with my power. That meant I let go of the vampires behind us. I heard a snarl and then a scuffle before the Guardians had the two vampires in hand. While I held Viktor, he stared into my eyes. I could feel his need for me. It pounded at me like someone trying to break through a door.

James said something to me, but I couldn't hear him over the pounding in my head. I laid Viktor down on the floor as gently as I could, but the pain had him crying out again. He passed out, and the pounding slowed down to a manageable level.

When I looked up, Marek was staring at where my hands were. I looked down and saw that I was cradling Viktor's head. I was covered in his blood, but the thing that upset Marek was that I was showing compassion for Viktor.

I got back to my feet just as James brought in a stretcher. He was followed by a team of EMT's that I recognized. The fact I recognized EMT's said a lot about my current life.

"They've got him," James assured me.

I nodded and looked down at Viktor, lying helpless on the floor. I couldn't help the sting of pain in my heart. He was mine, and he was broken. I felt an urge to hold him and offer him my blood. It freaked me out.

The team picked Viktor up with their power instead of lifting him with their hands. He still cried out, and I ran to him. I grabbed his hand and locked my power around him. He stopped yelling and looked up at me while I helped move him onto the stretcher. His lips curved up into a small smile.

"Thank you, Master," He said, then passed out again.

The room was silent for too long. I looked up to find all eyes on me except for Marek. He was staring a hole right through Viktor's forehead.

"What are you waiting for? Get him to the hospital and put his pieces back where they belong." I yelled.

The EMT's scrambled to roll Viktor out of the room. I couldn't ignore the pain on his face as they moved him. I needed to go with him.

I looked over at Marek, and he looked back with his usual stoic expression.

"*I need to go with him,*" I said through the bond.

"*I know,*" He said and turned away.

I looked back at Natalie. She was cradled in Caden's arms, looking at Viktor like he was dead. Marek was busy taking charge of the Guardians, so I took charge of Natalie.

"Caden. Take Natalie to the penthouse and watch her until I come to get her." I said.

"Yes, ma'am." He said.

He looked at Marek as he moved Natalie toward the door. Marek nodded as if to confirm my order. It didn't look like Caden needed the confirmation.

I met Marek's eyes, then turned and followed Viktor.

Chapter Twenty-Three

I sat on a tiny wooden chair staring at Viktor while he slept. It had taken the surgeon six hours to put him back together. They had needed me several times during the surgery to keep him calm. It turns out that it is challenging to sedate a master vampire, but if you happen to have their master handy, they can put the vampire under a suggestion to remain still.

That was something I learned tonight. I was Viktor's master. He had called me that name a few times, and after how everyone reacted to me, it was clear I had earned that status as if I was a vampire.

Viktor looked peaceful now as he slept. The pain was still present, but it was fading as the hours passed. I was having a hard time putting this new selfless Viktor in my mind with the cruel Viktor I knew so well. I half expected him to jump off the bed and come at me any moment.

Two Guardians stood outside the door, one for Viktor and one for me. The door was locked up tight so that Viktor couldn't escape. I'm not sure how effective that would be considering he tore the door off his cell in the detention area last night.

Viktor whimpered softly, and his brow furrowed slightly. I reached out and took his hand. It was smeared with blood as was my own. The moment our skin touched; I was pulled into his dream.

Viktor flew through the air and hit a brick wall. The force of the hit knocked several bricks loose, and they fell on top of him. His thoughts were a swirl of panic for Natalie. He couldn't let her be harmed or taken.

He picked himself up and rushed toward his attacker again, only to be thrown back on the ground.

"Give up, Viktor," a female vampire said with a thick Spanish accent.

The vampire looked wild, but it was clear that she was also beautiful. Her long dark blonde hair fell below her waist, and her voluptuous body was barely contained in a spaghetti strap silk dress. Viktor wasn't distracted by her beauty at all. He was more concerned with her temper.

"I don't know where he is, Magdalena," Viktor replied.

"Liar! You work with him on the Council. You know where he is." She yelled.

Her deep brown eyes were wild and tinged with red.

"For the last time, I don't work on the Council. I'm called in occasionally to consult. I don't know him well enough to be acquainted with where he makes his home or spends his time." Viktor said, exasperated.

She backhanded him, and his mouth filled with blood. He spit the blood out on the ground and wiped his lips with the back of his hand. He looked up at the woman, and surges of anger filled him. If she wasn't ancient, he could and would tear her head off. Unfortunately, because she is an ancient, that is much easier said than done.

Old vampires like her tended to lose their minds if they didn't stay grounded. Most ancients had covens filled with vampires made in every century to help them all adapt. This one was clearly insane, although she did have at least several vampires under her control.

"I may know where he will be. If you agree not to harm my pet, I will tell you." Viktor offered.

She narrowed her eyes at him like she was trying to decide if she should believe him.

"You are sure you know where he will be?" She asked.

"Yes," Viktor said.

"She could be useful after I find him. Marek takes a lot of interest in her sister." She said, flashing a smile at Viktor.

"Magdalena, please." He said with gritted teeth.

"Very well. If your information proves useful, I will leave your pet alone." She said.

It wasn't exactly what he asked for, but he knew it was all he was going to get.

"My son is introducing his newest vampire to society next week. Marek has been invited to attend on behalf of the Council of Guardians. He hasn't missed an event on behalf of the Council in years. You will find him there." Viktor said.

"Now, Viktor, that was not so hard." She said purring.

She pulled him into her and kissed him on the cheek. He remained stiff in her arms, but she didn't seem to notice. When she pulled back, she was smiling.

"You will tell me if anything changes. I will not be kept from him, or I will come for you again." She threatened.

"I understand," He said, bowing low to her.

The vision dissolved, and I was left looking down at a man who sold Marek out to some vampire named Magdalena. Viktor opened his eyes and looked confused. I still held his hand and dropped it as soon as I realized it.

"You were holding my hand?" Viktor asked with a smile.

"You had a bad dream," I said.

His brow wrinkled, and he looked like he was trying to remember. He tried to sit up, but I stopped him.

"You have more stitches in you than a patchwork quilt. You need to stay still until you heal." I said, holding him down with a hand on his shoulder.

He looked at my hand and then at the IV attached to his arm. He moved to pull it out, but I stopped him again.

"Viktor, stop it," I said sternly.

He stilled instantly.

"I don't want to be here," he said.

"Neither do I, but here we are," I said.

I started to pull away, but he grabbed my hand, keeping me from putting distance between us.

"Where is your Guardian shadow?" Viktor asked.

He stroked my hand with his thumb, and it felt good. Good enough to pull my hand away.

"They are all busy dealing with the little invasion that happened last night," I said, sitting back down in the tiny chair.

"Last night? How long have I been here?" He asked.

"You were in surgery all night. You have only been in this room for a couple hours." I said, feeling irritable.

"Whose blood is in this bag?" Viktor asked.

I laughed. Not because it was funny but because I had asked the same thing the last time I was in this hospital.

"Why is that funny?" He asked.

"It isn't. I'm tired. You seem better, and I need to catch up with what happened while I was in here with you." I said.

"Did you stay with me the whole time?" He asked, confused.

"I did," I admitted with a sigh.

"Did you sleep?" He asked.

"No," I said.

"Take my blood. You will feel better," Viktor said, raising his arm to his lips.

I stopped him before he bit himself.

"Viktor, you hardly have enough blood to fill your own veins.

Besides, I don't need your blood." I said.

"Don't need it or don't want it?" He asked.

"Both," I said, but it came out a whisper.

I didn't crave his blood exactly, but I have developed a taste for vampire blood since Marek first fed it to me. There is a fine line between needing it like medicine and taking it because it is pleasurable.

He took my hand and noticed the bloodstains. He flicked his tongue out and licked my fingers.

"Grosse Viktor, stop it," I said, pulling my hand back.

"Why is my blood all over you?" He asked.

"Because you were an idiot and tried to help Natalie while you were injured. You passed out in my arms." I said, remembering how I had been so concerned about him. It was a strange feeling to be worried about Viktor.

"It was convenient you were there." He said smirking a bit

"You are clearly feeling better, and I have to check on my sister," I said, standing up.

"Thank you for staying with me. Will you please let me know how dear Natalie is?" He said, and he actually sounded sincere.

"I will. Get some rest, Viktor." I said, knocking on the door to be let out.

James pulled it open and stepped aside. As soon as the door closed, the other Guardian on duty bolted the door. They both bowed to me, and then James motioned for me to lead the way.

"Is my sister in the penthouse?" I asked.

"She waits for you as directed. Caden is with her." He replied.

I figured she was okay if she was still with Caden. They seemed to have become fast friends.

"Where is Marek?" I asked, although I could tell where he was without much effort.

"He is attending to the questioning of the survivors from the raid." He said, moving down the hall with me.

"Still?" I asked. "He must be tired."

James gave me a look, "Have you met him?"

I laughed, and it felt good.

"Thank you, James. I needed to laugh." I said, looking at him.

"What did Viktor have to say?" James asked.

"Not much. I expect you will ring it out of him later." I said.

"I will try," James said, smiling.

"Marek's shut me out since I left with Viktor. Do you think he is upset with me?" I asked.

James turned to me and took my hands.

"I am not getting between the two of you, Ember. He isn't used to having someone to come home to." He said.

"I wasn't at home last night. I was sitting by the bedside of another vampire." I said.

"He understands." James insisted.

He pulled my hand into the crook of his arm and led me to the residential wing. There were now doors entering the hall where the elevators are. They must have been installed overnight. Marek had been busy.

We were silent on the ride up to the penthouse. I tried to poke at the bond with Marek, but it remained mostly blocked. I pushed aside the frustration I felt and readied myself to deal with my sister.

Guards stood outside the door when we arrived. I dismissed them and turned to James.

"Please wait here. I want to speak with my sister alone." I said.

"Ember," James said, stopping me. "Giving orders suits you. You should do it more often."

I looked at him, confused for a moment then realized he was

complimenting me. He bowed and stood at attention next to the door. I smiled at him and squeezed his arm.

I walked into the penthouse and called for Nat. She came running to me.

"How is Viktor? Tell me he's okay." She insisted.

"He is fine. It takes more than that to take out a master vampire." I said, reassuring her.

"I can feel his pain, is he really getting better?" She asked.

"Yes, and the pain is waning by the hour," I assured her.

"Madame," Caden bowed to me.

"Caden, thank you for looking after Nat. I didn't realize it would take so long." I said.

"She is a pleasure madame. Your sister is a joy to be around." He said, smiling at her.

"Will you please leave us alone for now, Caden? I will call you in if you are needed." I said.

He bowed and left swiftly.

"That was rude, Em. You didn't have to dismiss him." Natalie said.

"Natalie, he is a Guardian. He is not my friend. Responding to orders is how they operate. Listen, I'd like you to go down to Viktor and sit with him until he is well enough to talk. Please take Caden with you as your personal guard. I don't want you to go anywhere alone." I said.

"That sounds like an order," She said.

"Will you go?" I asked.

"Of course, I will. I would have gone last night, but you wouldn't let me." She said with tears in her eyes and stormed out of the penthouse.

I let out a breath I hadn't realized I was holding. Natalie didn't even realize that she was finally not locked up and hidden away.

I had to hope she would recognize that and let go of her anger.

I sat down on the couch to rest for a moment. I wanted to go see Marek. I've wanted to go to him all night. I still had blood on my hands, but I couldn't bring myself to wash it off. I let my eyes fall closed. It felt good to be still.

I awoke sometime later to the sound of men talking. I knew the voices well, and it made me smile. I missed Marek so much my chest hurt.

I yawned, and their attention turned to me. James nodded at me then went out the door. Marek walked toward me.

"How long have I been asleep?" I asked.

"James said Natalie stormed out about two hours ago," Marek said.

I rubbed my eyes as I stood up. I stumbled toward him, and his eyes landed on my hands.

"Your hands are covered in blood, my love," Marek said, pulling me closer so he could look at me.

"I was too tired to wash up after talking to Nat," I said.

"Here," He pulled me into the kitchen and brought me to the sink.

The water was warm, and his hands soft. He rinsed Viktor's blood from my skin and massaged away the pain of the evening. As he dried me off, I leaned into him. I could feel the link between us again, open and full.

"I missed you," I said, putting my arms around his neck and pulling him close.

I kissed him and felt a spark of desire burning between us.

"I hear Viktor is healing well." He said, pulling away.

"Are you angry about that?" I asked, following him to the living room.

"The compound was attacked. I'm certainly not happy." He said, avoiding the question.

Marek sat down on the couch, and I sat next to him. He was distant. Marek turned to me, and I saw it in his eyes. He was hurting. It was more than the raid.

"What's wrong?" I asked.

"Were you up all night?" He asked, tucking some hair behind my ear.

He was deflecting all my questions. It wasn't a good sign.

"I was. The surgeon needed my help with Viktor during the surgery. I didn't realize how hard it is to sedate a master vampire." I said.

"I am glad you were able to help," Marek said.

"You don't sound glad," I said, pushing.

"I am not angry exactly," He said, scrunching up his face as if he were confused.

His confusion filled our bond

"You've been blocking me, which we agreed not to do. I assumed that meant you didn't want me to know what you were feeling." I said.

He pulled me into his arms.

"I could not be angry with you for doing your duty as a master." He said, kissing the top of my head.

I snuggled into his arms and took comfort in the feel of him. I didn't believe him. He was mad, but I chose to ignore it for now.

"It sounds so strange to be called a master. Is that even what I am?" I asked, looking up at him.

He looked at me with love in his eyes.

"You are the master of my heart. It seems appropriate." He said with a smirk.

"Cheesy, but I love you for it," I said, leaning in to kiss him.

He kissed me back, and I fell into his affection like I needed it to breathe. In fact, I think I did need it to breathe. His touch brought me to life in a way that only he could.

"How was your night? I have no idea what happened after I left." I said.

Marek tensed slightly. I only noticed because I was currently draped so tightly around him.

"There were seven vampires captured alive. We lost two of our own, but my team took down twenty of theirs, so I am pleased with their performance. We have too many in the hospital, but the fact they survived is good." He said.

"Did you find out who sent them or anything else about why they were here?" I asked.

"It was a vampire behind it, but they would not give us a name. From what I can tell, he is an ancient. That narrows it down, although it leaves more questions than I would like." He said.

"She," I said.

"What do you mean?" He asked, confused.

"I think it's a she," I said. "When I was waiting for Viktor to regain consciousness, I fell into one of his dreams. He was fighting with a vampire named Magdalena, and she wanted to know where you were."

Marek stiffened, and I felt his shock at hearing that name.

"That is not possible. Magdalena is dead. She was killed many years ago." Marek said sure what he was saying was true.

"Voluptuous woman with a thick Spanish accent?" I asked.

"That sounds like her," He said, scrunching up his face.

"Who is she?" I asked.

"She is danger personified, but I do not know how she could be alive." He said with evident confusion.

"She came after Viktor and threatened him until he told her what she wanted to know," I said.

"Did he tell you she was involved with what happened last

night?" He asked, carefully.

"I didn't push him to talk about it. He acted like he didn't know what I was referring to, which is typical Viktor. Although he could have been confused. He seemed pretty groggy after the surgery." I said.

"I need to get under this right away," Marek said, looking stressed.

"She threatened Viktor with his vampire pet and her sister. I assume she was referring to Natalie and me, but I can't be sure until I speak with him. Magdalena wanted to find you for some reason." I said.

He ran his hands through his hair in frustration, pausing with his hands steepled at his chin. It was the most distressed I had ever seen him. I wondered if it was because I could feel all his emotions or if he was opening up to me more now that we had merged powers.

This ancient vampire's interest in Marek made me uneasy. I could handle threats to my own person, but threats to him made my hackles rise.

"I could use your expertise on this," Marek said. "I need to speak with Sabastian to get his buy-in, but I would like for you to work for me heading up the research team. This is going to be a highly secret mission, and I trust you more than James and Caden combined."

"Work for you, work for you? As in, you are my boss?" I asked, confused, and anxious regarding him being my boss.

"Technically, Sabastian would be your boss, meaning you and I would be partners. It would provide a good salary and an apartment in this building. Although you wouldn't need the apartment since you will be living here with me." He said, smiling.

"It's a tempting offer..." I said, thinking hard about any reason why I wouldn't do it.

While I pondered it, Marek sent a text message off to Sabastian and received a quick "hire her now, at any cost" message. I guess he saw the value in having me as part of the team.

Marek explained that currently, he ran the team with additional leadership from James and Caden but that they were being pulled in too many directions. He needed someone to take over, make improvements, and expand the operations. It was a bonus that he knew he could trust me implicitly.

The thought of running my own team within the Guardians was very appealing. It helped that I had worked with the team a little already, so I knew who I would be managing. I peppered Marek with more questions until I realized I had made up my mind.

"I'll do it," I said to his delight.

Although delight for Marek looked more like mild amusement to others.

"Now that we have forged an alliance in work and in love. What shall we do next?" He asked.

"Make love," I said without hesitation. "And preferably without interruption this time or someone is going to lose a limb."

Marek laughed, "The team is not used to me being occupied by anything other than work."

"You are mine vampire, they need to pick their battles," I said.

"And you, my love, are mine," He said, leaning in to kiss me.

Marek claimed my lips, and the world fell away around us. Lost in the feel of him, I began to imagine what it was going to be like living and working with him. I couldn't think of how I could possibly be happier. As long as I had him by my side, I felt invincible.

Clothing started to come off, and the heat built between us in the most pleasant of ways. I was about to suggest we go into the bedroom when a knock came at the door.

"I'm going to have to tear their arm off," I said, frustrated. "That will teach them to leave us alone."

Marek just smirked and rebuttoned his shirt at top speed. He was opening the door as I pulled my t-shirt on and straightened my pants.

"I'm sorry to interrupt," James said, looking contrite.

"What is it?" Marek asked.

James filled him in on the emergency, and then Marek looked at me.

"We will be right down. Let the team know they will be meeting their new leader." He said.

James looked confused until he realized Marek was referring to me. He smiled a big lopsided grin then turned away. Marek closed the door and sped over to me.

"Oof!" I said as the air was knocked out of my lungs by Marek tackling me.

He started removing my clothing as he kissed me.

"What are you doing?" I asked, confused.

"Protecting James from losing an arm," He said deadpan.

I laughed hard and then kissed him back. Making a life with him was going to be an adventure, and I couldn't ask for anything more.

The end, for now...

Ember Summers' next adventure:

An ancient vampire has set her sights on Marek and will do any-thing to get him back, including taking out the woman he loves. Ember won't just stand by and let it happen. Her bond with Marek has only grown as time has gone by and having merged their powers means that when Ember and Marek are together, no one can stop them.

Follow Nichole M. Bridges and get updates on her latest novels by going to her website at www.nmbridges.com.